The Lady is a Thief

The Lady is Mine, Book One

AIMEE NICOLE WALKER

The Lady is a Thief
(The Lady is Mine, #1)
Copyright © 2017 Aimee Nicole Walker

ISBN: 978-1-948273-02-2

aimeenicolewalker@blogspot.com

Cover photograph © Wander Aguiar—www.wanderaguiar.com
Cover art © Jay Aheer of Simply Defined Art—www.simplydefinedart.com

Editing provided by Pam Ebeler of Undivided Editing—www.undividedediting.com
Proofreading provided by Judy Zweifel of Judy's Proofreading—www.judysproofreading.com
Interior Design and Formatting provided by Stacey Blake of Champagne Book Design—www.champagnebookdesign.com

Copyright and Trademark Acknowledgments

The author acknowledges the copyrights and trademarked status and trademark owners of the trademarks and copyrights mentioned in this work of fiction.

Dedication

Mom,

Not a day passes that I don't miss you and wish I could hear your voice just one more time. Though you may be gone, I carry you in my heart. Always.

The Lady is a Thief

The Lady is Mine

Chapter One

Maegan Miracle

HAVE YOU EVER OPENED YOUR EYES FIRST THING IN THE morning and had a feeling wash over you that something big was about to go down? I'm not talking about a killer sale on high-heeled boots at Nordstrom's either; I'm talking about a life-altering event. It's happened to me a few times in my life and each time something big had actually occurred. Now, I'm not implying that I'm psychic, but I've learned to listen to my gut. I usually had an indication of whether the surprise was good or bad, but that wasn't the case on that particular morning. Why? Could the event be both good and bad for me? Was the universe still undecided?

I dismissed it all together as I rolled over and burrowed deeper in my blankets. It was my day off after all, and I decided it would be a lazy one. I envisioned myself leisurely drinking coffee while I caught up with my friends by text or social media. I would follow that up with an indulgent French toast brunch for one then a long, luxurious bath before I headed over to Curl Up and Dye for my hair and manicure appointment.

Lulu, my faithful French bulldog, snored obnoxiously loud when I nuzzled my nose behind her ear and attempted to cuddle her. It was her signature move when I irritated her while she was trying to sleep in late, and her diva-like shenanigans never failed to make me smile.

"Mama's precious angel," I whispered and kissed the velvety softness of her dark gray ear. Lulu's response to my lovey-dovey words and affection was snoring even louder. "Okay, then. I guess I'll be forced to eat all the bacon by myself."

Lulu rolled over onto her back, presenting her tummy to me, and looked up at me with her big, dark eyes. She knew damn well she had me wrapped around her paw and she wasn't remotely sorry. Lulu was a gray-and-white Frenchie, which wasn't that unusual, but her markings were unique all to her. Her ears and the top of her head were dark gray while the bottom half of her head beneath her eyes was all white, making it look like she wore a mask. Her pointy ears and dark gray mask made her look like Bat Dog. Yes, I hummed the *Batman* theme song every time she did something amazing, which was every day, of course.

Lulu was a gift from my twin brother, Milo, on my twenty-ninth birthday the previous year. I wasn't sure if he wanted to celebrate our last year in our twenties, commiserate because we're both pathetically single, or he just knew that I needed a healthy outlet for all the love bubbling inside me. Regardless of his reasons, Lulu was the best thing to ever happen to me. Yes, she was pampered and spoiled, but she returned that love to me by wagging her nub of a tail and prancing when I came home each day. I hadn't realized how quiet my house was or how lonely I'd grown until Lulu came into my life and filled the void. Milo smugly took all the credit for my happier state of mind, of course.

"Uncle Milo is right sometimes—okay, often—but we can't flatter him too much if we want to keep him grounded," I told Lulu.

My phone rang on my nightstand, jarring me out of my lazy cuddles with my dog. I raised up on my elbow and reached over Lulu to grab my phone. "Speak of the devil, and he'll dial you up before a decent time on your only day off," I said before I answered the phone.

2

"Good morning, Thing One."

"Get your lazy ass out of bed, Thing Two," Milo replied.

"Just how do you know I'm still lazing about in bed?"

"Twink link."

It was true that I was closer to Milo than any other person on the planet, including our parents. I mean, we did share a uterus for nearly forty weeks before we were pushed into the cold, cruel world against our will. We could feel each other's emotions through what we call our twin link—or twink link, as Milo called it—but I doubted I released an emotion strong enough to reach Milo that morning.

"What do you really want?" I asked dryly.

"French toast brunch, of course." Had I become that predictable? "Maegan, you make French toast every Wednesday. Most people do extravagance on Saturday or Sunday mornings, but not my sister."

"I have two businesses to run on the weekends and quit answering questions I don't ask aloud. It's just fucking creepy." I sat fully up in bed because I was no longer in the mood to cuddle under the blankets.

"*We* have two businesses to run," Milo corrected sassily. "I'm right beside you in the trenches, sister."

While it was true that Milo was my business partner at Books and Brew and Curious Things, we approached our businesses differently. Our stores were something that Milo did, but they were how I defined myself. Milo worked as many hours as me, but at the end of the day, he turned it off and went home. For me, the businesses were my life. When I wasn't at work, I spent my free time trying to create new ideas to make our stores stronger and even more appealing. I read articles about name branding and books on how to provide a positive environment for employees. I spent evenings looking at recipes for the next best baked good or combing through dark, dingy places trying to find the perfect curiosity to sell. Our success as business owners was my biggest source of pride.

We had started out renting one of four commercial spaces in our building and opened a coffee and pastry shop called The Brew. The other three window fronts were empty, and we bought the building from our landlord as soon as we saved enough capital to convince a banker to take a chance on us. We knocked down a wall between our coffee shop and one of the empty spaces to expand the space to include a bookstore and changed the name to Books and Brew. We initially planned to rent the other two places, but Milo talked me into turning my passion for selling antiques and oddities online into a brick-and-mortar store. The fourth space we did rent to Memphis, who opened a comic book and vinyl record store.

Milo didn't get excited about digging through attics and basements in homes to find the good stuff before they were sold at estate or auction sales, but Memphis loved it as much as I did. Together, we found some amazing treasures for our stores. He hadn't lived in Blissville for very long, but it felt like we'd known him our entire lives. Milo and I each had our own little circle of friends where we did our individual thing, but Memphis was someone we both enjoyed hanging out with, and he was so easy to love it wasn't funny. I thought it was too bad that Memphis and Milo weren't attracted to one another because they would make a gorgeous couple. I wanted at least one of the Miracle twins—that never stopped sounding funny—to find their happily ever after. Memphis had once joked that Milo was too nice and he only knew how to fall for bad boys, and although Milo would never admit it, I knew damn well which guy still owned his heart.

"Earth to Maegan," Milo said impatiently, cutting into my thoughts.

"Yes, Milo. *We* have two businesses to run. Wednesdays are my lazy days," I reminded him.

Milo snorted. "You can't do lazy if you tried. I bet you're planning to sip coffee and catch up with your friends, make your fancy French toast, crispy bacon, and fluffy scrambled eggs, and then take a long enough shower to use up all the hot water in your tank before you get your nails and hair done later this afternoon. How close am I?"

"Eerily close but I was hoping to take a long, hot bath and read a book."

"Well, I do know you pretty damn well," Milo quipped, "which is why I know that none of those things were going to happen."

"Wrong," I said defiantly, but I noticed my words lacked real conviction.

"You would've picked up your phone to catch up with your friends and ended up looking at some business article or finding a new recipe to try instead. That would've led to another article or a link to an upcoming estate sale or auction that would require you to make phone calls so that you could get a crack at the goods before anyone else." I wanted to argue that he was wrong, but he was so accurate it was spooky. "You would've ended up making a dash to one or more locations to find *the item* because you were sure it would only take *thirty minutes*. Then you'd end up losing track of time, requiring you to race back to town and pull up to the salon so fast that pedestrians would dive for safety."

"Okay, so maybe you've seen this show a few times."

"I've lived it for thirty years," Milo corrected. "So, I'm doing you a favor by coming over so you at least get your beloved French toast brunch because I'm confident that you would've settled for peanut butter crackers."

"Doing me a favor, huh?"

"I'm altruistic, Mae," Milo said dramatically. I pictured him sitting in his house covering his heart and blinking his big blue eyes innocently. "Someone has to save you from yourself."

"And if you just happen to benefit in the process then that's okay too, right?"

Milo sighed heavily. "You wound me."

"Give me twenty minutes to shower and get dressed."

"I'll give you thirty in case you want to work in a little…"

"Stop talking, Milo."

"I'll be able to tell if you do," he teased, knowing that it creeped me out. People actually asked us if we could feel each other having sex through our link. The answer was a grateful "hell no" each time. What kind of perverts asked that anyway?

"No French toast for you," I said, mimicking the soup Nazi from *Seinfeld*.

"We will see you in twenty minutes," Milo said.

"*We?* Did you have an overnight guest or is this a split personality day? If so, which extra personality are you bringing? Diva Divine or Fanny Flair?"

"Ha ha ha. I love how you give my multiple personalities drag queen names," Milo said dryly. "If you must know, I'm picking up Memphis on the way over. Don't make the bacon too crispy, Maegan. I'd hate to chip one of my perfect teeth. We don't like chewy bacon either." He hung up without saying goodbye, leaving me to stare at my phone in disbelief.

"Uncle Milo is an asshole," I told Lulu. She let out a loud snore while looking right at me. "Fine, but you're getting up to go pee as soon as I get out of the shower."

I didn't linger in the shower taking care of the business that Milo alluded to either. Unfortunately, I made it a quick shower rather than a long, luxurious bath.

As I stepped out to towel off, I heard the loud roar of my new neighbor's ginormous truck as he came home from work. I had yet to meet the man, or at least I assumed it was a guy based on his ride. Sure, women drove trucks, but they seldom drove trucks bigger than they needed. Maybe I was judging the guy harshly, but what did he need with a truck that tall with side mirrors that were bigger than my head? I'd understand if he was a farmer, but we lived in town, and this joker worked at night. I heard him fire up that diesel beast each evening about the time I drifted to sleep and he roared back home each morning when I was in the shower. I was curious about his identity, but not enough to do something about it.

As cold as it was in mid-January, Lulu got her business done and returned to the door quickly. I loved having a fenced yard on mornings like those so that I could watch from inside while she safely did her business. Cold weather didn't seem to bother her, but I threatened to move to Florida at least once a day during the months of December through March.

Milo and Memphis showed up right on time, and I started making breakfast for the three of us while they entertained me with their good-natured bickering back and forth. They honestly sounded like a couple who'd been married for twenty years or longer. It was too bad we couldn't convince our hearts and bodies who to be attracted to because Memphis made Milo laugh and smile as no one else did. That heat and attraction I saw in Milo's eyes when he looked at Andy Mason during unguarded moments was missing when he smiled at Memphis across my kitchen table.

"Beefcake Andy sure has some talented hands," Memphis said out of the blue.

I dropped my spatula on the floor while Milo choked on the coffee he'd just sipped from his cup. Memphis winked playfully at me as he pounded on Milo's back while he sputtered and coughed. I had tried to encourage Milo to patch things up with Andy, who stared at my brother like he hung the moon when Milo wasn't looking, but I had never tried to kill him in the process.

"Asshole," Milo said to Memphis, his scratchy voice sounding like he had gargled a mouthful of rocks.

"Yes, I do have one of those, and it's divine," Memphis said nonplussed while he blinked his eyes innocently. "What's with the name calling? I was just trying to tell you guys how Andy came over last night and used his big, strong hands to fix… things."

Milo glared at him for several heartbeats before he responded. "I fucking hate you."

"You fucking love me," Memphis countered. He shook his head and continued. "You're acting as if *I* was the thing Andy fixed, and I assure you that's not the case at all. I had a leaking pipe beneath the bathroom sink, and my bedroom closet door kept sticking badly. Andy fixed those things for me."

"Well, isn't Andy just the jack of all trades," Milo said bitterly.

"Oh, and I bet he masters quite a few of them," I said then bumped Memphis's fist when he raised it in the air. "Not that you're thinking about all the things that Beefcake Andy can do to you with his big, meaty paws, Milo."

"Stop calling him Beefcake Andy. It sounds barbaric. Andy might work with his hands and drive a truck, but he's not some knuckle-dragging Neanderthal who should be reduced down to his body and dick size."

"Who said anything about his dick?" I asked. "I believe the big and meaty reference was to his paws, as in hands, not his cock and balls." Memphis threw his head back and laughed.

Milo's face turned an interesting shade of red before he mumbled and said, "Both of you can shut the hell up." A wicked smile spread slowly across his face then he added, "Unless you want to discuss *your* sex lives."

"Who was talking about sex?" Memphis asked. "I'm pretty sure I said he fixed my closet door and bathroom pipe. Besides, no one wants to hear about my pathetic sex life. Hell, I can't even get lucky in my dreams."

I snorted. "Same here." I shook my head over the sad trio that we made. The bacon grease on the stove popped and burned the flesh on my hand closest to the skillet. "Damn, that hurt."

"It's fate," Milo said from behind me.

I remembered that *feeling* I had when I first woke up. I was pretty sure that getting splattered with bacon grease wasn't the surprise that life had in store for me that day, but was it a sign of crappy things to come? It seemed that way when I dropped my keys in a puddle of dirty melted snow on my way to the salon. I had half a notion to go back inside my house and hide from whatever fate had in store for me, but one did not miss a hair appointment with Joshua

Roman-Wyatt. A person had to book his services at least eight weeks in advance.

Once I got to Curl Up and Dye, all my tension faded away because I knew I was going to get a scalp massage that rivaled sex, a beautiful hair style that always made me feel like a million dollars, catch up on the latest town gossip, and I'd walk out of there with freshly painted nails that would make me happy every time I looked down at them.

I wasn't wrong either. Josh worked his magic with two different shades of blonde and a contrasting shade of brown that made the blonde look more vibrant. As for the gossip, I learned that Mr. Jacobi was trying to pass a kidney stone, Mrs. Danvers was testing the latest beauty cream from an infomercial she saw during late night reruns of *I Love Lucy*, and Nadine Beaumont finally left that worthless, piece of shit husband of hers. Rocky Beaumont, former town mayor and current town slut, was finally getting his just desserts.

My mood had completely turned around by the time I left the salon. I might've sacrificed four hours of my day off, but it was worth every second. I was convinced my luck had also turned around because Becker, a local realtor, called on my way home to tell me I had first crack at the Renzo estate. The older couple had recently passed away within months of each other and their son, Thom, was looking to sell the property since he had moved away after graduation and had no desire to return to Blissville. It was the best opportunity presented to me in a long time, and I couldn't wait to see what treasures were in store for me in that old house.

I know it sounds like I have questionable character, but I'm a good person. I swear! I don't wish death on people, and I certainly don't try to take advantage of the grieving families I work with, in fact, the opposite is true. The reason I'm successful at procuring first crack at the items is because I've earned the reputation as someone who is respectful to the families and honest in my dealings. I'm very proud of that too.

It was already dark by the time I left the salon, and I was ready to make myself a cup of hot cocoa and settle in my recliner with my book and Lulu curled up on my lap. Well, best laid plans and yada yada yada because Lulu had an upset stomach and wanted to eat grass. I decided to let my girl do her thing while I went upstairs and put on my pjs. Here's a quirk about me. I own more pajamas than I do anything else and in every style you can imagine. I have everything from the sexy frilly shit that never gets to see play time, because neither do I, to the floor-length nightgowns like my ninety-year-old nana wears, and everything in between.

That night, I grabbed my favorite pair of Betty Boop pjs. The top was a baseball T-shirt with a white torso and a sassy, sexy Betty in the center, and long, red sleeves. It was a little thin for winter, but so soft against my skin and it wasn't like I was going to be camping outside. I wasn't expecting company either so I decided braless was perfectly acceptable. The pj bottoms were made from the softest red and black flannel that hugged my lower half in a warm embrace. It was the perfect outfit for lazing about for the rest of the evening.

Once I got back downstairs, I looked out the window of my kitchen door to check on Lulu's progress. My heart raced in my chest when I didn't see her. I whipped the door open and used that whisper-yell technique to call her name.

"Lulu! Stop fooling around and get in here."

I stepped onto the back porch in my bare feet when I didn't see or hear her. I turned my head to the right and saw that the gate was hanging wide open.

"Oh my God!" My baby!

I darted back inside the house and pulled the emergency flashlight from the junk drawer next to the refrigerator. I ran back outside and was grateful that the batteries still worked because I didn't think to check them. There were only two things in the house that I could be sure always had batteries—my remote control for the television and my vibrator. *Hey! A girl must have her priorities straight in life.* I ran through the open gate and swept the weak beam of light from left to right as I looked for my precious dog. Too bad there wasn't snow on the ground or I could've followed her footprints.

"Lulu!" I didn't bother trying to be quiet. I heard the fear in my voice grow each time I called her name. "Come on, baby girl. Where are you?"

As soon as I crossed into my new neighbor's back yard, a bright spotlight came on, blinding me instantly.

"Fuck!" I yelled as I tried covering my eyes with my free hand.

I heard the back door fly open hard enough to smash into the side of the house. "Who's there?"

Oh, fuck! That hot, gravelly, just-woke-up voice sent shivers down my spine and made my lady bits clench in straight-up need. Damn, that voice would whisper the dirtiest shit in your ears while he pounded you from behind. I bet he would yank my hair and bite my neck. *Whoa! What's happening here?* My reactions to his angry voice shocked me enough that I dropped my flashlight.

I shaded my eyes and looked in the direction of the back porch, but due to the bright lights behind him, all I could see was a dark silhouette. And what an amazing silhouette it was too. If he wasn't naked then he was pretty damn close because I couldn't see any hint of clothing hugging his thickly muscled thighs, broad shoulders, or bulging biceps that tapered into massively strong-looking forearms that…

"Is that a fucking gun?"

Chapter Two

Elijah Markham

ALL I WANTED WAS SOME FUCKING SLEEP AFTER SPENDING the entire night writing up my last fucking report for my last motherfucking assignment. I'd spent the last four years working undercover operations for the Columbus Police Department and finally got a chance at a promotion. Unfortunately for me, the new job was in Blissville, Ohio, which was more than an hour south, and my old police captain wasn't inclined to turn me loose until my investigation was completed. I couldn't really blame him because switching out undercover cops in an eighteen-month investigation was asking to blow shit wide open or get someone killed. I used it as motivation to wrap things up all nice and tight, so I could get on with my life.

In my eagerness to begin my fresh start, I might've pushed myself beyond human limitations after accepting the position on the BPD, but taking down Axel Washington and his damn drug and gun-running motorcycle gang was so fucking worth it. Across the country, more and more gangs were popping up following the popularity of a certain cable television show. I confess to watching a few episodes myself to get an idea of what to expect before I went undercover, but

I can honestly say that Axel Washington was no bad boy wannabe; he was the real-fucking-deal.

Needless to say, I was exhausted by the time I pulled into the driveway of my rented house. I was grateful that I didn't have to report to my new captain until the following Monday, so I could attempt to get settled and catch up on all the sleep I'd missed before I would start my new job. I could already tell that I was going to like working for Captain Roman-Wyatt. My new partner, Adrian Goode, seemed like he was going to be a riot to work with. I just wanted to be at my best on day one and that was going to take some serious decompressing after the hellhole I'd just climbed out of the previous night.

I crashed hard the minute I got home and didn't wake up until about seven in the evening when I heard the familiar sounds of my neighbor letting her dog out. It was hard to tell the woman's age because she always did that whisper-yell thing, but I liked to pretend that she was a hot blonde with a rocking body—nicely curved hips, narrow waist, and large, luscious tits. It never failed to make my piss hard-on even harder, which took even longer for me to pee. I was tempted to peek out my bedroom window that overlooked her back yard on more than one occasion, but I didn't want to ruin my spank bank fantasy material.

Once I relieved my bladder, my stomach started making its unhappiness known. I'd survived on fast food for so long that I couldn't remember the last time I had a decent meal. I knew I should take a shower, get dressed, and go to the diner in town, but that required more energy than I possessed. I decided my stomach could wait and returned to bed, knowing that the neighbor lady's dog wouldn't be outside too long in the cold. I was certain that Lulu was some tiny lap dog and not a big, hairy Saint Bernard that would want to frolic around in the cold temps. There was something different about her voice, but I was too tired to give it much thought beyond it sounded louder and less whispery than usual.

I'd just lain back down and shut my eyes when my motion-sensor lights on the back of the house turned on and bright, white light flooded my back yard and one of my bedroom windows along the back wall. Those LED lights didn't fuck around and neither did I.

Instinctively, I grabbed my gun and ran down the steps and out the back door not caring that I was wearing nothing but a pair of boxer briefs. I half expected to see one of the motorcycle gang's family members standing in my back yard, but instead it was a vision greater than any I could conjure up and beat off to. The only thing dangerous-looking on my visitor was her pointy nipples poking through her cotton. They looked hard enough to cut glass, but I was willing to risk my safety if she wanted to get up close and personal with my mouth. That was a welcoming committee I could fucking get used to in a heartbeat.

"Is that a fucking gun?" she asked angrily through lips so plush and sensual that I easily imagined them wrapped around my cock.

"Uh…" My ability to communicate had drained south along with my blood to my dick, which I could feel thickening behind my underwear. My brain wasn't capable of saying much, but my dick was very expressive about what it wanted.

"Why in fuck's sake are you holding a gun in your hand?" She placed both hands on her hips, which only pushed her glorious tits out even more. Fuck! It had been so long since I'd had my hands on a set like hers that I worried I'd come in my underwear. In my experience, most people—especially women—shy away from a person holding a gun. Not this chick; she marched forward in angry strides that made her boobs bounce and sway hypnotically. My mouth went dry, which was terrible if I wanted to wrap my lips around those nipples and tease them with my tongue, which I desperately did. It was the neighborly thing to do when they were shouting, "Welcome to the neighborhood," like that.

I heard a crunch seconds before she let out a jagged gasp and stopped in her tracks. "Mother fuck!" Oh, beautiful and cursed like a sailor. My heart pounded a little harder in my chest. My raging hard-on was all but forgotten when she lifted her leg, and I saw blood in the arch of her dainty, bare foot.

I charged forward because that's what white knights do, right? Of course, she hadn't forgotten about the gun and quickly dropped her foot to take a step back away from danger. When she did, her foot landed on the flashlight she had dropped. The cylindrical object rolled, knocking her off balance and sent her tumbling backward. She cracked her head on the frozen ground and went immediately still.

"Fuck!" I tucked my gun into the waistband of my boxer briefs since I didn't exactly have anywhere else to put it. "Miss, are you okay?" I asked, dropping down to my knees beside her. I quickly assessed that she was breathing fine and had just knocked herself out. I heard a soft jingle of metal clicking together a moment before a gray-and-white dog ran over to the prone woman and began licking her face. I would've known it was Lulu by the sparkling collar alone, but she had a pink bone-shaped name tag that spelled her name in crystals—or diamonds for all I knew.

I slipped my arms beneath the blonde bombshell and easily lifted her off the ground. "Come on, Lulu. Let's check out your human to make sure she's okay."

As if she understood, Lulu raced me up the steps and waited at the back door for me. I carefully shifted the bundle of pure sex in my arms, and opened it so we could go inside where it was warm. I hadn't realized how cold I was until I lifted her freezing body into my arms. It was a miracle that I could get an erection in icy temperatures, but then I looked at the angelic face and hot body of the intruder as I laid her gently on the sofa. I covered her with the flannel blanket I kept thrown over the back because the furnace in the house was temperamental at times and it came in handy. I missed seeing her lush form, but only a creepy asshole would lust after her body while she was unconscious. I would wait and openly lust over her once she came around.

I ran upstairs to get some first aid supplies and a pair of my socks. *What the hell had she been doing in bare feet?* Oh man, I started to worry that she was a nutter, a real bunny burner like in *Fatal Attraction*. A sexy woman who would lure me into her tight, hot pussy then turn my entire world upside down. I didn't have a wife to threaten or a bunny to boil, but I was really attached to my cock and balls—figuratively and literally.

I sat at the end of the couch, peeled back the blanket from her legs, and lifted Sleeping Beauty's injured foot onto my lap. I tried to be gentle when I pressed the antiseptic wipe to her foot, but it must've stung like a mofo because she jackknifed into a sitting position and jerked her foot suddenly, tagging me hard in the balls.

"Dammit!" I roared as my boys wept from the abuse. I cupped my nads and willed myself not to puke all over the floor. At least I didn't have to worry about embarrassing myself with an erection. "Fuck!"

"Oh, I'm so sorry." Her dog barked beside the couch and the little vixen forgot all about me. "My baby!" She leaned over and scooped Lulu up, placing kisses all over her face and cooing to her. I got my first good look at the dog and thought she was pretty damn cute for an ankle biter, especially the way it looked like she was wearing a Batman mask. My guest must've suddenly realized she was in an unfamiliar house because she set the dog on her lap and looked around the room before she turned her large, luminous, and very green eyes on me. She blinked several times like maybe she was imagining things.

"Hi." No one would ever accuse me of being smooth.

"Hi." Her voice was a little broken and breathy like I would expect it to be when—*if*—I slid my dick inside her. She blinked a few more times and the long, dark eyelashes framing her eyes were quite captivating. She glanced down to where I was still cupping my boys to prevent a further beatdown, but they recovered fast and so did the sleeping giant. "Um, you must be my new neighbor. The one with a gun." She looked around for it.

"It's tucked in my underwear," I lamely said in a gritty voice rem-iniscent of Clint Eastwood's old western movies. I wanted to tell her to go ahead and make my day, but I didn't think she would be open to my suggestion right then. Worse, she might think I was a pain slut and drive her heel into my crotch again. If I didn't know that my cock was leaking from excitement over her sexiness, I would've said it was crying at the thought of getting maimed again.

"Where you keep all your big guns," she teased. Then her face turned an adorable shade of pink that made the freckles on her nose stand out. "Forgive my boldness; I take some getting used to—or so I'm told." I couldn't disagree more. I liked the way her eyes raked over my body appreciatively and boldly lingered on my crotch as if she was trying to see what was behind door number one. "I'm Maegan Miracle. I live next door to you."

She extended her hand and I tried to look down at it, but my eyes locked on her bountiful breasts again when the blanket fell to her lap. Fuck me! That shirt was paper thin and I could see the dusky rose color of her nipples straining against the fabric. I was a sex-starved man on the verge of humiliating myself in front of her.

I cleared my throat and removed one hand off my crotch so I could shake her hand. Her lips quirked up into a sly grin when she saw me shift my other hand to cover as much cock as I could. God, my dick was raging hard and I had never been so happy as I was right then that I had huge hands. Let her think I was modest because it was better than her knowing the pervert I really was.

"I'm Elijah Markham," I replied, still sounding like a Hollywood gunslinger. *Was that a faint tremble I felt in her hand, and did I see a slight shiver work through her body?*

Maegan released my hand and scooped her dog back up. She looked down at her precious dog and saw the way her nips poked through the fabric. I was surprised it wasn't painful. I wanted to reach across the distance between us and cup the lush flesh in my hands and massage them warm to ease any discomfort she had, but I wisely stayed where I sat and just stared. *Like that was any better.*

"Oh my God!" She yanked the blanket up to cover her chest and looked at me like I was a complete monster. Hey! She was just trying to get a glimpse of my goods too. Who the hell did she think she was to look all pissed off? I didn't ask her and her pointy nips to come over here and tease me to an erection. I was so glad I didn't say that out loud when I realized how creepy it sounded. "I gotta go." She swung her legs around and moved to stand, but fell back onto the couch the minute she put pressure on her injured foot.

"Let me look at that for you, Maegan. I promise to be a good boy."

She snorted but twisted back around so that her foot was once again resting on my thigh. "I think there's something in my foot."

I cupped her heel in the palm of one hand and gingerly ran my thumb over her arch. "I was just trying to clean it so I could see the damage before you woke up." She gasped but it wasn't a sound of pain. I looked away from her foot and saw that her eyes were locked on my crotch.

I could've been a nice guy and not commented, but that wasn't my style. Maybe I was that man once upon a time before life dealt me one low blow after the other, but not anymore. I was brash, rough, and sometimes crude, but people knew where they stood with me. "He likes you too."

Maegan's eyes darted up to mine. "Holy fuck!" she said before she covered her face with both hands. "I'm going to die from mortification."

"Why? Because you noticed my dick? I don't feel a bit embarrassed for admiring your tits. They are fucking spectacular and you should be proud of them."

"Oh my God!" Maegan said, but her body shook with laughter. "This can't be happening to me. I must be unconscious in your back yard still."

"Well, if this is a dream, I'd be helping you out of your pajamas to check to see if there are any other bruises or cuts that need my attention." She peeked around her hands. I saw one eye narrow in a warning for me to not even think about trying it. "No?" I asked. She shook her head. "Fine." I picked up the sterile wipe and cleaned her foot as delicately as I could, but she didn't let out a peep. I suspected it was because she was too busy looking over my body to notice the pain. That wasn't me being a conceded douche; I could feel her glance caressing over my skin so intently that it felt like her touch ghosting across my skin.

My dick couldn't have gotten any harder if she whipped her shirt over her head and let me touch her girls. Okay, that was a bold-faced lie, but I was hard, and I wasn't ashamed of the way my body reacted to her. Her uninjured foot moved a little restlessly against my thigh, giving me the impression that just maybe she was rubbing her thighs together in excitement. Damn, I wanted it to be so.

I wanted to look up her body until our eyes met, but I knew better than to chance it. She really did have a nasty piece of wood from the snapped limb embedded in her foot and deserved to have my focus there and not my obsession to know if she was bare beneath her pj pants too.

"I'm going to work the splinter out with a pair of tweezers. I'll be as gentle as I can."

"I'm a tough girl. I can take…. Ow! Fuck! I thought you said work it out; not dig it out with a rusty pocket knife." She jerked her foot out of my hand and sat back up again. "Give it to me," she said, holding her palm out. I placed the tweezers in her hand and tried my best not to stare at her chest while she worked the sliver of wood free. Okay, so she was a lot more delicate about it than I had been. She flexed her foot and rotated her ankle. "That's much better."

"Let me clean it for you," I offered. She wanted to argue, but for some reason I wanted to prove to her that I could be gentle and not just an overzealous klutz with big hands, eager dick, and a filthy mind. I wanted her to know that I did have some finesse, but I refused to entertain why it was important to me. She was just my neighbor, nothing more.

"Okay, but I'm watching you."

I glanced up and noticed her eyes were not on my hands and what they were doing, but were instead raking over my body again. Damn, the girl was something. Whew! I needed to get my mind out of the gutter. A woman who smelled and looked as feminine as she did, probably wouldn't appreciate the raw, gutter-like thoughts that came to my mind. I'd save that for after she left and could relieve the pressure building in my balls while fantasizing about a different turn of events for her visit. *I have her cup of sugar right here. My cup fucking runneth over.* Although, I was pretty sure I took a lot of liberties with that phrase from the bible.

"So, what brought you to my back yard?" I asked her.

"Someone left my gate open. Lulu escaped when I went upstairs to change into my pajamas after I got home." She stroked her beloved dog while she spoke, and I imagined those long fingers with bright red nail polish working my dick instead. Damn, I had it bad, but then her answer finally penetrated through the lusty fog in my brain.

"Does someone often open your gate like that?"

My thoughts had turned suspicious, it must've been obvious to Maegan. "It was probably one of the neighbor boys cutting through my yard to get to his friend's house. They don't usually leave the gate open." Maegan tipped her head to the side and studied me. "Do you always brandish a gun anytime someone enters your yard? And when did you install that horrible light with the motion sensor?"

"I'm a cop so suspicion is my middle name," I replied. "I installed that light the first night I moved in. It pays to be cautious."

"A cop, huh? Are you the new detective Gabe hired?" My surprise must've shown on my face because she just offered me a crooked grin before she said, "Small town. Everyone knows everything."

"Good to know."

"Anyway, thanks for not shooting me," she said wryly. Her smart remark might've been partially responsible for my pressing the bandage against her foot a little harder than either of us anticipated. "Brute." She let out a frustrated sigh as she inspected my nursing job. "Can I borrow that pair of socks to walk home in?"

"I can do better than that. Wait here."

I half expected her to be gone when I tromped back down the stairs with a pair of slippers in my hand, because what smart woman wouldn't have bolted in her place, but she sat on my sofa all wrapped up in my blanket looking like she belonged there. I made sure to shove that thought aside faster than I'd retreat upstairs to jerk off as soon as she went home.

"This is really kind of you to let me borrow these," Maegan said as she slid her feet inside the fur-lined slippers my mom sent me for Christmas.

"No problem," I told her. "How's your head? Maybe I should check your pupils to see if they're dilated."

"I'm okay," she replied, waving me off. "I know a concussion when I feel one, and that's not the case here."

"Been roughed up a few times?" I asked as she rose to her feet. She started to take the blanket off her shoulders. I couldn't handle seeing her breasts again, and I didn't want anyone else seeing them either, although I wasn't sure who would be out and about on a cold night like that one. "Bring it back when you return my slippers."

Maegan smiled in relief, and I knew that I had said the right thing for once that evening. She took a tentative step forward to test how her foot felt before she put her full weight on it. She must've been okay because she pivoted back around to face me. "I've had my fair share of collisions on the soccer field and softball diamond over the years," she said in response to my question about her familiarity with concussions. Maegan looked down at her little dog and said, "Come, Lulu," as she began walking toward the kitchen door.

"It was nice to meet you, Elijah. Welcome to Blissville." Her voice was breathy again, sounding a lot like that cartoon character she wore on her paper-thin pajama shirt.

"See you around, Freckles."

I shut the door behind her after she left and stood there for several moments. A wide smile spread across my face as I realized, that for the first time in my life, the reality of something—or someone in this case—might possibly turn out to be better than my fantasy.

Chapter Three

"**A**RE YOU WALKING FUNNY?" MILO ASKED AS HE followed me through the door that separated Books and Brew and Curious Things.

"No," I said with a scoff.

"Yes, you are," Milo countered. "Oh my God! I recognize that awkward gait. If I didn't know better, I'd say you've been well and pleasantly had. More than once too."

"Shut up!" I wanted Milo to go back to the coffee shop so that I could have a few minutes to myself before my store opened. Technically, it was both of ours, but Milo couldn't tell the difference between real China and the cheap knockoffs. I turned to face my brother with hands on hips and an irritated expression on my face.

"It's true, isn't it? Who was it?" Milo tipped his head to the side and pressed a finger to his lips as he considered the eligible bachelors in Blissville. There weren't many straight ones left, so it didn't take him long. Unfortunately, he drew the wrong conclusions. "Maegan Rochelle Miracle! Are you screwing Clayton Callahan again?"

Clayton was the older brother of one of my best friends, Vanessa. There are a lot of romance books where the heroine falls hard for her best friend's older brother. Who hasn't crushed on their friend's brother? Well, my history with Clayton had the opposite of a happi-ly-ever-after ending. I crushed hard on that guy all through school and well beyond; he used it to his advantage by stringing me along whenever he and his high school girlfriend, Amanda, were having problems. He would flirt with me and tell me he wished Amanda was more like me. He gave me just enough hope to string me along with-out crossing a line until last year.

He and Amanda actually broke up or took a break—depending on who told the story—and Clayton jumped on the opportunity to make Amanda jealous by romancing yours truly. He just didn't let me in on the game at the time. A few dates that led to him sleeping over at my place was enough to bring Amanda to her senses. I was left out in the cold with a broken heart and shattered self-esteem, while Clayton and Amanda realized they never wanted to be apart again. In fact, they were so adamant that they got engaged. Clayton left my bed in the morning and put an engagement ring on Amanda's fin-ger that very same night. It was a miracle that my friendship with Vanessa stayed intact, but she wisely admitted that Clayton's actions were wrong. I didn't ask her to choose sides; I simply asked her not to defend his douche bag actions. She never did.

"Please," I said, rolling my eyes. "Trust me when I tell you he doesn't have what it takes to make a girl limp. Besides, I sure as hell wouldn't hook up with the slime ball while he was engaged to Amanda. I can't stand her."

"Oh, so you haven't heard the latest gossip yet. That's so amazing since you were at the hair salon last night." Milo rubbed his hands together gleefully. "It pays to be the one to open the coffee shop be-cause you get the gossip first." Milo and I took turns being the early bird to keep things fair and prevent burnout. "The engagement is off! I don't know what pencil dick did, but it must've been bad because Amanda publicly threw his ring at him across the table in the diner last night during the supper rush. It's the talk of the town."

"Huh," I said then took inventory of how the news made me feel. I would've expected to feel a little bit of triumph, but I felt… nothing. I had well and truly put their bullshit behind me after more than a decade.

"So, you can expect dickless to wander—or is it dickless wander—showing up here trying to win Amanda back by making her jealous again."

"Not going to happen."

Milo tilted his head while he studied me. He must've believed me because he changed the subject. Sort of. "So, who were you banging, if not Clayton?"

"I wasn't banging anyone." Well, no one in the flesh anyway. "One of the neighbor kids must've left the gate open yesterday because Lulu escaped. I stepped on a stick in the new neighbor's yard and got a nasty splinter. That's why I'm walking funny." It was only partially a lie.

"You went out barefoot in January?"

"My baby was missing." The part of me that told Milo everything wanted to share the rest of the story, but for some reason it didn't feel right. Nothing special happened the night before with Elijah, yet it felt that way. Was he the big surprise I felt when I woke the day before? *Oh, he was big all right.*

Freckles. Who knew such a simple nickname could make me shiver. I had more passion with my vibrator while thinking about Elijah Markham than I'd ever known with a real man. Damn, those dark eyes of his raking over my body made me insanely horny. I couldn't stop thinking about the way he stared at my breasts through my top. I wondered if he was even aware that he licked his lips more than once like he was practicing what he wanted to do with my nipples, or maybe it was an automatic thing for him. I hardly got any sleep the night before because as soon as one orgasm faded from my body, my mind would conjure up something else about him that amped my lust right back up again. I gave my vibrator a workout like it had never seen before and ended up with sore thigh muscles and most likely a bruised cervix. Every twinge and ache made me think of Elijah, and I wanted to go back home and do it all over again, preferably with him in my bed.

I had never seen thighs as big and strong as his, or biceps either for that matter. His carved chest and washboard abs were something I'd only seen on a romance novel cover or men's fitness magazine. Men like him didn't live in Blissville—well, not straight ones anyway. And that bulge in his tight boxer briefs captured and held my attention. Jesus fuck, I wasn't a size queen, but I craved trying him on for size. I wanted to press my toes against the flesh hidden beneath the cotton to see if he was as hard as he looked. Just recalling it made my mouth water to suck and taste him.

I never considered myself to be an overly sexual woman, but there was something about him that called to me and made me want to be brave, bold, and daring. *Let's not forget horny!* I needed, not wanted, to know the feel of his scruff scraping against my inner thighs or over the smooth lips of my…

"Earth to Maegan." Milo snapped his fingers to get my attention. "I don't believe for one second that you're walking funny because of a splinter, but I'm going to let you keep your little secret for now." Milo's expression went from humorous to serious in a flash. "Just promise me that you'll send Clayton Callahan packing when he shows up here today hoping you'll pick up where you left off last year. You deserve so much better than him, Mae. Someday you're going to know it."

"A snowball stands a better chance in hell than Clayton Callahan does in my life," I assured him. "Get on back and man your station so I can have my moment of peace before my day starts." I did a shooing motion with my hands that earned an irritated huff from Milo before he pivoted and did as I requested.

I went to my small office in the rear of the shop and gingerly sat in my chair behind the antique desk I bought at an auction last year. I enjoyed my coffee and pastry I snatched from next door while I went through my emails and paid bills. I looked at the notes that my part-time employee left for me about items that customers requested yesterday. Bonnie was a retired teacher who wanted to earn some extra spending money, which suited me because I could keep my operating expenses lower. The arrangement worked out great for both of us, and I truly enjoyed her company.

I smiled when I saw the list of items my clients sought: pocket watch from WWII era, antique cameo broach, and antique China in a blue-and-white pattern. I received more of those requests each week; I loved the thrill of the hunt and the joy my clients expressed when I came through for them. Included with the request was the timeframe and budget my clients had, which is important. I didn't mind working hard, but I preferred to work smart. There's no need spending fifteen hours looking for something that their budget couldn't afford. There had been times that I helped them find something similar in their price range.

I immediately set to work putting out feelers with contacts I'd made over the years, because some of those items were harder to find than others. Once I finished that, I set up my register and flipped the sign on the door from closed to open. The morning started off slow, so I was glad when Vanessa dropped in at lunchtime to visit. Of course, I could tell by the wry smile on her face that her visit wasn't purely social.

"You look different," Van said, tipping her head to the side to check me out from head to toe. "Oh my God! You've had sex!"

"For fuck's sake," I said, grabbing her arm and tugging her toward my office. I stood sideways in the doorway so I could keep an eye on the shop and have more privacy to talk to my friend. "I have not!" Well, sort of. "You don't need to warn me that your idiot brother is on the prowl either because my idiot brother already told me what happened."

"I don't want to see you get hurt like that ever again, Mae." Vanessa reached over and rubbed my arm. "I'll kill him if I must."

"Sweetie, that ugly-ass orange color would look terrible with your skin tone." I received the smile I was looking for and continued. "Besides, I'm way over him by now."

"So, who is he then?" Vanessa asked. "You're putting out vibes that a woman only emits after a night of amazing sex."

"It's not like that, Van." Damn, I wanted it to be. I sure as hell wasn't going to tell her about grinding on a vibrating substitute all night long.

"I don't believe you, Mae." She shook her head before glancing at her watch. "I'm sorry to cut this visit so short, but I did want to give you a heads-up that Clayton was off his leash."

"Thank you, Van. I love you." It was true. I had loved her since the day we met in pre-school. The only person who knew me better than Vanessa was Milo.

"Chicks before dicks," she called over her back as she left the shop.

Milo came over and supervised my store long enough for me to run to the diner to grab some carryout lunch for us. We talked about expanding our menu to include deli sandwiches and various side dishes during lunch hours, but we didn't think there was enough need for it yet. Besides, the best way to make enemies in a small town was to pull business away from someone who's already established. I'd rather stay on Edson and Emma's good side because I didn't want them spitting in my food.

"Emma's meatloaf is the best," Milo said once we gathered in my office to eat. "Don't tell Mama or Grandmama I said that."

"Your secret is safe with me," I said before I took my first bite of savory chicken, dumplings, and real mashed potatoes. "Damn, I'm going to ask Emma to marry me."

"Maybe she'll adopt us," Milo said, tucking into the baked macaroni and cheese he ordered as a side dish.

I heard the little bell over the door jingle letting me know that someone had entered my shop. The last thing I wanted to do was stop eating, but duty called. I closed the lid on my takeout carton and gave Milo a look that warned him to keep his fork to himself. I knew how many dumplings were left.

The welcoming smile I had plastered on my face wilted when I stepped out of my office and I saw who disgraced me with his presence. "Clayton," I said tersely.

"Maegan, you look beautiful."

I wanted to go back inside my office, soundly shut the door, and finish eating, but I wouldn't give him the satisfaction of knowing he still ruffled my feathers. Instead, I marched across the room until we were nearly toe to toe. I crossed my arms over my chest and gave him the same look I'd just given Milo. I meant business, and I wouldn't suffer his foolishness much longer than it took for him to tell me why he came, as if I didn't already know. "What do you want?" Succinct and direct to the point; it was the only way to deal with people like him.

"Is that any tone to use on the guy who will be taking you to dinner tonight?"

Did this sack of shit actually think I was pathetic enough to go on a date with him after what he'd done to me last year? Looking at him right then, I couldn't even remember why I was even attracted to him in the first place. His height and looks were average and nothing to get excited over. He certainly didn't have the rugged, bad boy look and his shoulders weren't as broad as a linebacker's. I never called Clayton's name in the throes of passion—not with a vibrator, and definitely not with him, because he was the kind of lover who wasn't a member of the Ladies First Club. Not to sound cruel, but he was a three-pump-chump. Afterward, he had the audacity to blame his short performance on me. He'd never had someone so tight and hot, yada yada yada. As if that was going to impress me.

"I'm not going anywhere with you, Clayton. Not tonight and not ever."

"Darling, is this attitude left over from the little misunderstanding

29

we had last year?" His smarmy voice made me want to puke. Misunderstanding? *Is that what sleazebags called it these days?* "Come out with me tonight, so I can make it up to you." That pleading expression on his face was everything I dreamed of for years, but not anymore.

"Sloppy seconds just aren't my style, Clayton. Move along before this gets really embarrassing for you."

"Maegan…"

"I believe the lady asked you to leave." *Elijah!*

Oh God! That voice! I nearly spontaneously orgasmed right on the spot. I didn't risk turning around and looking at him for fear of making an ass of myself. I kept my eyes on Clayton's surprised face instead. I waited for his eyes to return to me so that he saw how serious I was. "I did ask you to leave, and I meant it."

"I'll call you later."

"No, you won't," Elijah and I said at the same time.

"Who the fuck are you?" Clayton asked the newcomer. *He's the man who can make me come without trying.*

I felt the heat radiating off Elijah's body as he approached and heard leather shifting before I felt the pressure of his hand on my shoulder. I closed my eyes because it felt so right.

"Who I am isn't important," Elijah said in a deadly calm voice. "Leave this store and do not bother her again."

"See you around, Maegan," Clayton said as he beat a hasty retreat out the door. I figured his next move was to call his sister and demand to know who Elijah was to me. I gave it ten minutes tops before Vanessa dialed my cell phone and eleven minutes before she called the shop's landline when I didn't answer my cell.

I expected Elijah to drop his hand once Clayton left, but he didn't. Instead, he massaged my neck in small circles with his thumb. A small whimper escaped my parted lips and my head fell forward, giving him more access. A warm chuckle rumbled out of his chest and he raised his other hand to my neck and deepened his massage.

"Don't stop," I whispered, not recognizing the husky voice as my own.

"I've been wanting to hear you say that since the moment we met."

I was ready to drag him into my office when I heard someone clear their throat followed by, "Aren't you going to introduce me to your *friend*, Maegan?"

Fuck! Milo!

Chapter Four

Elijah

I HAD PLANNED TO TEST OUT THE DINER THAT EVERYONE AT THE police department raved about when a display of pastries in a picture window caught my attention. I looked at the artfully painted name on the large picture window. Books and Brew. A customer walked out the door as I walked by and the delicious aroma of coffee and pastries made my mouth water. I knew exactly where I was going to stop on my way back to my truck.

I glanced through the window at the business next to the coffee shop and bookstore and caught sight of something I wanted to taste more than diner foods, sugary sweets, or even rich java brews. Maegan. Fuck me! I thought she looked adorable and sexy in her pajamas the night before, but that sexy librarian thing she was rocking sent my lust into hyperdrive. I jerked to a stop and watched as she strode angrily toward a guy in her store. The blonde curls she had piled on top of her head bounced with every step as did her amazing tits that strained against the pale pink sweater set she wore. Her long legs were encased in black tights beneath a black and floral print skirt that hugged her hips and legs to just below midthigh. The chunky black heels she wore gave her a few more inches of height.

Jesus, I wanted to push that skirt up her hips, rip those tights and panties off and bury my dick so far inside her. Lust clawed at my guts and my pulse pounded like the fucking tribal drums they used to play before going into battle. My tempo wasn't a battle cry though, it was a call to mate, to possess, and claim. So help me, the skin on my dick would be raw if I didn't get my hands on her soon.

Maegan marched right up to the guy in a way that made me think she was going to slug him, but instead she crossed her arms over her chest, which pushed her glorious boobs higher. The only thing preventing me from popping full wood was the changes of expression in her face as the guy started talking. I didn't need to overhear them to know what was going on. The guy was trying to sweet talk his way into her panties, and Maegan wanted no part of it. I didn't want him to have any fucking part of it either. I was the one who would make Maegan soak her panties, and I was the man who would pull them down her legs.

Rage filled me at the thought of that man, or any other, touching Maegan. Everything about her posture was screaming no, but the douche canoe wasn't getting it. I hated men like him with a passion. I jerked the door open forcefully but the two of them were so engrossed in their conversation that they didn't hear me.

"Sloppy seconds just aren't my style, Clayton. Move along before this gets really embarrassing for you." Maegan had the trifecta working in her favor: intelligence, sexy, and feisty. I wanted it all to myself. *Take a fucking hike, Clayton.*

"Maegan…"

"I believe the lady asked you to leave," I said firmly. Maegan stiffened but didn't turn around.

"I'll call you later."

"No, you won't," Maegan and I said at the same time.

"Who the fuck are you?" the dumbass demanded to know.

I don't know why I did it, because I didn't have the right to touch her in such a familiar way, but I walked to her and placed my hand on her shoulder. Maegan relaxed immediately beneath my touch.

"Who I am isn't important," I said in the most menacing voice I could muster. "Leave this store and do not bother her again."

"See you around, Maegan," the tool said as he beat a hasty retreat out the door.

Drop your hand and step back. Drop your hand and step back. Did I do those things? No. I liked my hand on her body and battled the urge to let it roam freely over her soft curves. Instead of pulling back, I gently dug my thumb in her neck and massaged small circles. The tension melted away as her body warmed beneath my touch, releasing the scent of her perfume or body wash. Maegan's outfit was ladylike and demure, but her sultry fragrance screamed of long nights filled with hard fucking and back clawing.

A tiny whimper escaped her lips and her head fell forward invitingly. My second hand joined the first and I dug my thumbs a little deeper in her soft skin on either side of her neck, eliciting a long moan from her. My dick was on high alert and if Maegan took a half-step back her ass would've encountered the proof of just how much I wanted her.

I had a succinct feeling that Maegan was multifaceted like a high-quality diamond. I caught a glimpse of her vulnerability the night before and the force of her strength as she faced down someone much bigger than her the very next morning. She didn't need my assistance, but she accepted it without complaint. She wore a spicy fragrance beneath elegant clothes. Maegan's light green eyes were both honest and mysterious at the same time. She was a beautiful riddle that I desperately wanted to solve, but not too fast. I wanted to take my time uncovering all the facets of Maegan Miracle, starting with her body.

"Don't stop," she said huskily.

"I've been wanting to hear you say that since the moment we met."

A delicate shiver worked its way through her body. I knew

without a doubt where this was heading. The only question was how long it took us to get there.

"Aren't you going to introduce me to your *friend*, Maegan?"

She stiffened then stepped out from beneath my hands, breaking the contact as sharply as the interloper broke our connection. Maegan turned around and looked at me for the first time since I walked into the shop. She smiled sweetly, but the heat in her eyes told me how affected she was by my touch.

"Um, hellooo," the guy said. "Earth to Mae." She turned her head and pinned the guy with a death glare so fierce that I expected laser beams to shoot out of her eyes and zap him into oblivion.

I chuckled then turned to assess my potential competition. He was a few inches taller than Maegan, but still shorter than my six-four height. He had medium-brown hair styled in a boyband fashion and guileless blue eyes that twinkled with mirth.

"Well, I guess it's up to me to do the introductions." He sort of muscled his way between us and held out his hand in greeting. "I'm Milo Miracle, Maegan's older, dashing brother."

"Elijah Markham," I said, shaking his hand. "Maegan's new neighbor."

"Oh, so you're responsible for my sister walking funny today," he said. *Brother. Good to know.*

"Excuse me?" I asked.

Maegan made a noise like she was choking on air. "I'm going to kill you, Milo." I should've told her it wasn't wise to threaten someone in my presence, but I was having too good of a time. I wished that I was the reason Maegan was walking funny, although I didn't want her to actually be injured, if you know what I mean.

"She told me about chasing Lulu into your yard and stepping on a stick in her bare feet. She had a splinter and that was the reason why she was limping earlier."

"Maybe I should look at it. Is it infected?"

"Are you a doctor?" Milo asked.

"Cop," I replied absently.

"You're Adrian's new partner," Milo observed out loud, but neither Maegan nor I were paying him much attention.

"Were there any red streaks around the wound."

"I'm fine, Elijah," Maegan said softly. "I promise." She looked at her brother once more and rolled her eyes. "Milo is exaggerating as divas are prone to do."

"Diva? Me?" He batted his eyelashes.

"Excuse me," said a timid voice from the doorway that led to Books and Brew. "Milo, the espresso machine is acting up again."

"I'll be right there, Sara," Milo said before he turned his inquisitive gaze on me again. "Well, it's nice to meet you. I'm sure I'll see you around... town."

"Nice meeting you too," I said to his retreating back before I zeroed in on Maegan. "Hi, Freckles."

"Hi," she said, sounding almost shy.

"Were you limping this morning?" I asked. I didn't notice her limping when she charged toward that doofus. It was possible that anger made her temporarily forget her injury.

"I'm fine." Her face flamed a deep red, and I couldn't imagine what part of my question made her so uncomfortable. I mean, if I asked her that after a night of sex... Maegan chewed her bottom lip and slid her pearl necklace between her thumb and forefinger as she diverted her eyes away from mine.

Fuck me! Maegan Miracle spent the night having very filthy thoughts about me then did something about it. Jesus, my dick got impossibly hard at the thought of her pleasuring herself after getting turned on by the sight of my body. How many times? Once? Twice? I jerked off four times and each time I fantasized about a new position I would take her in.

I slid my finger beneath her chin and tipped her head so that I could look into her eyes. I was back to wondering how long before I knew every inch of her delectable body. The answering heat I saw in her eyes said not long. *Don't be a dick, Elijah. Make conversation and quit staring down at her cleavage. Act like you have some fucking class.*

"I couldn't sleep from wanting you. Oh, Freckles, the things I want to do to you would scare you to death." *Real classy, asshole.* I stopped just shy of telling her I practically pulled the skin off my dick.

Her bottom lip quivered but not from fear. Her pink tongue darted out to lick the plump flesh and I groaned embarrassingly loud. More than anything in the world, right then all I wanted was a small taste of her. I looked around and saw that we were still alone and there was an empty office in the back of the store. I grabbed her hand and tugged her inside.

I shut the door and backed her up against it then lowered my head until my lips were centimeters away from hers. "I hope your boss doesn't mind us using the office, but I won't go another minute without knowing how you taste." I wasn't a total caveman for crying out loud; I gave her the chance to tell me to get lost.

"She's a real bitch sometimes, but she'd kick my ass if I didn't take advantage of the opportunity."

Maegan slid her hands in my hair, pulling me the rest of the way until our lips met—tentatively at first while we learned the texture of each other's flesh. I put my hands on either side of her head, caging her against the door. Maegan's lips trembled shyly until I leaned my full weight against her body and she felt how badly I wanted her. Then she turned into a wildcat who literally left claw marks on my scalp as she raked her nails through my hair. She boldly slid her tongue against my lips seeking entrance. When I opened to her, she pulled her tongue back out teasingly. I pulled back and looked down into her wicked eyes. She smiled seductively and pressed her pelvis against my erection, seeking friction.

I dropped my arms, cupped her round ass, and lifted her in the air. Maegan cried out in delight as she wrapped her legs around my waist. Her cries turned into guttural moans as I ground my hard-on against her crotch. I felt her heat and smelled her arousal. I knew damn well she'd be dripping wet if I slid my fingers beneath her panties.

Maegan grabbed my head and gave me the most blistering hot kiss I'd ever had as she rode my cock, seeking her pleasure. Fuck! I worried I would blow my load because no woman had ever made me so hot and horny so fast. We alternated between rubbing our tongues together or Maegan sucking my tongue into her mouth like it was my cock. The only noise was our choppy panting and the creaking my leather jacket made when she gripped my shoulders for leverage and rode my dick harder. Fuck! What would happen when I finally spread this girl beneath me in the bed?

Maegan ripped her mouth from mine, leaned her head against the door, and came hard silently with her mouth hanging open and a startled look in her eyes. If I didn't know better, I would say that Maegan just shocked herself, but why? Was it her bold behavior or the orgasm itself that caught her by surprise?

"I can't believe I just dry humped you in my office," she rasped. She sounded like she had been trapped in a desert for a day with no water. "I should be embarrassed, but I'm not."

"I'm not complaining," I said, gently pushing back the damp tendrils of hair that stuck to her face. Then I realized what she said. We were in *her* office. "So, you're the boss, huh?" I asked casually like I didn't want to drop to my knees and pull her tights down so I could lick her juices from her hot cunt.

"Yep. Milo and I own both businesses and lease the third space to our friend," she said proudly. She made no attempt to wiggle out of my arms and had returned her hands to my hair. I was a sweaty mess in the small confines of her office, but she didn't seem to mind. She looked me straight in the eye and said, "I couldn't sleep from wanting you either."

I groaned and leaned my head forward, resting it against her collarbone. It got me closer to the glorious treasure I couldn't wait to get my hands, lips, and dick on. Yeah, I wanted to squeeze her tits together and slide my dick in and out of the tight tunnel they made. I wasn't sure how much further Maegan was going to take things in her business, but I took a chance and slid one of my hands between her parted legs to stroke over her soaked tights.

"You smell so fucking good, Maegan. I can't wait to taste you." I acted like it was a foregone conclusion and she didn't challenge me. In fact, she whimpered and pushed against me. I don't know what would've happened next had the little bell over her door not jingled.

"Fuck!" she whispered and wiggled free from my hold. She straightened her clothes and ran her hand over her hair. "Do I look like I just had an orgasm in my office?"

"Yes."

"Oh my!" She placed her hands over her cheeks like she was trying to cool her heated skin. She looked and sounded like a prim librarian again, which did nothing to deflate my raging hard-on. It had the reverse effect. "I got to get out there."

"Do you have a bathroom?"

"Uh, yes. It's right around the corner." She looked down at my bulging crotch, licking her lips. I saw the confliction in her eyes and the desire to return the favor, but her customer wasn't going anywhere.

"Yoo-hoo," the female customer hollered out. "Maegan, are you in there?"

"I'll be right out, Mrs. Tanbury." She inhaled deeply and released it slowly. "Are you free for dinner tonight?"

"Fuck, yes."

"Is six thirty too late to eat?"

"No," I told her. "Maegan," I said stopping her before she could leave. "I like dessert first."

"Fuck, yes," she whispered back before she opened the door and disappeared. "What can I do for you, Mrs. Tanbury?" She didn't sound like a woman who'd just came apart in my arms and dampened the front of my pants.

I gave Maegan a few minutes to create a diversion by pulling the woman into a conversation before I slipped out of her office and walked to her bathroom. The space was small, clean, and completely feminine. It smelled of whatever deliciousness she put on her soft skin. My dick was so fucking hard it hurt when I released it from the confines of my jeans and underwear. Jerking off in Maegan's bathroom wasn't how I wanted to come, but it would do until I got her alone later that night.

I took my swollen flesh in my hands and pumped it while thinking of Maegan's lips and the way I wanted to fuck her mouth. I fantasized about pulling out right before I came and painting her fair skin with a different kind of pearl necklace. It didn't take many strokes before I shot my load in the wad of tissues I yanked from the container on the vanity. Once the room stopped spinning, I washed my hands and tucked my dick away.

Maegan was still with the elderly customer when I walked back into the store. She caught my eye as I walked past. Maegan blushed prettily and I knew she was thinking about what I'd just done in her bathroom. There was no shame in my game, so I winked playfully before I walked out of her store and into the harsh winter afternoon. Not even freezing temperatures could douse the heat simmering inside me.

Tonight, Freckles.

Chapter Five

Maegan

MY CHEEKS HEATED WITH EMBARRASSMENT EVERY TIME I thought about the way I shamelessly rode Elijah's erection in my office, which meant my face stayed red all fucking day long. I couldn't believe I'd been so bold, or came so fast, or so hard. Pleasure had ripped through me so intense that my lungs froze and robbed me of the ability to even groan. Remembering his dirty talk and knowing he jerked off in my bathroom kept me aroused all damn day long also. My nipples felt chaffed from rubbing against their lace prison, and I thought the only thing that would make them feel better was Elijah's lips and tongue.

What had I been thinking? My store could've been impacted negatively had anyone caught us. My businesses were everything to me, and I couldn't afford to act so stupidly again.

"Want to grab a bite to eat with me?" Milo asked as I locked the door to my shop and stepped into the alley behind our businesses. Books and Brew would be open for a few more hours, but the night crew had it under control.

"Um, I can't tonight," I replied. "How about tomorrow night?"

"What are you doing tonight? Or shall I ask whom?"

"Milo." I said his name in the same exasperated tone our mother had used on us since we were born.

"Fine," he said, raising his hands in surrender. Then he hooked his arm around my neck and pulled me into a hug. "Just be careful."

"I will."

I let Lulu out to do her thing as soon as I got home then looked through my refrigerator to see what I could whip together for dinner. My options were on the thin side since I was a few days away from my next grocery trip. I glanced at the clock and thought I had enough time for a quick trip to the store to grab something a little more appealing than breakfast for dinner. A knock sounded on my back door, and I saw Elijah standing on the porch.

Oh my God! He was an hour early! I had planned on taking a shower and shaving my legs, even though I'd done it just two days prior, reapply my makeup, and put on something a little sexier than what I wore to work that day. *Although he seemed to like it just fine.*

I stood staring at him through the window, unable to walk toward him or run, until he held up a pizza box and a six-pack of bottled beer—the good stuff. His wicked smile said he was ten steps ahead of me. I returned his smile when I opened the door.

"You're a little early," I said, leaning against the doorjamb. I didn't want to appear too eager to ride his cock again. I figured the guy should work for it a little.

"I couldn't stop thinking about you. Invite me in, Freckles."

His gravelly voice weakened my knees, but I managed to step back so he could enter. Once again, I found myself pushed up against a door as soon as Elijah put the pizza box and beer on the counter.

"I bet you had plans to shower, didn't you?" I thought his question was a little strange until he spoke again. "I didn't want you to wash the scent of your orgasm off your cunt. I wanted to taste it."

"I was hoping you could give me another one," I said, confidently pushing my hips against his like I tried seducing men every single day.

"That's a promise, Freckles, but I still want to taste the first one."

It felt like slow motion as he lowered himself to his knees. Power surged through me, kicking my lust into overdrive at seeing such a strong, powerful man at my feet. Elijah only broke eye contact when he removed my black leather, high-heeled Mary Janes. Then his hot gaze journeyed slowly from my stocking-clad feet up to meet my eyes, lingering on the juncture between my thighs and my breasts, of course.

His tongue darted out to moisten his lips, and I squeezed my thighs together, hoping that my wet pussy lips lived up to the expectation I saw in his eyes. Elijah placed his hands at the back of my knees and slowly inched them up until they reached the hem of my skirt. He bunched the material in his large hands and kept moving upwards until my skirt was wrapped around my waist.

Elijah broke eye contact again when he pressed his nose against my pubis and inhaled deeply into his nose. He closed his eyes and growled in the back of his throat, making my pussy even wetter. When Elijah reopened his eyelids, his dark brown eyes were nearly black with lust. My lips parted and a shaky breath staggered out when he reached for the waistband of my tights. Like with lifting my skirt, Elijah took his time pulling them down over my hips and revealing the delicate pink lace of my thong. He stopped once my tights were midthigh and pressed his nose against the lace.

"Fuck me," he whispered reverently. I felt his hot breath against my sensitive pussy lips.

"I plan on it," I answered boldly.

"You're going to be the death of me, Freckles."

"It will be a glorious death though," I promised. *Where had that come from? When did I start guaranteeing a good time like a promise written on a bathroom stall?*

Elijah finished pulling my tights off and tossed them over his shoulder. "You're a walking contradiction," he said as he traced the lines of the flower petals tattooed on upper thigh with his finger.

"Beneath that demure, elegant outfit lives a woman who is bold and raw in her desires." Elijah slowly rose to his feet, his body brushing against mine. "Take me to your room, Freckles."

I didn't bother pushing my skirt back down; I rather liked the idea of him checking out my ass when I walked up the steps in front of him. I was damn proud of my ass. I took him by the hand and led him up the steps, but we didn't make it to the top before he released my hand and grabbed my hips, halting my progress.

Elijah dropped to his knees on two steps beneath mine. "Bend over, brace your hands on the stairs, and spread your legs."

I did what he asked and felt the coolness of the air on my pussy when Elijah pulled the thin strip of lace to the side exposing the most intimate part of me. Goose bumps pebbled across my skin when I felt the heat of his breath on my bare lips. My body was both hot and cold at the same time as I waited for him to make his next move. When it came, I should've been mortified, but I had never in my life been so damn turned on.

Elijah licked a path from the top of my ass to my clit then practically buried his nose between my ass cheeks so he could work my pussy with his tongue. He started out with teasing little licks along the folds of my lips, then my clit, before he speared my cunt with his tongue.

"Elijah," I whispered hoarsely. Nothing in my life had ever felt so good. My stomach clenched tight with a pending orgasm. Instead of shrinking away in horror over my wanton behavior, I pushed back against his seeking tongue.

For the first time in my life, I embraced the rawness and boldness that seemed to drive him wild. I wanted to come with Elijah's tongue in my pussy, and I was going to get it. He reached between my thighs and began rubbing little circles against my swollen, nerve-laden clit. I didn't whimper and plead, I growled and demanded, "More."

Elijah gripped my panties in his hands and ripped them as easily as tearing a blade of grass in two. My body tightened all over as he worked me closer and closer to my orgasm with his deft tongue and finger. The position pulled my hamstrings tight, but I knew my legs were shaking from pleasure, not pain.

He pulled back suddenly, stood up, and then playfully swatted my ass. "Up the stairs," he gruffly said.

I stood up too fast and was a bit dizzy. I didn't want to continue up the stairs; I wanted to come.

"I'm going to strip you bare, lay you down, then bury my head between your thighs until you come. I thought you might appreciate a more comfortable location."

That was enough to get me going again. When we reached my room, I turned to face him. I put my hand on his chest to halt his progress. He unleashed a side of me I never knew existed, and I was giving the horny bitch free reign. I slid my hands between my legs and teased my clit before I delved my fingers between my lips, coating my fingers with my wetness.

The wildness I saw in his eyes spurred me on, and I continued to toy with myself in front of him. I used just enough pressure to tease and arouse, but not enough to make myself come. I saw in his eyes when he reached the breaking point. Elijah opened his mouth to protest his treatment, but I silenced him by pressing one of my wet fingers against his lips.

Elijah growled and grabbed my wrist before I could pull it back. He sucked the two digits I'd used to finger myself into his mouth. His eyes never left mine as he cleaned my fingers thoroughly.

"My turn."

He whipped my skirt down my legs and I stood there bare from the waist down. It felt dirty, raw, and so fucking thrilling that my heart thundered hard in my chest, drowning out any sort of protest the practical side of me might've voiced. He was a complete stranger after all—one that made me burn with the desire to fuck like I've never known. My eyes dared him to do his worst.

Elijah slowly pulled my sweater set over my head like he was savoring every inch of my skin that he revealed. Then I stood before him wearing a lacy bra that hid nothing from his eyes, a pearl necklace, and a wanton smile. He placed his hands on my hips and left them there while he feasted his eyes on my cleavage. I started to reach for the clasp between my breasts, but his words stopped me.

"Leave it." Elijah's voice was rough and his features were as hard as stone from arousal. His cock strained beneath his jeans, and I couldn't wait to feel him pounding inside me.

Elijah walked me backwards and laid me on the bed but he still didn't move to uncover the breasts he couldn't stop staring at. He cupped my knees and spread my legs wide, but didn't go down on me. Instead, he situated his fully clothed body between them, lowered his head, and teased a taut nipple through the lace with his tongue. Feeling his hot breath against my sensitive nipples had me bucking beneath him. I wanted to feel that mouth even lower. I cried out when he sucked the lace-covered nipple hard into his mouth.

I dug my nails into his skin, but his flannel shirt acted as a buffer. Elijah grunted his pleasure then turned his attention to my other breast. I dug my heels into the bed and pushed my pelvis against his stomach. The friction was enough to make my eyes roll back into my head. It wouldn't take much to set me off after the tongue-lashing he gave me on the staircase.

"Don't you dare come without my tongue in your pussy," he said darkly as he pushed my breasts together. Elijah lowered his head and licked the swells that rose above the lace cups before he nestled his nose in the valley between them. Without warning, he gripped the fabric and tore it too. I gasped at the sting of the lace scraping against my skin, but it was all forgotten when nothing stood between his mouth and my bare flesh.

Elijah ravaged my breasts in the best possible way. My nipples were licked, sucked, nibbled, and even scraped with his scruffy chin until Elijah had his fill. Then he released them and locked his eyes on mine as he scooted down my body.

"Ready to come?"

"Gee, I'm not… Fuck!" I yelled when Elijah sucked my swollen clit into his mouth at the same time he slid a finger inside my soaking cunt. It was like he had the GPS coordinates to my G-spot because he nailed it on the first try. A second finger joined the first and he worked me in and out, driving me out of my mind. "Oh… Oh… Fuck!" Elijah pulled his fingers out of me and pressed that hand against my stomach to hold me still while he speared my opening with his tongue. His nose bumped against my clit, sending me spiraling over the edge. Every muscle in my body pulled tight as I arched my back off the bed. My orgasm flowed through my body like a heat wave, starting below my belly button then spreading up and down my body. I didn't even try to stave off my response to him. I bucked my hips against his face as my pussy spasmed around his tongue.

Elijah sucked and laved between my legs like it was the best thing he'd ever had until the last spasm faded. My body's descent from pleasure was like a feather drifting on a breeze, slow and airy. Then I looked into the hungriest dark eyes I'd ever seen and knew we were just getting started.

He rose to his knees and yanked his flannel shirt off his strong shoulders and down his long arms. I jackknifed to a sitting position and grabbed the hem of his black T-shirt and tugged upward. Elijah reached behind him and grabbed the neck of the shirt and whipped it over his head, leaving me eye level with that sexy chest and stomach I'd thought so much about since I first laid my eyes on it.

I leaned forward and teased his navel with my tongue while I boldly cupped him through his jeans. I looked up into his eyes while I worked his button loose, pulled his zipper down, and licked the skin just above the waistband of his underwear. He tasted bold and spicy; I couldn't wait to sample the rest of him. I gave Elijah a dose of his own medicine when I placed my nose against his underwear and breathed him in. Lord, his arousal triggered mine to fire back up again. I sucked the head of his dick through the cotton and tasted his salty essence on my tongue. The groans I pulled from him told me how much he liked it, so I continued to tease him, noting the circle of wetness on his underwear was spreading and getting bigger the more excited he became.

Elijah put his hand on my neck and slid it up into my hair, clinching my curls in a fist, but not hard enough to hurt me. I knew what he wanted; and I was going to give it to him.

Chapter Six

Elijah

GODDAMN! MAEGAN MIRACLE EXERTING HER POWER OVER me and making me squirm was the sexiest thing I'd ever seen. The look in her eyes spoke volumes; she had me right where she wanted me and she planned to enjoy every second of my torture.

She took her time working my pants to midthigh before reaching for the waistband of my underwear. Maegan unwrapped me like a highly-anticipated present, slowly revealing the head of my dick then the long, thick shaft, which sprung forward proudly to greet her when she freed it from its prison. Maegan tucked my underwear beneath my sac and stared at me with wide eyes.

"Oh my."

Look, I don't mean to sound like an arrogant prick, but a man knows when he's hung. I was huge everywhere so it only made sense that my dick was proportionate to my body. I worked several hours a week to maintain a hard physique, and I didn't have to be narcissistic to know that I looked good. I didn't need to be a psychic either to know that Maegan's reaction was delight and not fear.

"I need you to touch me now, Freckles."

Maegan tore her gaze away from my cock and looked into my eyes. Her wicked smile said that she heard the hint of desperation in my voice. Instead of reaching for my cock that bobbed between our bodies, she cupped my heavy sac in her hand and firmly massaged my balls. Maegan broke eye contact and pressed her mouth to my sternum then kissed a path along the swell of my pectoral muscle as she massaged and tugged on my boys. My fists flexed in her hair as I fought the urge to take control, but I held back. I couldn't say why, but I almost felt like I was being tested, and failure wasn't an option here. Instead of pushing Maegan's head down toward my dick, or pulling her up toward my nipples, I let her start back in the center of my chest and repeat the same exploration on the other side while I breathed heavily through my nose like a horse who'd been rode hard.

Damn, I wanted to be rode hard and put away wet—so fucking wet. *Be patient. Don't rush her.*

"You're beautiful," Maegan whispered reverently against my skin in between her tiny kisses that created huge sparks. "Flawless."

I'd received my fair share of compliments from the ladies, but no one had ever called me beautiful. Maegan's praise meant more to me than any I'd ever received; it made me want to beat my chest. Just when I thought I couldn't take another second without her tongue on my heated flesh, she eased her tongue out between her lush lips, curled it upward, and teased my hard nipple. Around and around, she swirled her tongue around the pebbled flesh, moaning like my flesh was the best thing she'd ever tasted.

"You're killing me, darlin'."

"I haven't even started yet, *darlin'*."

I had a feeling I was going to love her brand of torture, but my hands were no longer willing to remain idle. I slid them down her sleek back and cupped her luscious ass in both hands and squeezed. It was hard to say what my favorite part of Maegan was—her tight ass, delectable pussy, or her bountiful tits. I was going to need many rounds of energetic sex before I could choose, and even then, it might prove to be too difficult of a task.

I teased the crack of her ass with my middle finger, pressing playfully against her furled hole with each pass. Maegan didn't shy away from my boldness, she embraced it and stepped up her game too by reaching behind my balls to tease my taint. If she kept it up, I would splatter her tits with cum long before I wanted to.

As much as I loved the feel of her pink tongue rasping over my nipples, I was ready for her to wrap those lips around my cock. I scooted out of her grasp, stood up, and shucked my jeans, underwear, socks, and shoes. I wrapped my hand around my cock and began slow, steady strokes that threatened my sanity. I swiped my finger over my leaking slit, gathering my slick pre-cum then smeared it on her full bottom lip.

Maegan's eyes widened in surprise, but her tongue darted out to capture the proof of my excitement from her lip. I brought my thumb up to her mouth and rubbed her wet lips before I slid the tip of my thumb into her mouth. "Suck me."

Maegan's chuckle vibrated against my thumb, but she wrapped her lips tightly around my digit and worked it in and out of her mouth. My eyes nearly rolled in the back of my head from anticipation of having her suck my dick into her mouth just like that. Maegan pulled off my thumb, curled her tongue around the tip, then sucked it back in again.

In her bright green eyes, I saw her challenge me to take what I wanted. "Lie on your bed, and I'll give you just what you need." I retrieved the condoms I tucked away in my wallet and tossed them on the bed.

She did as I commanded, spreading her legs and toying with her wet cunt in a way that made me insane to sink my dick inside her tight heat. Damn, I wanted to pound that pussy, but instead of suiting up and claiming that hot haven for my own, I straddled her chest and rubbed my seeping cock against her mouth.

Maegan's tongue darted out to lick the slick trail I left behind. I continued to paint her lips with my spunk while she licked them like it was a tasty lip gloss she couldn't help but devour the second she put it on.

"Open for me, Freckles."

She smiled devilishly before she opened wide enough for me to ease my swollen head inside. Maegan wrapped her lips tightly around the crown and sucked, rubbing her tongue against that sensitive spot beneath the crown.

My entire body shook from restraining myself, fighting the natural urge to push my cock as far into her mouth as she could take. Burying my cock in her throat was the single most important thing in my life right then, but I wouldn't sacrifice the trust I saw in her luminous eyes. So, I waited until her lips softened then eased my erection further inside her wet, hot mouth. Maegan's tongue provided mind-blowing friction against the underside of my cock, making it nearly impossible to hold back when I wanted to rut until I came down her throat.

I rocked my hips forward and back, in and out, while Maegan sucked and moaned around my flesh like she couldn't get enough of my cock. It took everything I had in me to pull out of her mouth, but there was so much I wanted to do to her before I busted a nut. I wasn't some randy teenage boy who couldn't control myself; I was the man who was going to give Maegan the lay of her life.

My cock glistened with her saliva when I withdrew it from her mouth. I scooted back a little further, took her glorious tits in my hands, and pushed them together. I thrust my cock between the large, firm mounds while circling her nipples with my thumbs.

"So fucking hot," I said, watching the head of my dick disappear into her cleavage and pop out the top. My body shook hard with want and need. I felt my orgasm building inside me and there was no fucking way I was coming anywhere other than inside her pussy our first time together.

I released her perfect mounds to reach for a foil packet, making quick work of tearing it open with my teeth and rolling it onto my cock. Then I was between her legs with my swollen dick in my hands, rubbing and teasing her cunt instead of pushing hard inside her like I wanted.

I released my cock to part the lips of her pussy and tease her opening with my thumbs. "Fucking t-t-tease," Maegan stammered between gritted teeth. "Fuck me, dammit!"

"So impatient, Freckles."

"Fuck me, Elijah!"

I buried my cock in her pussy in one hard push. Maegan cried out in ecstasy and dug her fingernails in my ass, pulling me deeper inside her hot channel. I knew I wouldn't last long and wanted to see her come apart beneath me with my dick inside her pussy. Making her scream my name took precedence over my own needs. I reared back and slammed inside her again and again. I didn't have to worry about trying to read her signs, she made her desire known.

"Yes! Fuck me, Elijah!" She pulled my head down for a hot kiss, but ripped her mouth away so she could groan loudly. "Right there… Oh my God! I've never… Yes! Fuck, yes!"

Her pussy spasmed around my cock, and I couldn't hold back another second. I pinned her hands above her head as white-heat burned me from head to toe and bolts of both pleasure and pain zapped my balls. I finally knew what it meant by something hurting so good.

"You feel so goddamned good," I gruffly said as the pleasure built, pulling my body taut. And like with a rubber band, my body snapped when the pressure became too much. "Maegan!" I roared her name, rutting inside her and riding out my orgasm as I flooded the condom.

I collapsed on top of her but braced the bulk of my weight on my elbows. I loved the feel of her lush tits pushing into my chest as she labored to catch her breath. I reluctantly pulled my softening dick out of her tight heat, but I needed to dispose of the condom.

"There." Maegan pointed to a trash can beside her nightstand. She lay sprawled across her bed wearing nothing but that pearl necklace and a satisfied smile. Seeing her looking so deliriously happy made me want to strut my stuff, but it would take a while before I had the strength in my legs to pull it off. She looked pretty damned pleased with herself too, as she should. "I'm going to be walking funny for a week after the orgasms you gave me last night and tonight."

"How many?"

"A lady never tells."

"There was nothing ladylike about you just now when you demanded I fuck you. So, Freckles, tell me. How many times did I make you come?" Finding out became my number-one mission and I wasn't above playing dirty to get the answer.

"About every four hours throughout the night," Maegan said. "I would come, fall asleep, dream of you, then wake up hot and sweaty with a throbbing clit that wouldn't let me rest until I rubbed one out again. How about you? Did you jerk off last night while thinking about me?" So much fucking boldness, and not a drop of shame for the way she felt. She was pure perfection.

"Until I thought I would pull my skin off. Damn, Freckles, you wind me up." A thought suddenly occurred to me. "Did you touch yourself after I left your shop?"

"No, but I wanted to."

"Jesus, your honesty and the way you go after what you want is so damn sexy," I told her, brushing the damp hair off her forehead.

"I don't believe in lies and games." Maegan ran her finger across my collarbone then below to the jagged scar on my left shoulder that I received in a bar fight during my wilder days. I could tell she wanted to know about it, but didn't ask. Instead she raised her head and pressed a gentle kiss on the ugly, raised skin. "What you see is what you get with me, Elijah."

"I like what I see." It was true. There wasn't anything about her that I didn't like. Seeing the sexy tattoos she hid beneath her clothes intrigued me. The one on her thigh was my favorite because I pictured myself tracing every detail of the flowers and vines with my tongue before I licked and sucked a path to her delicious pussy. What stood out more to me in my post-coital bliss was how badly I wanted to get to know Maegan. What was her favorite music, food, and movies. Did she like sports? Did she prefer television or movies? Batman or Superman?

It had been a long time since I wanted to know something about a woman other than how good she was in bed. Normally, I showed up, we both came, and then I went home. I never repeated sex with the same woman. It was one and done; no exceptions. I wasn't relationship material—not anymore. Maegan was different; she made me want to linger in her bed and… cuddle. *Fuck!*

"You're starting to freak out. Why?"

"I am not," I said, but it sounded pretty weak.

"Your body is tense, and I can hear you thinking," Maegan countered. "You're not worried that I'm going to start making demands on your time, are you? I'm not even sure I like you beyond your magnificent body and magic cock."

"Magic cock," I scoffed.

"Trust me, sexy. It was pure magic for me." She tweaked my nipple. "Seriously, relax and don't worry that you'll find me waiting on your front porch for you to come home from work or start stalking you around town."

"What do you want from me?" I asked after a few moments of awkward silence. I was almost afraid to hear the answer. I was going to be unhappy if she said she wanted nothing, but I wasn't going to be happy if she said she wanted to date. The only thing I could offer her was sex, but Maegan didn't strike me as fuck buddy material.

"Sex and pizza."

"More sex?" I asked to clarify.

"If you do," she said, sounding nervous for the first time that night.

Did I want repeat sex with Maegan? "Yes. Yes, I do."

"Mmmmm. Soooo good, Elijah." Maegan was as vocal about her love of food as she was about her love for my cock, which stirred when it couldn't tell the difference between sex and food moans. "Damn, that hit the spot." *Oh, I planned to hit that spot again and again and again.*

I set my beer on her coffee table and looked at Maegan. Her hair was piled on top of her head in a messy bun with rebellious strands escaping and framing her face. I would've thought it was artfully done had I not watched her do it in less than a minute. My flannel shirt looked so much better on her than it did me, especially when it was closed by the one button between her tits. She'd put on a pair of panties she called boy shorts. They looked like boxer briefs for women and they were my new favorite thing in the world for the way they snugly fit her ass and made her legs look even longer.

With any luck, I'd be peeling those bad boys off her legs and throwing them over my shoulder. The thought of underwear jarred a memory of me tearing hers off. "I owe you a set of bra and panties."

"Don't worry about it," she said, waving her hand. "But I need to know if you plan to make a habit of it, so I can take advantage of the semi-annual sale next month and stock up."

My breath froze in my throat. Next month was… next month. I knew where I would be living and working, but I had no idea if I would still be ripping underwear off Maegan. I wasn't sure how to answer her, because I didn't want to hurt her feelings. Sensing my internal struggle, Maegan reached over and covered my hand with hers.

"Forget I said that. I wasn't trying to trap you into anything. It was just a casual observation. Okay?"

"Yeah," I said, nodding. "I like you, Maegan, and I don't want to hurt you."

"Then don't." She made it sound so simple, but nothing was easy when it came to human emotions. Maegan smiled sweetly at me. "I only ask that you're honest with me. If I can't handle the truth, then that's on me. I can't stand dishonesty or games. Be upfront and truthful, and I promise you that we won't have any problems."

"Yeah, I can handle that." Only time would tell if that would work between us.

"Good."

We fell silent when Maegan dug into her second slice of pizza, and I resumed drinking my beer. Even though we were virtually strangers, it was a comfortable silence rather than the awkward one you'd expect. I had no idea where the fuck this was going between us, but for the first time in a long time, I wanted to pull someone close instead of walking away without a backward glance.

It was scary shit.

Chapter Seven

Maegan

"**G**OOD AFTERNOON, MY LOVELY GIRL." JACKIE MIRACLE entered Curious Things with a flourish that left no doubt as to where Milo inherited his flair for the dramatic. She walked to me briskly, yet graciously, and kissed the air near my cheeks. *Somebody's been watching her favorite black-and-white films again.* "You look beautiful, Maegan."

I looked down at my tan tweed jacket, high-necked ivory blouse complete with a frilly bow in the front, navy-blue pencil skirt, and brown, knee-high boots that had a respectable size heel to them. I'd worn the same outfit plenty of times before and never received such high praise.

"It's not the outfit; it's the woman beneath it," my mom declared, clearly seeing the confusion I felt over her remark. "There's something different about you. Same beautiful clothes, same beautiful face with intelligent, green eyes, and adorable freckles, yet something is different."

Growing up, I hated my freckles. When I was little, my mother had told me that my freckles were left behind after angels kissed my nose and cheeks. I had looked at Milo and demanded to know why the angels didn't kiss him. Milo had started crying and wanted to know why the angels were mad at him. I said it was because he had boy cooties, of course. Mom just told him that the angels had blessed him with a different kind of sparkle. Milo demanded to know what kind, and she said he'd figure it out someday.

I spent my teen years and early twenties trying to cover my freckles with foundation. Yet, Elijah found them cute and gave me an endearing nickname, and suddenly I was smiling when I looked at them in the mirror. *Angel kisses, indeed.* Ugh! I didn't want to become one of those women who allowed a man to determine their worth, not even one as sexy as my new neighbor. Not that I wanted to go back to hating my freckles, I just wished that I could've concluded that they were cute on my own.

The twinkle in my mother's eyes told me that Milo had been blabbing about my visitor yesterday. She was probably already working on the seating chart for the wedding rehearsal dinner before Elijah crept back across his yard in the pre-dawn light after an amazing round of oral sex. I loved the consideration Elijah showed to my tender pussy, who saw more action since I first met Elijah than probably the entire previous year. His "kiss and make it feel better" motto was one that could easily become an addiction. Of course, I wouldn't be telling my mother any of that.

"Don't pry, Mother. It's unbecoming of a lady."

How many times had I heard that phrase growing up? "Walk, don't run, Maegan." "Speak in softer tones, Maegan." "Stop beating the boys at all the games, Maegan. They don't like that." It went on and on until I was afraid to be myself. I crafted and molded myself into the image my mother wanted for me, but I was fucking miserable. I wanted to laugh heartily, run wild with the boys, and throw my game for no one. We butted heads, my mother and I, fighting fiercely during the first two years of high school, but that all changed my junior year when reality dealt me a hateful blow. Then she was everything I needed and more—my mom, my best friend, my advocate, and my hero. I pushed those thoughts aside because they often led me back to a dark place I hoped to never revisit.

"But 'being a lady is boring,'" she repeated back to me before pulling me into a hug. "It's not nice to remind your mother of her past foolishness." There wasn't an ounce of scorn in her voice. She dropped her Jackie O pretense and kissed my cheeks for real. "I love you so much, Maegan. I only want you to be happy."

"I am happy." I pulled out of her embrace and looked into green eyes that were identical to mine. "Look at me and really see me, Mom. I am very happy. I have an amazing family, the best friends a girl could ask for, and a career that I love." It was more than most people had, and I'd humbly accepted it as my fate years ago.

An image of a dark-haired Adonis with sexy, brown eyes sprawled in my bed while I worked his cock with my mouth or fist sprung to mind, reminding me of how right he felt in my bed and body. *Don't get your hopes up, Maegan. It was just one night. Don't forget how tense he was after that first mind-blowing orgasm subsided. He was ready to bolt. Keep your guard up!*

"So, what do I owe this pleasure?"

"Can't a mother just want to have lunch with her daughter?"

"Yes, I suppose she could." I knew better though. "Bonnie, I'm going to head out to lunch with my mom. I won't be long. Would you like for me to bring you something back?"

"Don't you worry about me, Maegan. I brought my lunch, but thank you for asking me. Take as long as you'd like since you'll be rooting around in some dank cellar or musty attic tonight," Bonnie replied.

"Cellar? Attic?" My mom sounded pretty damn disappointed that my life didn't drastically change the second that tall, dark, and sexy entered my world. "That's how you plan to spend your Friday night?"

"Part of it," I answered. I had no idea if, or when, I would see Elijah again. I was no longer the kind of girl who sat around their house waiting for Prince Charming to ride up on his white steed and save the day. I had a business to run, memories to make, and amazing treasures to sort through with my trusty sidekick, Memphis.

"I can't wait to hear what you find. It always amazes me how some things never go out of style and everything else seems to come back in to style eventually." My mom waved her hand in the air to encompass my shop. "You really have a beautiful, unique store, Maegan. Your father and I are so very proud of you and Milo."

"Thanks, Mom. That means the world to us."

"It's obvious that you're not going to reveal any secrets to me about your new neighbor, so how about you tell me the latest between Andy and Milo. Are those two still circling each other?"

I think Milo and I were doomed to be miserable the minute we both fell for our best friend's older brother. It works great in books and movies, but not so much in real life. I limped away from the experience a little tattered and bruised but with my dignity intact. Milo was an entirely different story. He and Andy had dated during high school and seemed so in love. Milo was crushed when Andy broke things off when he went to college. I thought he moved on with his life until Andy moved back to Blissville two years ago bringing an air of mystery with him. He was also less cocky and proud, which made him even more attractive to Milo. But like my mom said, they circled each other as they both waited for the other man to make the first move.

"Oh yeah, and it's hilarious." I was so grateful to have her focus off me that I happily threw Milo under the bus and ran over his ass. "They think they're being discreet, but they're anything but."

"It's too bad they can't work past their differences." She sighed dreamily as we stepped out into the cold, winter day. "They make such a beautiful couple." She wasn't wrong. "Hmmm," my mother said as she looked up toward the second story of our buildings.

"What?"

"It's tragic that you have all that wasted space on the second

61

story. I understand you need storage space, but you have a basement beneath the buildings you could use for that. The second-story spaces have separate rear entrances because they used to be apartments years ago. Have you and Milo given thought to remodeling the space to make them into apartments again? There's significant income earning potential there."

"And we just happen to know a single, hunky carpenter."

"I never even thought about that," she said with wide-eyed innocence.

"We have talked about it, but we thought it would be best to try and recoup some of the money we spent remodeling the first-floor window fronts." I tipped my head to the side. "But there's not a lot of work that needs completed and we would start recouping money right away."

My mom looped her arm in mine as we started walking toward the diner. "I agree. Let me know what Milo says about the idea."

I knew exactly how he was going to respond, so I needed to wait for the right moment.

"He's joining us for lunch, so that would be a perfect time."

"No!" Milo shook his head vehemently. "It's too soon after the other renovations."

"Why don't we get an estimate to see how much work and money is involved before we rule it out?" I asked calmly. Mom was just trying to snag a son-in-law by hook or crook from one of her kids, but I was thinking of the earning potential.

"Mae," Milo said, imitating our mother's vexation like a pro. "Why are you pushing so hard for this? I've seen our profit and loss statements. We're doing good, so why can't that be enough?"

I didn't know why, but it wasn't. I was always trying to wrangle some new goal or dream. I'd achieve one thing and set off in search of the next without enjoying the spoils from my previous conquest. I chalked it up to my personality rather than looking for deeper meanings, because I didn't want to dwell on things I couldn't change. Mom gave me the perfect excuse to push this idea harder than I normally would.

"If we were flipping houses, maybe I could see the risk, but you're talking about apartments. There's often high turnover with tenants and a lot of ugliness that comes along with being landlords."

I sat up straighter in my chair. "Flipping houses?"

"Now you did it," our mother said, grinning like the cat that ate the canary Sylvester would be so jealous. I almost expected to see yellow feathers fall out when she opened her mouth to speak again. "It's too bad you guys don't know a carpenter who could take on big projects like that." *Smooth, Mom!*

"What are you talking about?" Milo asked. "Have you forgotten about Andy? He could do it with one arm tied behind his back." It was nice to see him drop his pretense to stick up for his ex. I thought we might be making some progress in our Milo Still Loves Andy mission.

"What can I do with my hands tied behind my back?"

A nicer sister would've told her twin that his heart's desire was in earshot, but I was desperate to see one of us happy for fuck's sake.

"Hello, Andy." My mom once again channeled Jackie O when she rose to her feet to greet Andy. "It's good to see you."

"You too, Mrs. Miracle," Andy said, smiling at my mom as she sat back down. Then he pinned Milo with a questioning look. "You were saying?"

"Milo is thinking about flipping houses," I announced. Milo's eyes nearly bugged out of his head before they narrowed to mere slits in a warning for me to shut up. "My mom mentioned that we would need a carpenter who could take on big jobs like that. Milo said you were man enough—excuse me, carpenter enough—to get the job done."

"Did he?" Andy asked uncertainly. "Hmmm."

"I wanted to renovate the spaces above the shops to make them into apartments again, but Milo wasn't impressed," I told Andy. "He mentioned flipping houses as an alternative."

"Flipping houses takes a lot of capital unless you get really lucky and find a diamond in the rough."

"I'm good at digging until I find the good stuff," I assured Andy. "Why don't we get a ballpark cost analysis for both types of projects. Can we do that?"

"Sure, but it'll be a really rough estimate since I don't know the details on a specific house you're looking to flip." He tipped his head to the side and thought a minute. "I actually have a house in mind. How about I come by tonight to look at the spaces above the shop so I can work up an estimate?"

"That's great, Andy. I'm not available tonight, but Milo is free to let you into his—our—back door." Milo's face flamed red with embarrassment, and I knew he couldn't wait to get even with me.

"What? You don't have a date?" Andy asked Milo.

Milo tore his eyes from mine and looked at Andy as if seeing him for the first time. Did he know he rubbed his tongue along his bottom lip or that Andy couldn't seem to look away from the slight back and forth action.

"Nope," Milo finally said.

"Huh. What time do you want me? To come over," Andy hastily clarified.

My mom sat straighter in her chair and winked at me. I sipped my Coke and watched the various shades of red color spread across Milo's face as his emotions seemed to run the gamut between embarrassment, need, and everything in between. Still, Milo was a cool customer.

"Meet me at Books and Brew at five thirty, and I'll give you the key to look around at your leisure."

"Okay," Andy said like it was no big deal, but I saw the flash of disappointment in his eyes. Milo would've seen it had he looked at

Andy to gauge his reaction. "See you tonight, Milo. Have a good afternoon, ladies."

Nothing was said for several minutes after Andy left until Milo set his fork down and looked up from his plate. "You both will pay dearly for this."

"What?" Mom and I asked innocently at the same time.

"I mentioned turning the second story into apartments not that long ago," I said defensively. "This isn't new."

Milo batted his eyelashes and fanned his face dramatically. "I do declare, Milo. I wish you could find yourself a strapping stud for a carpenter. Oh, I know! Beefcake Andy!"

Okay, once was a fluke, but twice was fate.

"Strapping stud, huh? It's nice to know that you still notice, Milo." Andy chuckled as my brother squirmed in his chair. "Beefcake Andy is a new one though. It's kinda catchy. I was trying to come up with a slogan the other day. The best I could come up with was Handy Andy, but I like yours much better. Perhaps I should change the name of my business and slap that on my T-shirt," he pondered out loud.

"Really, Maegan?" Milo demanded, giving me the same death glare that Dad received from Mom on many occasions. "Not even a little hint that he's standing behind me *again*?" All coolness from earlier was gone as Milo looked back at Andy. "Forget something, Just Andy?"

"Actually, yes," Andy said. All traces of humor slid from his face. "I forgot that I have a prior commitment tonight and won't be able to meet you after all."

"I'm sure you do," Milo replied dryly.

"It's not what you think, Milo. Anyway," Andy said in frustration, "I would cancel if I could, but…"

"I'd never dream of asking you to cancel your plans on a Friday night. We'll do this some other time."

"Milo…"

My brother pinned Andy with a look that expressed how firmly he'd shut that door. "I'll call you next week."

"Are you two happy?" Milo asked once Andy walked away dejectedly. "I can't remember the last time I felt this humiliated."

"Seventh grade," I suggested. "You forgot the words to the song you picked to sing in the variety show."

"Oh my goodness!" My mom threw her head back and laughed. "You practiced that song every day in the bathroom mirror for a solid month. How could you forget the words?"

Milo grinned wryly then shrugged. "Nerves. Performance Anxiety. It happens in more places than the bedroom, you know."

"Divine intervention," I added. "You told them you were going to sing Bette Midler's 'The Rose' then planned to sing 'Like a Virgin' instead. It's a good thing you got stage fright or you would've risked a suspension from school."

"Were you planning to imitate masturbation on a makeshift bed?" Mom asked.

"Who said anything about pretending?"

Mom and I laughed riotously at Milo's response. I could easily imagine the horror on the staff's face if Milo had pulled off his plan—pun intended.

"I'm so happy that I entertain the women in my life," Milo said huffily.

"I'm sorry, Milo. Let me make it up to you."

"How?" he asked cautiously.

"I know just how you really want to spend your Friday night."

"I'm not crawling around in people's dirt and dust to find 'treasures' with you and Memphis." I thought his little air quotes were adorable.

"Oh, come on," I cajoled. "You always have a fun time when you come with us."

"True, but I'll still pass."

"Okay, you can stay home and pine after—"

"Fine, as long as you promise not to bring *him* up."

"Deal." I extended my hand across the table so we could shake on it. I didn't point out that his part of the deal was ambiguous. He didn't specify a timeframe, so I decided to bide my time. Our mom didn't agree to anything of the sort and chose every opportunity to work Andy aka Handy Andy, Beefcake Andy, and Just Andy into the conversation during the remainder of our lunch.

Chapter Eight

Elijah

I WAS IN UNCHARTERED TERRITORY WITH MAEGAN. WELL, THAT was only partially true. I'd sailed the waters before, but it had been a very long time, and my boat ran ashore with catastrophic results. The fact that I didn't want to wash Maegan's scent off my body prompted me to haul my ass to the shower at the ass crack of dawn and do just that.

She's just a piece of ass, Eli. Beautiful, sexy, and alluring, but still just a piece of ass. Don't ever forget it. Don't trust her.

No matter how much my brain urged me to be cautious, my heart—and dick—recalled every single second of the night I spent with her. Running the bar of soap over my flesh reminded me of all the places on my body she touched, kissed, sucked, or licked. Maegan was a very inquisitive girl and the only part of me that she didn't know intimately were the spaces between my toes. Everything else, and I do mean *everything*, had at least been traced or touched by her teasing fingers. As if to mock me, the claw marks she left on my back and ass cheeks stung when I stepped beneath the scalding spray.

I'd never had to pop ibuprofen after sex before, but then again, I wasn't sure what we experienced could be reduced to such a simple word. Every muscle on my body ached from extended tightening and flexing beneath her ministrations. There was so much more than an exchange of body fluids going on, which was the real reason for my panic. That, plus the confession that slid from her lips in the dark.

"Wow, this has never happened to me."

"Multiple orgasms?"

"No, an orgasm with another person."

She had to be fucking with my mind, right? No other guy had managed to make her scream their names? Were they fucking idiots? Were they selfish pricks, or did they just not have any skill in the sack? Man, her words blew my mind. And what was my response to this discovery?

"Huh." *Yep, but it gets better.* "Well, you're welcome." Hey, the lady ignited my soul and I was grappling with everything she made me feel and want.

I waited for the huffy breath and scathing remark—possibly a slap to the face—but Maegan showed me again that she was as unpredictable as choosing the winning lottery numbers. She laughed deep and hard in the darkness, so hard it shook her bed. I couldn't see Maegan, but if I could, I knew her head would be thrown back as laughter rolled out of her. I suspected that Maegan put her full heart, body, and soul into everything she did.

She didn't giggle, she laughed. Maegan didn't make love, she fucked. I instinctively knew that Maegan didn't give her heart easily, but when she did, she gave her whole heart—not just tattered fragments. I was the exact opposite; all I had to offer were shards of the man I used to be, and not many were willing to risk cutting themselves by getting too close. My heart—or was it my dick—wanted me to take a chance on Maegan because she was strong enough to glue the pieces of my shattered soul together again.

Run. Get out now!

Fuck. The strain from wanting to pull Maegan close and push her away created a seesaw effect on my nerves, causing pressure to build inside my head and chest until it felt like I might explode. I flopped down on my bed after toweling off, both grateful and sad that my bed didn't smell like her. *We could rectify that in a heartbeat.* My dick started to swell at just the thought of having that sexy wildcat in my bed. My skin started tingling where she had scored me, making me think she was a sorceress who'd cast a spell. It was like she was sending a message through the marks she left behind. If they could talk, they would have said, "I dare you to try and forget me, Elijah."

Resist!

Lack of sleep from the previous two nights caught up to me, and I fell into a hard and fast sleep. I should've known the riotous emotions would follow me into my dreams and wreak havoc, but the intensity of the memories that flitted through my brain like a cruel kaleidoscope caught me off guard—ambushed me as surely as the Taliban had.

"I'm going to love you forever, Elijah." We were eight years old and I had carved our initials in a tree like some lovesick sap.

"I, Elijah Donovan Markham, take thee, Brandy Lynn Rogers, to be my lawfully wedded wife…" It was supposed to be the happiest day of our lives.

"This war might separate us physically, Elijah, but I'll be right there in your heart. You'll never be alone. Do you hear me? When you get home, I promise to be the first thing you see. It's you and me forever just like we said when we were kids." Words that lifted my battered soul and eased the guilt I felt over leaving her alone.

"I miss you so much, baby, but your family has made me feel so loved." It comforted me to know that my family was taking care of my girl while I was away.

I ignored my gut instinct and blamed the missed calls and decrease in letters from her on everything and everyone but my wife. There was no way that my Brandy would do the things that seasoned soldiers warned me about, not my girl. Her heart was still as pure as when she gave her body to me after homecoming our sophomore year of high school. Elijah and Brandy. Names that went together from the moment we were born, which was only a few days apart. Our mothers were best friends, so we were raised together, took family vacations together, and learned about love together.

A person didn't think of me without thinking of Brandy, and vice versa. I held onto that knowledge when fear clawed at my guts in the middle of the night when loneliness descended on me like a suffering smog, or when the bombs exploded and the world burned to the ground around me, threatening to consume me too. Brandy was my constant, my guaranteed prize at the end of the ugliest fight. Knowing she would be there to meet me with open arms was the only thing that got me through the year-long separation.

Except she wasn't there when I got off the plane at the base. "She's not feeling well," my mama calmly said, but I knew it had to be serious for her to miss my homecoming. She told me she had bought a special dress to wear and everything, but of course, that was before she started withdrawing from me. Fear lashed at my insides, leaving me bloody and raw as I went in search of her. Brandy wasn't in the apartment we shared. She wasn't at her mama's house. None of her friends would tell me where I could find her. I was beside myself with grief and panic. *What the fuck was going on?*

She ended up being in the last place I expected to find her. I'd gone to his house knowing he'd get drunk and commiserate with me, not stopping to think it was weird that he wasn't there to greet me with Mom and Dad either. Jack was my big brother, my hero. I knew something was wrong by the expression on his face when he opened the door, but I swear to God, nothing could've prepared me for the shock I faced.

"You need to remain calm, Elijah," he said, his hands up in surrender. "She's in no condition for the fight you probably want to have right now. Take it out on me; I deserve it."

"What the fuck are you talking about, Jack?"

That's when he realized that no one had told me yet. He hid in

71

his house, expecting our parents or mutual friends to tell me what he'd done to me. My own motherfucking brother. Wife-fucking was the accurate adjective, but not nearly as nasty enough for the crime he committed against me. The fucking coward shook with fear as he confessed to what he'd done.

"Is she here?" I asked, shoving past him. "Brandy! You fucking whore!" I screamed. "Come out here and face me."

"She can't, Elijah." Jack grabbed my arm to stop me from going into his bedroom. I wheeled on him and punched him in the fucking mouth. I left him holding his hand to his busted lips while I charged into the bedroom, nearly ripping the door down in the process.

"Elijah," Brandy said weakly, tears streaming down her face. I used to think she was so beautiful, an angel sent from above, but right then I knew I was looking into the eyes of someone as evil as they came. Then my eyes dropped to her swollen stomach and it felt like someone had kicked me in mine. "I never meant for this to happen. I never wanted to hurt you. It just… happened."

"You never meant to spread your legs for my brother, Brandy? How does that accidentally happen?" She started to sob, but I wouldn't be deterred by her guilt. She wasn't sorry; she was ashamed. "What happened to forever, Brandy? What happened to the promises you made to me? Vows to be faithful? Was it always a lie? Is Jack the first one you fucked behind my back or just another sorry sucker that fell for your honey trap?"

"It wasn't like that," she said, pleading with her voice and eyes for me to understand something that would never make sense to me. "I'm so sorry."

"Please, Elijah," Jack said from the doorway. "She's on complete bed rest because of a high-risk pregnancy. It's too soon, and our son won't survive if Brandy goes into labor now. She can't take this kind of stress, brother."

"Don't you call me that, Jack. You're fucking dead to me," I snarled. His cautionary words had the effect he wanted though, because no matter how much I hated them, I would never want to cause harm to their unborn son.

"Take it out on me, br… Elijah. I deserve it; I can take it. Please leave her alone."

"Outside now," I commanded.

Jack followed me, head held high, and took his ass-whooping on his front lawn without trying to defend himself or even deflect my blows. It was a good start, but it did nothing to slake the blood-lust pumping through my veins. The sky opened and pelted me with rain, but even that couldn't diminish the fires raging through me. I left Jack lying nearly unconscious on his front lawn in the pouring rain and drove to the nearest bar to find trouble. I found it fast. I took on three of them who were as angry about life as I was and willing to fight back.

I woke up in the hospital a few days later thinking I'd been in some sort of accident and Brandy's betrayal with Jack was nothing more than a bad dream. One look into my mother's eyes told me otherwise. Anger rose swift and hard inside me. "Get out." She should've told me instead of letting me find out like that. Tears streamed down my face as I recalled seeing Brandy's pregnant stomach because she was supposed to cradle my babies beneath her heart, not my… Jack's.

"Son," my father, Jack Sr., said in his thunderous voice. I didn't know he was even in the room. "Don't take this out on your mother."

"Why didn't you tell me?" I asked between racking sobs.

"We didn't know how." My mom reached for my hands, but I jerked away from her.

"Don't touch me."

"Do not talk to your mother like that," my father snarled. The gunnery sergeant was as gritty and badass as they came, except when it came to my mama. "What happened to you is terrible, but we can't undo it. We just need to find a way to move forward. Adapt and improvise."

"How easily would you have adapted and improvised if mom

fucked Uncle Stan while you were in Vietnam?"

My father's growl snarled in his throat, and he balled his fist in preparation to fight me. It was obvious just hearing the words brought out a murderous rage in my father's heart. "You can't even stand hearing the words, so you try to imagine seeing it with your own eyes, Jack." He stopped being my father in that moment. "You can shove 'adapt and improvise' up your ass, Jack, and both of you can get the fuck out of here."

"No, Elijah," my mom said tearfully then turned to my father. "Stop being such a hard-ass. What they did to Elijah is inconceivable."

"Jack is our son too, Brenda. Are we supposed to cast him aside over Brandy's infidelity?"

"Did she drug him before she fucked him?" I asked sourly. Don't get me wrong, I was furious over Brandy's betrayal, but it wasn't hers alone. It took two to fuck me over. His precious namesake owned half of the blame too, but he didn't want to hear that. Jack could do no wrong in his eyes, not even getting my wife pregnant while I fought a war. I had begged my whole life for the man's attention, even joined the military to follow in his footsteps hoping it would make him proud. It was a hateful reality to know that he'd choose a lying, phi-landering asshole for a kid over me. "Don't give him a pass because he's your firstborn and namesake." I left off favorite, even though it applied as well.

"I'd think someone in as much pain as you're surely in would be a little smarter," he sneered at me. "You don't get to suck us into a war between brothers over a piece of faithless ass."

"I also don't have to give a shit about a parent who can't spare an ounce of compassion for his son who just had his motherfuck-ing world turned upside down! Get out!" My blood pressure soared, making the pain in my head throb worse, and sounding the alarms for the nurses. "I don't need you! I don't need anyone! Get out!"

My mom cried harder with every word I shouted, but I couldn't stop myself. Right then I felt she was as complicit as the others in my betrayal because of her silence. "Please forgive me," she whispered as the nurses shoved past her and administered mind-and pain-numbing medications that helped me slide into a blissful, dark hole.

Something yanked me from my turbulent sleep; I came out swinging and snarling as piercing pain seized my heart. I rubbed my hand over my chest, but it did nothing to alleviate the agony that those memories elicited in me. I eventually repaired my fractured relationship with my mom, but in the past ten years, I hadn't stepped foot in their house, or talked to my father, Jack, or his wife. I knew that Jack and Brandy had a few kids together, but I'd never met them.

I heard Maegan's metal gate slowly creak open from beneath my window, putting me on high alert. I eased out from beneath the covers and softly walked to the window.

"I wonder if she's home?" a teenage boy asked hopefully.

"You're just hoping to get a glimpse of her tits," a sullen teenage girl replied. I imagined her eyes were rolling up in the back of her head.

The entire thing would've been funny if I'd been in the right mood. I yanked my curtain open and peered down at the two kids as they entered Maegan's gate and headed across her yard. Sure enough, they left the gate hanging wide open.

Fury lit my ass up, and I jerked the window open. "Hey, assholes! Close her fucking gate! You left it open the other night and Lulu got out. Luckily she didn't get hit by a motherfucking car."

"Oh no!" the girl said, covering her mouth. Her eyes widened when she saw my bare chest, and her face turned pink for reasons other than embarrassment.

The boy wasn't nearly as impressed. He puffed up like a fucking rooster and challenged me with a look before he opened his mouth. "Who the hell are you? The gate police?"

I grabbed my wallet off the dresser and flipped it open for him to see my Blissville Police Department badge. "Gate Detective," I clarified, "but I'll answer to Detective Markham also." I closed my wallet and pointed at the punk. "Stop creeping around here trying to get a glimpse of Ms. Miracle's tits! That's fucking pervy and the first step to becoming a serial killer." Okay, that was probably overkill because any straight dude with a pulse would want a peep at Maegan's tits.

The girl's giggle was muffled by her gloves, but we both still heard it. Her male companion didn't find anything funny about the exchange and stomped back out of Maegan's yard.

"We're sorry, Detective Markham," the girl said.

I nodded. "Don't cut through her yard anymore. It's rude."

"Yes, sir," she said, closing the gate and scrambling after her friend. She caught up to him two houses down, and I smiled when they started to argue and gesture toward my window.

I closed the window and curtains then returned to my bed. A smile spread across my face over the incident until I realized the real reason for my ire wasn't that the boy wanted to see Maegan's tits, it was because I didn't want anyone else besides me seeing them. Ever.

Fuck! Nothing good would come from this.

Chapter Nine

Maegan

"**T**HIS IS SO GROSS," MILO SAID SHUDDERING. "I CAN'T believe Thom Renzo didn't think to put bulbs in the sockets so that we could at least have better light than just our flashlights."

"Think of it as a grand adventure," Memphis said excitedly.

Sweeping my flashlight from left to right, I stepped forward into the cellar. "You can go back upstairs if you're bothered by dirt and dust, Milo. Memphis and I will be at this awhile." There were boxes stacked on top of boxes in every direction. I had learned long ago that the pack rat gene wasn't isolated to a specific income class. I had a feeling that the Renzo estate was going to be the jackpot, but it would require both grit and patience. One of those traits came more natural to me than the other.

Patience was especially hard to come by after the week I had. It started off with Thom Renzo putting me off for a week after he'd already given me the green light. He waited until Milo, Memphis, and I were on our way to his parents' home the previous Friday before he canceled our appointment through the real estate agent. I was immediately suspicious because Becker said that he wouldn't confirm another date when I could come out. It sounded shady to me, but I tried to look on the bright side instead of thinking that the squirrelly fucker gave someone else first crack at the good stuff.

Friday night at home wasn't a depressing option though when I lived next to an extraordinarily sexy man who rocked my world in ways I never dreamed possible. After the way we connected, I was sure he would be just as eager to have me again as I was him. Elijah had told me that he was off duty until Monday and I figured there was no better way for him to pass a cold winter weekend than getting naked and burying his dick inside me. Hell, I couldn't wipe the grin off my face as I dropped Milo and Memphis off at their homes because I was certain of the way I'd spend the night. I pictured a strong, powerful body between my legs, or beneath me, hot kisses that stretched into hours, and more orgasms than I could count.

Except, his house was dark and his truck was gone when I pulled into my driveway. I didn't let that deter me. I took a shower and made sure all of me was smooth and soft everywhere before I slid into my Wonder Woman pajamas. I didn't want to be too obvious that I was attempting to seduce him, so I went without a bra since he seemed to like that the first time, and situated my silk pj pants low on my hips so he could get a peek at the belly button ring I slid into place. I thought the little flash of silver would capture his attention and make him want to put his mouth on my stomach before he kissed a path lower.

I settled in my recliner beneath his blanket that I had failed to return to him and waited for the rumble of his ginormous truck. Hours ticked by, giving me too much time to think. Had I dreamt him? I pushed my pajama bottoms down enough to see the love bite he left on my mound above my clit. *Nope, he was real.* Just looking at it turned me on, but I refrained from making myself come. I knew that whatever he gave me would be a hundred times better than anything I did solo.

The rumble never came Friday night, nor did it come during

anytime on Saturday. Elijah didn't return home until late Sunday evening. Of course, I didn't sit my sappy ass in that chair with his blanket the entire weekend. I wasn't that girl anymore dammit! I was mature, and I had a busy life. I didn't sit around and pine after a man. No, I did fun things and… *Who am I trying to fool?* I worked long hours Saturday and Sunday so that I wouldn't pine after Elijah's dick. When I wasn't working, I was wrapped in that stupid fucking blanket with Lulu while I beat myself up for being so damn stupid. Again.

It was just sex, Maegan. Earth-shattering, life-affirming, saw-fireworks-behind-my-eyelids sex, but still sex. Don't confuse that with real affection just because he made you come.

That might've been true, but that didn't squelch the arousal that crested inside me when I smelled him on my sheets and pillowcase. Nor did it stop me from pretending it was his hands or lips teasing my nipples and clit or his dick inside me instead of a vibrator when my lust from knowing he was nearby made it too hard to sleep Sunday night.

Monday dawned bright and sunny, even though it was nip-hardening cold. The thought occurred to me that I should walk my ass over to Elijah's house and offer him a free Danish and coffee as a welcome to the Blissville PD, but I heard him leaving while I was in the shower. Sure, I was disappointed but convinced I'd have the chance to talk to him that evening.

I wasn't wrong. Elijah was taking his trash can to the curb for Tuesday trash pickup when I pulled into my driveway. I got out of my SUV with a big smile on my face, but it melted when I saw the hesitation in his eyes during his tepid greeting. A sinking feeling took root in my stomach that Elijah had deliberately avoided me all weekend, and he couldn't have been more obvious that my attention wasn't welcome.

I was proud of the way I handled myself though. I didn't flip him off or give him a reason he could use to justify his abrupt change in attitude toward me. I offered him a small smile and wished him a nice evening, even though I wanted to kick over his trash can. Once inside, I allowed myself to feel the disappointment; in fact, I embraced the sting of rejection and used it as fuel. I marched up to my room, stripped my bed and tossed it all in the washing machine. I should've washed the blanket I borrowed from him too, but I wasn't quite ready to wash his scent off everything just yet. I planned to return it to Elijah after enough time passed that I didn't look like I was using it as an excuse to see him.

I wasn't that girl. When it was over; it was over. I wouldn't beg him for attention nor would I leave my window open a crack to give him a taste of what he was missing. I nailed that window shut, knowing it was best to move on and find a guy who knew what he wanted and wasn't emotionally closed off. If that never happened, at least I had my friends, family, a career I loved, and my precious Lulu.

I stuck to my guns all week long and only masturbated to the memories of him twice, but I saw that as progress. My heart and mind were certain that I no longer wanted anything to do with Elijah Markham, but my body mourned his absence in our life. My clit pulsed every time I heard the rumble of his truck, but she wasn't running the show.

"I can handle dirt and dust," Milo said, pulling me back to reality. "It's the thought of finding a dead body that bothers me."

"Milo, there's nothing to be afraid of down—" A big, hairy spider dropped from the ceiling on its web right in front of my face. I screamed loud enough to wake the dead body if there was one, then followed it with "OH MY FUCKING GOD!" when the spider swung toward me instead of scampering to get away. I felt it crawl across my forehead and into my hair. "GET IT OUT! GET IT OUT! GET IT OUT!" I dropped my flashlight and did the crazy, spider-in-the-hair dance while thrashing my head around and shaking the strands furiously so the bastard would fall out.

"Hold still and I'll help you," Memphis said seriously. He tried to keep up with my constant turns to the left and right. I felt his hands on my head, but I just knew if I stopped moving the spider would crawl inside my ear and lay eggs that would eventually hatch and burrow inside my brain. Left, right, left again. I turned, pivoted, and circled around like I was doing the spider samba.

Memphis stepped forward and reached for my head again, but I turned and bumped him with my elbows, knocking his flashlight out of his hands too. Then I stumbled into the rest of the web, where I was certain the spider's family was waiting to pounce on me. I screamed and waved my arms around trying to get free while Memphis bobbed and weaved to avoid my fists and elbows.

"You're okay, Maegan," Memphis said soothingly. "Just calm down."

What did my twin brother do? He doubled over laughing at the spectacle I made, and in doing so, aimed his flashlight down toward the dirt-packed floor of the storage cellar. All three flashlight beams were aimed in different directions on the ground and not in the air where I was desperately trying to untangle myself from the killer, brain-eating spiders.

Milo's laughter died as quickly as it started. "Oh, fuck!"

"Oh my God! Are there more of them? How many? I can't see anything!"

"We have bigger problems than that one tiny spider, Maegan."

I wanted to argue that it was a huge, brain-devouring spider, but the seriousness of Milo's tone stopped me in my tracks. I looked in the direction I last saw him and followed his beam of light. "Is that blood?"

"Yes," Milo said. "A lot of it. And there's a trail leading back behind those boxes."

"Is someone down here with us?" Memphis asked, sounding like the lead guy on his favorite ghost hunting show.

"Let's go back upstairs and call nine-one-one," I said. I was no expert, but it wasn't likely that whoever lost that much blood was still alive to tell about it.

The three of us got upstairs as quickly as we could and waited for the police to arrive in my SUV. Unfortunately for me, the first of the BPD's finest to arrive on the scene was the last one that I wanted to see.

A few of the officers came to my SUV and informed us that Detective Markham wanted to separate us for individual interviews. Why couldn't he tell us that? We were put in three separate squad cars, but at least they left the engines running to keep us warm. I appreciated the gesture, but shock, fear, and isolation caused my body to shake so hard my teeth rattled. I watched as more officers showed up, followed by the crime scene guys, and our county coroner. That's when I realized the situation was as bad as I had feared.

I wanted to see Elijah and hear him tell me that I was going to be okay. Instead, he didn't look in my direction after his initial shock that I was at his crime scene. He just went about his investigation, which included talking to Milo and Memphis then sending them home in the back of their squad cars. I knew that neither of them chose to leave me by myself at the crime scene. Why isolate me? It was like Elijah was angry at me or something, but he would have to care about me for that to happen.

I felt my blood drain when the coroner loaded the black bag into the back of his van and drove off. There was only a scattering of officers and crime scene personnel on the scene by the time that Elijah could no longer delay talking to me. He approached the squad car with long, confident strides and pulled the rear passenger door open briskly. I expected him to ask me to step out of the car like he had Memphis and Milo, but instead, he climbed in beside me and shut the door.

Earlier, I would've been so grateful to have him sit beside me but not after an hour of waiting and being ignored. I was cold, afraid, and angry. I didn't want him to see me as weak, so I mentally held myself together. I imagined a warm blanket, but not his, wrapped tightly around me and willed my teeth to stop chattering. I felt his intense regard as he looked me over from head to toe, but I didn't dare look at him for risk of falling apart.

"What were you doing here tonight, Maegan?" Elijah finally asked.

"I'm sure Milo and Memphis told you." Yeah, my voice was as frosty as you'd expect it to be.

Elijah released a frustrated sigh then said, "I want to hear it from you."

"Thom Renzo sent me an email and gave me the okay to look through his parents' estate to see if there is anything I'd like to buy for my shop," I told him. "I was supposed to do it last week, but he canceled our appointment at the last minute."

"How'd you get in?"

"The email contained the code to the lockbox on the front door."

"Was he supposed to meet you here?" Elijah asked.

"He didn't say, but I assumed not since he provided the code and there was no other vehicle parked here."

"Hmmm." His response caused me to turn and look at him.

"What's that mean, Detective Markham?" He looked surprised that I addressed him formally.

"Is that typical for someone to trust you to go looking through their heirlooms by yourself?"

I turned in my seat to face him the best I could. "Are you implying that I'm not trustworthy?"

"Not at all," he replied, shaking his head. "I'm just asking if that's typical of someone to show you that much trust."

"I've earned a reputation as an honest and reliable business woman. I have never cheated anyone, and I'd never steal anything!"

"How do you feel about killing people?"

I'm sure my dramatically raised brows and slacked jaw made me look like a cartoon character. Nothing was funny about the situation.

"Right this minute, Detective?" I asked.

"You look mad enough to kill right now," he said. "Are you having murderous thoughts?"

"Toward you?" I crossed my arms over my chest, drawing his attention to my full breasts, even though they were hidden beneath a thick coat. "Why would you think that?" Did he think I was still pining after his cock, bemoaning the fact that his lips were no longer pressed against my pussy?

"It's just a vibe I'm picking up on."

"Hmmm, how astute of you."

"It does come in handy," he quipped. "Why don't you run me through your night, so that you can get home. I'm sure Lulu misses you."

He listened without interruption while jotting stuff down in his little notebook. When he was finished, he closed it and tucked it back inside his pocket. "So, the spider is responsible for your hair?"

"What?" I raised my hands up to my head and was horrified when they met what felt like a rat's nest. I scooted over and looked in the rearview mirror of the squad car and was horrified by my reflection. "Oh my God. Could this week get any worse?"

"Hey, your hair looks better than Thom Renzo's," Elijah said.

Just like that, the tenuous hold on my emotions snapped, and I burst into tears.

Chapter Ten

Elijah

W*AY TO GO, DETECTIVE DUMB FUCK!*

"OhmyGodIcantbelieveThomRenzoisdead!" Maegan strung all the words together before she took a stuttering breath and sobbed harder.

Had she been any other witness, I would've patted her on the shoulder and tried to calm her down. I knew what would happen if I touched Maegan in any way, and the techniques I would use to comfort her weren't taught at the police academy. I needed to stick with a hands-off approach with her.

"Maegan," I softly said, hoping the sound of my voice would get through to her. "I need you to take a few calming breaths and repeat what you just said."

"Oh my God," *gasp, gasp, gasp,* "I can't believe," *pant, pant, pant,* "Thom Renzo," *wheeze, wheeze, wheeze,* "is dead."

I won't lie to you, all that panting and gasping made me recall the animalistic way Maegan liked to fuck and get fucked. My dick started to rise and salute her under my jeans, but I ignored his demands to focus on the right thing to do. Maegan deserved better treatment than what I had showed her, and I planned to find the right time to apologize, but that wasn't during a murder investigation.

"Did you know him well?" I asked.

Maegan shook her head then took some calming breaths as she tried to pull herself together. "Not really. He went to the same school as us, but he always came across as a little… weird." I could tell she felt guilty for thinking it, let alone saying it about the recently departed. "He was kind of a loaner during most of high school."

Maegan, Milo, and Memphis's story all matched, and I believed that none of them took a blunt object to Thom Renzo's head. From the coroner's initial findings, he hadn't been dead long before the treasure hunters stumbled upon the blood trail. What they might've done was destroy valuable evidence like footprints in the dirt-covered stone floor.

She seemed so tiny and vulnerable in the back of the cruiser with her arms wrapped tightly around herself like she was physically trying to hold herself together. I realized that sending her brother and friend home was probably a mistake because she didn't look to be in any condition to drive. I hadn't been thinking clearly at the time. It had taken every ounce of willpower to stay away from the woman after I blew her off in my driveway earlier in the week. I hated the look of hurt I saw flash in her eyes before she covered it with a blinding but fake smile. She didn't deserve my callous treatment, and I wanted to apologize to her every day, but my self-preservation won out.

Then I get sent to my first crime scene and who is one of my witnesses? None other than the woman who had haunted my sleep since I first met her. I told myself I separated her from the two men to prevent them from influencing one another's statements, but I knew better. I wanted to be alone with her again, if only for a few minutes, in a controlled environment where I knew I wouldn't make an ass of myself over her again. Surely, I wouldn't kiss her lips and fondle her tits in the back of a patrolman's car, right? I put nothing past me when she was near. There was just something about her that made me want… so many things.

I reacted badly when I learned that Maegan probably arrived so soon after Renzo died because it scared the fuck out of me. The body had still been warm. What if she'd arrived just a little earlier? She could've been killed too! Was the killer still in the house when she arrived? I was worried about her safety and angry because she'd slipped beneath my defenses. I allowed my anger over what could've happened fuel shitty behavior towards her. Again.

Then, as if a switch had been flipped inside of her, the tears suddenly stopped and the expression on her face could only be described as furious. She went from vulnerable to fierce in a heartbeat and damn if that didn't turn me on even more.

"You're such an asshole, Elijah!"

"I am." It was confirmation, not a question, which caught her off guard. Maegan could only blink at me for a few seconds, but she recovered in magnificent fashion.

"If you think agreeing with me will save your sorry ass then you better come up with a better plan."

Regardless of her ire and crazy hair, I thought she had never looked more beautiful and hearing the word "come" slip from her mouth distracted me in ways I had hoped to avoid.

She saw, or at least sensed, my reaction to her, because she started yanking on the door handle to open it. She'd obviously never been in the back seat of a cruiser because they have the equivalent of child safety locks, but are used to prevent our detainees from escaping the car instead of toddlers. "Release me right fucking now."

"Oh, Freckles," I said before I could stop myself. "I want nothing more than to help us both release, but this isn't the time or place. I'm available later though."

"Arrogant bastard," she snarled, but I saw the heat flair in her eyes. She felt it too, and it wouldn't take much effort from me to get back to where we both wanted me—in her bed and between her beautiful, shapely legs.

"Don't forget it, Freckles." I tapped on the window and Officer

Jansen opened the door for me. I walked around the vehicle and opened the door so Maegan could return to her SUV. "Are you okay to drive? I could—"

Maegan raised her hand to cut me off. "Don't bother, Detective Markham." She looked over the top of the squad car and seemed surprised to see that Jansen was still there. He looked at Maegan as sappily as one of those cartoon characters with bulging hearts for eyes. "Tell your mama that I said hello, Brett."

"Will do," Jansen said. "Are you sure you feel okay to drive home? You've had a huge shock; I can take you if you want."

"That's so sweet of you, but—"

"She said she was fine, Officer." Jansen's eyes rounded in surprise at the gruffness in my voice.

"See you around, Mae." He walked toward the house to join the remaining officers on the scene.

Maegan rounded on me, hands on her hips and fire in her eyes. It seemed like I ended up deeper and deeper in the doghouse with every word I spoke or step I took. I thought it was for the best, but I still didn't like that she was getting the wrong impression about me.

"Mae, huh?" I thought it was cute.

"Only my friends and family are allowed to call me that, and you're neither of those things, Detective Markham. If there's nothing else you need, I'd like to leave now."

I needed plenty, but I wisely kept my response professional. "That's all for now. I know where you live if I think of something else." *Okay, reminding both of us about the hours spent in her bed wasn't the best idea either, especially when I acted like a jerk and pulled a disappearing act followed by the cold shoulder.* She looked at me in disbelief before she rolled her eyes and walked away. "Drive safely," I yelled to her retreating back. She responded by flipping me off.

I realized that I was good and fucked because I loved her moxie.

"Tell me what you know," Captain Roman-Wyatt said when I returned to the station after securing the crime scene.

"Someone was very angry at Thom Renzo, sir," I told him. "They hit him over the head with a heavy, blunt object causing him to stagger and fall. He wasn't immediately knocked out though because it appears that he pulled himself to his feet and shuffled further into the cellar before his killer finished him off. It was really bad, sir." I was grateful that Maegan, Milo, and Memphis went upstairs and called for help instead of following the trail of blood. I would not have wanted them to see Renzo's gruesome homicide. "It's unfortunate that the killer appears to have taken the murder weapon with him."

"What do we know about the last few hours of his life?" the captain asked.

"He made an arrangement with a local business owner to look through his parents' belongings to see if she wanted to buy anything for her store before the items were sold at an auction at a future date."

"Maegan?" he asked.

"Yes, Miss Miracle," I replied, hoping that addressing her formally would prevent me from thinking about how beautiful she looked naked beneath me, over me, or beside me. It didn't work nor did it prevent me from wanting to do it all over again as quickly as possible. "Miss Miracle claimed that she was supposed to meet Thom Renzo last week, but he'd canceled their appointment."

"Claimed? You don't believe her, Detective?"

"I do believe her, sir. That was a poor choice of words."

"Carry on," the captain said.

"She said that she received an email from Renzo today, telling her that she was good to come out this evening, he confirmed the time, and provided the code for the lockbox at the front door that contained the key.

"Miss Miracle didn't say this," because she was too pissed at me, "but Mr. Miracle said he thought the email in itself was odd. The previous communication with his sister was done through a realtor that both Renzo and Miss Miracle knew. He thought it seemed odd that suddenly Renzo emailed his sister randomly with little notice."

"What do you make of it?" the captain asked.

"By itself, nothing. I'll call the realtor and set up an interview. I'll also reach out to the auction house and see if I can track down Renzo's friends and put together a timeline of his last few days. I find it really odd that his car wasn't at the scene and I'd like to know how he arrived. His driver's license was issued in Kentucky so Wen is looking through the database to see what type of vehicle Renzo owned to issue a BOLO. We'll want to get inside his apartment as soon as possible to see what we can find for possible motives."

"Good start," he replied. "Your partner will be back from vacation on Monday. Nothing like a homicide to welcome you to our town. In the meantime, I'll contact someone at the Kentucky State Police to set up a time for them to meet us at his residence for the search." He shook his head. "I'm going to pair you with Officer Kevin Wen to assist you with the interviews since local potential witnesses will be more comfortable talking with him." *Instead of an outsider.*

"Sounds good, Captain. Maybe the first thing Wen can help me with is determining Renzo's next of kin, if one exists, for notification."

"I bet I know someone who can help you with that."

"Great," I said, happy for any help I could get.

"What are you doing tonight?"

I knew what—or should I say who—I wanted to do, but that option wasn't on the table, especially after my behavior earlier. "Nothing that I'm aware of, sir."

The captain held up a finger for me to wait while he dialed his cell phone. "Sunshine, I'm bringing home a guest for dinner." He listened for a second then laughed. "It's my new detective on the police force. He saw the worst our town had to offer today, so it's only fair that he sees the best." I wasn't sure exactly what his husband said, but it elicited a possessive growl out of the captain's throat that made me smile. "I was talking about your cooking."

While the captain verbally volleyed with his husband, I looked at the photos that sat on the credenza behind his desk. It was plain to see the two men were crazy in love with one another in each picture he proudly displayed. The newest photos included their twin son and daughter. I could see why the captain called his blond husband Sunshine. It wasn't just the color of his hair; it was the joy and love that radiated from him. I could only hear one side of the conversation, but I got the impression that Josh Roman-Wyatt was a real firecracker.

"See you in thirty minutes or less." He disconnected the call and looked at me. "Do you like country fried steak?"

"Love it," I replied.

"You're about to have the best country fried steak you'll ever put in your mouth."

"How will that get me closer to finding Thom Renzo's next of kin?" I asked curiously.

"My husband and I own the salon in town and he knows everything about everyone," the captain said.

Josh Roman-Wyatt was as sunny in person as he was in his photos, and the smells coming from his kitchen seemed to back up the captain's claim.

Josh greeted his husband with a peck on the lips. "Hello, Captain Crunch."

"Sunshine, you know that I hate that one."

"Well, I very well couldn't call you my personal favorite nickname since you brought one of your detectives home with you."

"I think I'd rather you call me Captain Underwear than Captain Crunch, regardless of who hears it."

"Fucknugget! Fucknugget!" a blue macaw squawked loudly from the solarium.

"Cockbadger! Cockbadger!" a scarlet macaw fired back.

"Dirty Birds!" the two husbands yelled.

"Big Daddy!" the scarlet said sweetly.

"Good girl, Sassy," the captain said.

"Slut!" the blue macaw squawked accusingly at his companion.

"Savage," Josh said in a warning tone. Then he turned to his husband. "Have you noticed that those crazy-ass birds have stopped cussing in front of the kids? It's like they know."

"They're crazy smart, Sunshine. I sleep with one eye open." The captain looked around the living room with a frown on his face. "Where are my angels?"

"Our little monsters are spending the weekend with their grandparents. They're staying with my folks tonight and yours tomorrow night. Two blissfully quiet nights at home," Josh said with a happy sigh. I noticed the merry little twinkle that sparkled in his eyes, and I figured they wouldn't be too unhappy if I ate my food and ran. In fact, judging by the looks the two men exchanged, they had forgotten I was in the house with them.

"Hey, good-looking. Want to suck my dick?" the bird Savage asked. I was pretty damn sure he was talking to me.

"Maybe some other time," I replied.

"Gabe, you need to do something about your bird," Josh told his husband.

To Josh, the captain said, "That's your bird." To me, he said, "I'm truly sorry, Elijah."

"Please don't apologize to me, sir. This is the most fun I've had in a long time."

"How about you drop the formalities and call me Gabe when you're a guest in our home?"

"I can try, sir." I grinned sheepishly because it seemed I would need to try a lot harder.

A timer buzzed in the kitchen and Josh announced it was time to eat. The captain hadn't been lying when he bragged about his husband's cooking. The country fried steak was crispy on the outside and juicy on the inside. Not even my grandmother's homemade gravy could top Josh's.

"Sunshine, Elijah needs some help with figuring out who Thom Renzo's next of kin is since his parents' preceded him in death," Gabe told his husband.

"I heard about that," Josh soberly said, setting his fork down. "There has always been an air of mystery surrounding the Renzos. They moved here mid to late eighties. They never socialized much with anyone in town, so we don't know much about them." That was pretty much what Maegan had said word for word. "Your best bet would be to talk to the local attorney in town who handles ninety-nine point nine percent of estate law for the Blissville residents."

I left the Roman-Wyatt house with a full stomach and the name and number for the attorney, so I called that a win-win situation. I tried not to look over at Maegan's house when I pulled into the driveway, but I failed. I sat looking up at her bedroom window where a thin crack of light showed beneath the shade she pulled down for privacy. I wanted to knock on her door and find out how she was holding up. I suspected her annoyance with me stiffened her resolve long enough to get home, but worried that her shock and fear returned the minute that wore off.

I don't know how long I sat there debating what to do, but I eventually squelched the desire to knock on her door. That was until I walked up my front porch steps and saw what had been neatly stacked by my front door. I should've been glad she returned my slippers and blanket when I wasn't home so that we avoided any awkwardness, so why then did it feel like she kicked me in the nuts?

"Oh, I don't think so, Freckles."

Chapter Eleven

Maegan

MAYBE IT WAS IMMATURE AS HELL, BUT I TOOK EXTREME pleasure in leaving Elijah's things on his porch for him to find when he returned home. My only regret was that I didn't have time to wash the blanket first because my scent was all over that thing. I didn't want him to know how many times I wrapped myself in that stupid thing while I pined after his sorry ass all frigging week long. On the other hand, I hoped he smelled me on that blanket and got a raging hard-on that never deflated. If I were capable of casting spells, I'd make it so he couldn't grip his cock and jerk off either. *What was I thinking? Spells?* Besides, he'd just hump the mattress or something until he came.

I pictured his ass muscles clenching tight as he rocked his hips back and forth seeking pleasure. God, I remember how hard his ass felt when I gripped it to pull him deeper inside me. *Dammit, Maegan. Why the hell did I have to start thinking about his thrusting hips?* The walls of my vagina clenched in protest of *not* being filled by Elijah. I did my best to distract myself with a book, but reading about the main characters having sex only made me want it more.

Fuck, even the sound of his stupid truck rumbling down the

road made my nipples tighten and tingle. Damn that man and his magic cock! I should be furious with the way he treated me instead of wanting to ride him like a carnival ride. I learned firsthand that trusting my heart to a player was just as dangerous as riding the tilt-o-whirl operated by some sketchy-looking pervert who kept hitting his flask in between hitting on the ladies.

"Calm your nips," I said to my aching breasts. "I'm not letting him back inside my house or pussy. He's one and done. Well, technically one night." *Fuck!* He had me talking to myself like a fucking loon. "I might as well just go adopt a house full of cats!"

Lulu barked her displeasure over the idea like she understood what I meant, or perhaps she just responded to my hysteria that was simmering just below the surface. I felt it rise every time I thought about how close we came to finding Thom Renzo's dead body. The only thing that saved me from giving into that panic right then and there was my desire to see Elijah's reaction when he saw I had returned his crappy stuff.

I tiptoed and watched him through the crack in the curtains in the dining room. All the lights were turned off and he couldn't see me, but I had a great view of his front porch that was illuminated by the light next to the door. That sucker was bright enough to light up a third of the street. I waited and waited for him to get out and walk to his porch, but he remained inside his truck. From my vantage point, I could only see the grill of the big monster. What was he doing? Was he thinking about me and wondering how I was doing? Did he want to knock on my door but was too afraid of giving me the wrong impression that he was human?

If I wanted to see inside his truck, all I had to do was look out the living room window, but those curtains were antique lace that offered no cover for me to hide behind. I was about to risk it when I heard the creaking of rusty hinges when he opened the door of his truck.

It's show time! No, I didn't think that in a Beetlejuice voice. Okay, maybe.

Elijah strolled to his porch in determined strides. In fact, I'd categorize it as angry, but what the hell did he have to feel mad about? I was the one he fucked over—literally and figuratively! His forward momentum slammed to a halt the second he locked eyes on the items I left for him to find. I had hoped to see a fraction of the frustration he made me feel, but all I saw was determination in his expression. He stood rigidly still for a few moments, and my brain conjured up all things I could do to ease the tension from his muscles.

I saw his mouth moving, but couldn't read his lips. An ornery smile slowly spread across his face then he pivoted and walked back down the porch steps. I thought he had moved with a purpose before, but that was nothing compared to the way his legs gobbled up the distance from his porch to mine. Even though he was out of sight after a few strides, I knew his destination was my front porch.

"Open up, Freckles," Elijah said as he pounded on the door hard enough to make it rattle in the frame. He didn't sound angry though; he sounded… horny.

Yes, my body cried out. I shook so hard from anticipation that I practically vibrated through the house instead of walked.

"I know you're awake. I saw your bedroom light on! Open up this door before I—"

I yanked the door open before he could finish what he was going to say. "Huff and puff and blow it down?" I asked sassily, finishing for him. His pulse pounded wildly in his neck, matching the tempo of my heart trying to beat its way out of my chest. "What the hell is your problem?"

"I got something for you to blow."

"You wish," I retorted.

Elijah's eyes lowered to my unbound breasts and stayed there. He wasn't the least bit ashamed that he was staring at my girls. Okay, so the nips were saluting his soldier, but that didn't make it right. What woman doesn't whip off her bra as soon as she comes home for the night? It wasn't some part of a grand scheme to lure that jackass back into my bed. *I'd settle for a wall-banging.*

I crossed my arms beneath my chest, but that only plumped them up more for him. Elijah's delighted smile should've pissed me off because I was not the kind of girl who opened her doors and legs for a guy at whim. What an asshole! Who did he think he was… *Oh, fucking forget it.* I grabbed his scarf and pulled him into my house and shut the door.

He outweighed me by a good hundred pounds, or more, so I wouldn't have budged him if he didn't really want to come inside. And I saw just how badly he wanted to *come inside* when his hungry eyes finally jerked up from my boobs to meet my gaze. Elijah placed his hands on my waist and began walking me further into the house.

I placed both my hands against his chest to halt our progress. "I just need to know one thing first," I told him.

"What is it, Freckles?" he asked hesitantly.

"Your ring size," I said then dramatically rolled my eyes when he widened his in alarm. "Relax, big guy. I'm not after your last name or inheritance; I'm only interested in your cock." *And balls, hands, and mouth.*

"Words that every man wants to hear as long as you're not holding a knife in your hand."

"Are you married?" I asked. "Or even separated? I can't be with you if either apply to your circumstances. We had that one night together then you freaked out and disappeared."

"I didn't freak out," Elijah denied. "I… okay maybe a little, but I am not married or even separated. I don't have a girlfriend tucked away someplace. I went to the cabin I inherited from my grandfather to do some thinking."

Thinking? More like hiding. I wanted to know what he *thought* about while there, but I didn't press him. I had told him I needed to know one thing and he answered my question without hesitation and even volunteered extra information. Elijah looked me straight on and didn't so much as blink as he waited for me to make up my mind about what I wanted to do next. He was giving me all the control and it went straight to my head. I whipped my shirt off and tossed it to the floor because there really wasn't much of a decision to make.

Elijah swallowed hard and I could see how difficult it was for him to keep his eyes locked on mine when he really wanted to feast them on my breasts. The good thing about the cold weather is how firm it made them feel. I reached up and cupped them, daring him to look away. I brushed my thumbs over sensitive nipples, relishing the feel of them hardening even more, as I started walking backward again. Elijah didn't follow immediately and I worried that I needed to practice my come-and-get-it expression in the mirror before I attempted it a second time.

Turned out that I had nothing to worry about because he closed the gap between us in one stride. Elijah snaked his arm out to hook around my waist and hauled me tight against him while he cupped a breast with his free hand.

"I'll take it from here, Freckles." Then he bent me backward over his arm that held me up and laved one eager peak before turning to its twin. "Damn, your tits are pretty and perfect. I've missed your eager cunt too."

Jesus! Since when did I ever let a man talk to me like that? Why was it so fucking hot? What was it about this man that made me excuse his crude treatment? I should've slapped his face but decided I'd rather ride it instead.

"You could've had access to this all week long if you weren't hell bent on being a dumbass."

Elijah tore his attention from my breasts to look into my eyes. "I'm too horny and grateful to argue with you because I did behave like a dumbass."

"I can think of a few ways you can properly apologize to me."

"Oh, I think I can too." Elijah stood to his full height and led me to the couch. "We'll get upstairs to your bed eventually, but for now, this couch will work fine for your first orgasm."

"First."

"I have a lot of apologizing to do, Freckles." Instead of laying me down on the cushions, he yanked my pj pants down my legs and pressed my ass against the arm of the couch. "Trust me?" I nodded my head even though I didn't understand where the trust came from. "That's my girl." *Oh, the little thrill that worked its way through my body over those three little words.*

Elijah placed his big hand in the center of my chest and pushed until my head, shoulders, and upper back rested on the seat of the couch. He dropped to his knees and placed his strong hands on my thighs, rubbing the tense muscles with his thumbs. Once I relaxed he spread my legs nice and wide so he could have unfettered access to my femininity. He placed his thumbs on my pussy lips and opened me further for visual exploration. Elijah must've liked what he saw because he licked his lips in what I hoped was fevered anticipation.

He kept his eyes locked on mine as he lowered his head toward my promise land. "Keep your eyes on me, Freckles. I want to see the fireworks in them when you come for me." *Arrogant ass.*

A hard shiver of lust and longing shook my body, making my pussy and clit throb intensely. "I think I just did."

Elijah lowered his head until it hovered just over my mound. "That was nothing." His huskily-spoken words ghosted over my bare flesh, raising goose bumps all over my body. "Play with your tits while I eat your pussy."

My arms were stretched out over my head resting on the couch as I submitted my body to him, but at his command, I immediately pulled them down to cup the rounded underside of my breasts, pinching my nipples between my forefingers and thumbs. I tugged and twisted, working them like his mouth would, sending a zap of lightning straight to the clit where Elijah's tongue hovered. I couldn't tell if he was captivated by my actions or just being a clit tease, but I wasn't happy either way. I lifted my hips from the arm of the sofa putting his tongue right where I wanted it.

My boldness snapped Elijah back to action and he flicked his tongue over my swollen nub. Just that simple little tease and I was nearly ready to detonate. Then he flattened his tongue and licked a path from the bottom of my slit up to my clit. When he reached the bundle of nerves at the top, he eagerly sucked it into his mouth while he slid a stealthy finger inside my pussy. Elijah taunted the hot flesh of my core by sliding that finger in and out in a slow fuck, but never hitting that golden spot that would send me over the edge. He would suck my clit into his mouth then release it to tease it with his tongue.

"Oh!" I wanted to reach down and grip his hair and hold him right fucking there, but I didn't want to stop toying with my nipples either. It felt too good and I was already so close to coming.

Hotter than the tongue action going on between my legs was the dark, raw desire I saw in his eyes. This was a man who knew what he was doing to my body and loved every second of it. He was perfectly content taking his time drawing out my pleasure, making me hot and slippery wet for him. I wasn't interested in being denied another second, so I undulated my hips trying to get his deft tongue where I wanted it.

Elijah's dark chuckle rumbled from his chest, but he must've decided to take pity on a girl who was desperate to come. He crooked his finger, tapping my G-spot at the same time he sucked my sensitive clit into his mouth.

"Elijah!" I dropped one hand to grip his hair while I fucked his face, coming long and gloriously hard.

He stayed with me, licking and sucking until I became too sensitive. He lifted his head and stared into my eyes. Elijah smiled widely, his lips wet from my juices. "Oh, the things I'm going to do to you tonight, Freckles."

Then life said, "Hold my beer," when Elijah's cell phone rang.

"Don't answer it," I implored him. "A girl has needs, Elijah. You just got started." It was true. In one night, he'd ruined me for all other men. I'd gone from no orgasms to multiples and there was no coming back from that.

Elijah straightened up and reached for his phone. "Damn it," he grumbled. "I have to take this." He rose to his feet, paced away from me, and said, "Markham," into his phone. "Yeah, thanks, Wen. I'll be right there."

He turned to look at me with so much regret in his eyes. I could almost hear his straining hard-on weeping behind his zipper. He held out his hand and helped me sit up, which was good because there was no graceful way of getting out of that position. *Graceful! Snort!* I'd just fucked his face. *Lord, what had come over me?* I redressed quickly while trying to hide my embarrassment over my wanton behavior.

"I, uh, need to meet Officer Wen to do a death notification. He found Thom's next of kin." His cop mask was firmly back in place as well as his shield to keep me away.

Too damn bad for him that it didn't work. "Oh, that must be a really hard thing to do. I'm truly sorry, Elijah." I went to him and kissed him softly on the lips. I knew it could ruin the tenuous truce between us, but I didn't care. I wanted him to know he had a safe place to land if he needed one. "I'll be up for a few hours if you want to come back over later."

"Because you owe me an orgasm?" he asked, trying to steer us back into his comfort zone.

I followed Elijah to the front door. "No, because you have more ass kissing to do. That was only one orgasm," I told him.

He stopped with his hand on the door. "It was as powerful as two," he countered.

"Still, I don't feel sufficiently pacified yet."

Elijah opened the door and looked over his shoulder as he stepped onto my covered porch. "I'll be back, Freckles. It might not be tonight, but I'll be back."

"Be safe," I called after him as he jogged down the steps and across the lawn.

"Plan on it."

I went back inside prepared to nuke some popcorn and find something to watch on Netflix when my phone rang. As if life hadn't screwed with me enough already that evening, I saw that my mother was calling.

There was no sense in ignoring her call because she'd just call back. "Hello, Mama."

"You could've been killed!"

"Mama, I—"

"Don't you 'mama' me, young lady. I'm coming over there."

"Why? I'm okay. I didn't see anything." I'd already had this conversation with Milo and Memphis, who had both insisted they come over to my house. Memphis did it out of concern for me while Milo was only being nosy about the conversation I had with the oh-so-very-fucking-good-looking detective after he and Memphis left.

"You're my baby girl and you could've been killed tonight."

"Mama, that's an awful big leap. Why aren't you coddling Milo?"

"Who the hell said I wasn't? Where do you think I've been the last thirty minutes?" An image of Mom peppering Milo's face with kisses as she fussed over him made me smile. Not because Milo needed it, but because he was as independent as I was. I knew he hadn't called Mom, which meant she found out the old-fashioned way—word of mouth. Someone had burned up my mom's phone as soon as the cops showed up. I was adamant that I wanted to be alone, but then my mom brought out her big guns. "I baked brownies today."

"You and your brownies get on over here."

It was good to be loved. Of course, I like my prior plans of loving better. Well, sexing at least.

Chapter Twelve

Elijah

MY MOTTO OF DUTY FIRST HAD NEVER BEEN TESTED AS strongly as when I was kneeling between Maegan's parted legs tasting the pleasure that I gave her on my tongue and lips. I was moments away from sinking inside that tight, hot heat—the place I wanted to be all fucking week long—just as Wen called. I had to turn away from her luscious body so that I could concentrate on the conversation and not how hard my dick throbbed behind my zipper.

Maybe Wen's locating Thom Renzo's surviving uncle was fate because I was close to handing over my heart to Maegan Miracle. If this continued, I'd be looking around her antique shop for a pretty silver tray to put it on before presenting it to her. She was everything I wanted in a woman and more, but I had been tricked before into believing the woman my heart chose for me was the one I'd spend my life with. I had been more than happy with occasional hookups until I met Maegan. She made me want so much more than I trusted myself to accept. I wanted to give her more than I had to offer. That spelled disaster because one, or both, of us was going to get hurt if I allowed this *thing* between us to continue. It was better to break off all personal ties with her before things got out of hand.

You already tried that, moron. Yeah, well, I'd just have to try harder because I really believed I could be happy in Blissville if I could tamp down the urges that my beautiful neighbor brought out in me. I could hit up a bar or club in Cincinnati if I needed some company for the night. I found it amazing at how cold that idea left me when just a few weeks ago it would've heated my blood. *Resisting is futile, dumb fuck.*

I was glad the drive to the police station was a short one so that my brain had something to focus on other than Maegan's lush body and the sounds she made when she came. I could ignore my heart's demand that I give her a chance to prove that she was nothing like Brandy and focus on solving a homicide. The first step in solving a murder was to learn everything you could about the victim.

"Sorry for calling you out tonight," Kevin Wen said when I opened the passenger door of his cruiser. "I'm sure you had better things to do."

"Catching Renzo's killer is the only thing on my mind." A kaleidoscope of sexy and sweet Maegan images replayed in my brain, calling me out for being a liar. Fine, but I could turn that off to focus on nailing a criminal. *Then we can think about nailing…* "What do we know?" I asked Wen, cutting off my thoughts.

"Thom's uncle, Stanley Hubert, lives about twenty minutes from here in a rural part of Carter County. According to my mother, he's a confirmed bachelor and former ladies' man, if you will. I don't know what kind of relationship Stanley had with his sister's only son."

"It's a start," I told him. "We'll start there and kick over every rock until we find our guy."

"Or gal," Wen corrected.

"Or gal," I conceded.

It was black as pitch in the countryside, which was nothing new to me since I grew up in rural Franklin County, but it added an element of danger when showing up at someone's house unexpected.

The last thing I wanted was to look down the barrel of a trigger-happy landowner. I was pleased when we arrived at Stanley Hubert's house and there was plenty of exterior light illuminating our way to the front porch.

"This place isn't nearly as creepy as his sister's house," Wen softly muttered before he knocked on the front door. "That place looked like something you'd see in a gothic horror story. I'm surprised there aren't gargoyles."

Wen was in uniform and my badge hung around my neck in plain sight for Mr. Hubert to see when he looked through the glass after I rang the doorbell. When he opened the door, I saw awareness in his eyes.

"I guess you're here about Thom," he said. "Is it true?"

"I'm sorry to tell you that your nephew, Thom Renzo, was a victim of a homicide. We're sorry for your loss, Mr. Hubert," I told the elderly man.

"Do you need me to come down and identify the body?" he asked nervously.

"No, sir," Wen told him. "I went to school with Thom so I was able to do that for you." What we didn't tell the man was that our medical examiner, Dr. Melissa Chen, would also confirm the DB's identity with dental records. Every bone in Thom's face was broken so using his driver's license photo for comparison wasn't an option. Wen identified him by a tattoo on his forearm. I was glad we could spare Mr. Hubert from having to look at what remained of his nephew. "Can we ask you a few questions?"

"Okay," Mr. Hubert replied, stepping back so we could enter his house. "I just can't believe it." The elderly man slowly shook his head as he lowered himself into his recliner. "Who'd want to hurt Thom?"

Wen took a seat on the sofa and angled his body toward Mr. Hubert while I remained standing, taking a minute to check out Mr. Hubert's surrounding while Wen finished making small talk with the elderly man. Everything was dated, drab, and dreary. If I wanted to add another d word into the mix, I would've chosen dusty. Hubert himself dressed like Mr. Rogers and it was hard to imagine that he was once a ladies' man. What era? The seventies? Time had not been kind to the man, and I wondered how much of it had to do with the half-empty bottle of whiskey and the cigarette smoldering in the ashtray on the table beside his chair. How often did he go through a bottle? A day? A week? A month? How many packs of cigarettes did he puff through in a day?

You're looking at your future self if you're not careful. I could've argued that I rarely drank and never smoked, but I knew that my heart wasn't referring to his habits. The loneliness the man felt was a palpable thing that hung heavy and thick in the air. Sure, hearing that his nephew died so closely on the heels of his brother-in-law probably played a large part, but I sensed that his loneliness was an old friend, not a new acquaintance.

The thought was depressing as fuck so I quickly steered my thoughts back to the investigation. "When was the last time you spoke to Thom?"

"Not since his father's funeral." Mr. Hubert shook his head sadly. "I tried being closer to the boy, but he was just… odd."

"Odd? How so?" I followed up.

"I don't like to speak ill of the dead," Mr. Hubert replied.

"We need to find out who killed your nephew and the only way to do that is to look at everything, even when that makes us uncomfortable, sir," Wen told the grieving man.

"I'm not sure I'm the right person to be talking to since I feel like I don't know Thom anymore. We used to be close when he was a kid, but he drifted away once he got to high school. He ran around with the Sampson kid, who was nothing but trouble. I wasn't surprised at all when he was arrested for stealing drugs from the evidence locker when he was a deputy in Texas. He'd always been a sly one, and that mother of his always made excuses for him and covered up his bad behavior. Still, I don't think any of them were up to criminal mischief back then, mind you. They formed that awful band and were convinced they'd make it big. That was all Thom talked about during high school. He drove us nuts with 'our band' this and 'our band' that."

Wen had already explained the Sampson and Renzo connection to me at the station, but that seemed like a stretch. Sampson was arrested and turned over to the DEA two years ago, so it wasn't likely that he knew anything about Renzo's death. It had to be related to something else.

"As weird and as isolated as Thom had become over the last decade, it's really hard to imagine him making someone mad enough to kill him."

I'd seen kids get gunned down in the street for a pair of fucking shoes, so I discounted nothing. I saw no need to share my past experiences with him though. Instead, I asked, "Did your sister and brother-in-law own anything of value?"

"Something valuable enough to kill over? No, of course not. Why would you ask me that?"

"Thom had made arrangements with an auction house to sell the contents in the household, but he also set up a meeting with a local woman to give her first crack at the things she wanted to buy for her store. Is it possible there was a family heirloom worth a significant amount of money?"

"Was the local woman little Maegan Miracle?" Mr. Hubert asked. I didn't like the way he lit up a little and suddenly sat straighter in his chair. *Little Maegan Miracle?* Little as far as height maybe, but that woman was larger than life when it came to personality and sex appeal. *Yeah, IEDs could be little too, but look at the damage those bastards caused!*

"Yes, it was Miss Miracle. In fact, she and two other people were the ones who discovered Thom."

"Oh no!" He sounded horrified at the prospect, so I rushed to assure him that Maegan was okay.

"She didn't find Thom's body," I explained. "She saw the blood and called nine-one-one."

"Still, she must be traumatized."

An image of Maegan arched over the side of the couch and grinding her pussy against my face sprung to mind. If I wasn't careful, other things would get sprung. "She's a trooper, Mr. Hubert. What about an heirloom or anything else you can think of?"

Mr. Hubert scoffed. "The only thing Betsy and I inherited from our side of the family was high cholesterol, but I can't speak about Charlie's family. He was from Georgia, and I don't think I've seen his family since the day he married my sister. They met while attending the University of Kentucky. Charlie's family never approved of my sister or our family. We weren't good enough for them."

"You didn't see them at his funeral?" Wen asked.

"Not even then."

"Do you know if Thom was able to contact anyone from the Renzo side after his father passed?"

"Thom told me that they didn't bother with his dad while he was alive, nor did they show up for his mother's service. He said they didn't deserve to be notified that Charlie passed away. He didn't want false platitudes to ruin his father's memorial." I could understand his sentiment. "Charlie just gave up on life after Betsy passed away."

"Were their deaths close together?"

"A few months apart," he answered.

"Did either your sister or brother-in-law have any property disputes with anyone?" I asked.

"Nothing that they ever told me about, Detective. I'd surely tell you if I knew."

I'd be willing to accept that Thom's homicide had nothing to do with his parents' estate if it wasn't for the timing. Unfortunately, there was no one alive to ask about missing items from the estate. Unless, Maegan had knowledge of specific items that were no longer on the premises. She had expressed her eagerness to pick through the estate, but why? What did she know that Stanley Hubert didn't. I made a note to ask her the following morning. *Why wait until morning? She made it clear that I was welcome back there if I stopped freaking out.*

Wen and I asked a few additional questions, but we didn't learn anything of value. Hubert provided the name of the estate attorney who represented both of Thom's parents. I added his name to the list of people I wanted to interview the next day. I couldn't think of anything else to ask Mr. Hubert right then, so I expressed my condolences once more and thanked him for his time.

"What time do you want to get started tomorrow morning?" Wen asked once we were back in his car.

With Adrian gone on vacation until Monday, I was grateful to have his help. I was just sorry that I had to cut into his time off with his family. "Does nine o'clock work for you?" I asked.

"Yeah, that works okay for me."

It was almost eight in the evening by the time that Wen dropped me off at my truck. I thought about going to the diner for a piece of pie, but I didn't feel like company. *Liar.* I wanted company, but not the kind I'd find at the diner. I wouldn't mind spending some time with a certain blonde-haired minx but saw that she had company when I pulled onto our street. I'd never seen that silver Cadillac parked in her driveway before and couldn't help wondering if it was that putz I met in her shop. Instead of calling the station to have them run the license plates, I grabbed my blanket and slippers off the porch and went inside.

I thought about Stanley Hubert and the sadness that rolled off him in waves when I kicked back in my recliner to watch college hoops with a cold beer in my hand. Was that what I had to look forward to in the future? How were my circumstances any different than his? *Age and choice of alcohol.*

"I'm not lonely." *Liar.*

I fell asleep after halftime and didn't wake up again until after one in the morning. I didn't recall covering myself with the blanket that Maegan returned to me, but her fresh floral scent tickled my nose as soon as I opened my eyes. One of the anchormen on ESPN was talking about the biggest upset in college basketball history when I hit the remote to turn off the tv. Normally that would interest me, but my brain wasn't the only thing woken up by Maegan's perfume. My dick reminded me of how close we'd come to the promise land only to be denied by honor and duty. I knew damn well I wouldn't go back to sleep with a dick that hard.

I went upstairs and turned on the shower to let it run for a few minutes before I considered removing my clothes. I had learned quickly when I moved in that it took a long time for hot water to travel along the old pipes in my rental house. January wasn't the time of year to stand around naked and wait. The hot water heater was in the basement, but you'd have thought it was a good thousand feet beneath the earth for as long as it took. In the mornings, I could brush my teeth and shave my face before the water reached tepid temperatures.

I wasn't about to climb into a cold shower in the dead of winter, so I crossed the room and looked out my bedroom window to kill time. I tried to convince myself that it was to check out the neighborhood, but I released the curtain I'd pulled back the second I saw that Maegan's SUV was the only one parked in her driveway.

I felt the smile tugging at my lips as I made my way back to the bathroom because I knew where my first stop would be in the morning. I tested the water to make sure it was hot enough then stripped out of my clothes. Once beneath the hot spray, I gripped my cock and stroked it while thinking about all the naughty things I could do to Maegan on her sturdy-looking desk in her office. Then I recalled the sounds she made as she jerked and came apart beneath me earlier that night. It felt so real to me that I could almost taste her on my tongue again as I shot my load onto the black tile.

I braced one arm against the wall while I let the hot water beat down on my head, neck, and shoulders. I wished like hell Maegan was sleeping in my bed so I could kiss her awake and make love to her slowly since I took the edge off my desire. A week ago, I panicked because of the things that Maegan made me feel. And while I wasn't ready to completely throw caution to the wind, I wasn't willing to blow my second chance with her either.

Baby steps, Markham.

Chapter Thirteen

Maegan

"How long did Mom coddle you last night?" Milo asked after I arrived at work the next morning.

"Longer than I thought." I figured she was going to hang around for an hour tops, but she stuck around for four hours. "We watched a few chick flicks to soothe her nerves." Which meant that she was still there when Elijah's truck rumbled into his driveway. Did he wonder who was visiting? Did he care? *Stop it, Maegan.*

"You could've called me. I had nothing better to do on a Friday night," Milo whined.

"And whose fault is that, Milo?"

"Memphis had plans."

"I wasn't talking about Memphis and you know it." I pinned him with a dark look. "Andy had to cancel the week before, but I seem to remember him calling to tell you that he was available last night to look at the upstairs space."

"Well, it wasn't convenient for me. I had made a commitment to you—"

"Save your breath, Milo. It's okay to admit that you're afraid to be alone with Andy. You don't trust yourself around all that hunky flesh."

"The fuck you say. I'm not remotely interested in him, so Andy's 'hunky flesh' is completely safe from me," he rebutted, but I noticed that he avoided my penetrating gaze when he told that big fat lie. Instead, he placed pastries and donuts in the cases.

"Anyway, had I known she was going to stick around for four hours then I would've called you. I had hoped for a quiet night with a bubble bath and a good book after the night we had."

"Who's the liar now?" Milo demanded. His roundabout confession made me smile. Then my brother stood up straight and faced me. "Detective Markham was really worried about you last night. I think that's why he seemed so angry with you."

"Yeah, I know."

"Because he told you so?" Milo asked with a raised brow.

I swallowed hard and hoped my face wasn't too red when I pictured Elijah's dark head between my thighs. "In his own way."

"At least one of us is getting some," Milo said.

"I never—"

"You didn't have to, sister dear, nor did I need to rely on my twink link. Your emotions are broadcasted all over your face." Milo looked over my shoulder toward the front door. "You might want to get them under control too."

"Why?"

Someone rapped their knuckles confidently against the door even though we weren't due to open for another hour. It could've been one of our baristas who'd forgotten their key or an overeager, desperate customer, but I could tell by Milo's wry grin who stood on the other side of the glass.

I stuck my tongue out at Milo before I turned and locked eyes with Elijah. The sun had just started to rise and the peachy-pink sky was a beautiful backdrop to his rugged beauty. He stole my breath and I stood frozen in place for several heartbeats as I catalogued the scruff that covered his chin and his dark, penetrative stare. Those full lips tilted in a crooked smile as he pointed to the lock. Yeah, he knew the effect he had on me.

"Invite him in," Milo whispered behind me.

"You've been watching reruns of *True Blood* again, haven't you?"

"Maybe, but let the good detective in before his manly parts shrivel in the cold," Milo said. "It's rude to keep a man waiting." The last part was a perfect imitation of our mother.

I crossed the coffee shop and opened the door. "We're not open for an hour, Detective Markham."

"I'm not here for the pastries and coffee." He sniffed the air appreciatively. "Although, I wouldn't turn down an early morning treat."

"I remember how you like those."

Lust smoldered in Elijah's eyes until Milo cleared his throat, reminding us both that we weren't alone. Elijah blinked and broke the special connection we shared. The desire I saw in his eyes was replaced with a different kind of determination, which told me that his early morning visit was a professional one. "Good morning, Milo," Elijah said to my brother without taking his eyes off me.

"Would you like a pastry or a cup of coffee, Detective?"

"No, thanks," he replied, still not looking away from me. "I have a few follow-up questions for you."

"Okay. Would you like to talk in my office or—"

"We better stay here," he said softly. *Where it was safe.* He didn't say the words, but I saw them in his wry expression. We both knew what would happen if we took advantage of the privacy that my office afforded us.

"What can I do for you this morning?" I asked once we sat at an empty table. I was careful to keep my voice neutral and professional, but I saw the way Elijah's nostrils flared.

"Finding a motive will be crucial to solving Thom Renzo's homicide. I talked to his uncle last night and he wasn't aware of the Renzos owning valuable items, but I know that men are often clueless about these types of things. What about the estate interested you? Were you looking for something specific?"

"It wasn't the Renzos' belongings that grabbed my interest; it was the items left behind by the previous owners."

"Like something the Renzos found in the attic after they moved in?" Elijah asked.

"Well, that house itself is kind of folklore around here. You could tell it was old, right?"

"Yeah, it reminded me of something you'd see in *Scooby-Doo*."

"People swear up and down that it's haunted," I told Elijah. "It was originally built by Anthony Bliss who founded this town in eighteen thirty. Anthony was a progressive railroad tycoon who believed that Blissville could be a thriving depot because of its central location to bigger cities like Cincinnati, Dayton, and Columbus. He believed railroads were the key for both shipping and traveling. People thought he was crazy when he laid out this tract of land and named it after himself. He built the home here and moved his family from New York City. His vision became true and this tiny little community became a bustling trading town. At first, the railroads were used strictly for travel in Ohio, but eventually they expanded to include national railways."

"Huh, I never would've guessed that," Elijah said. "So, the Bliss family just up and abandoned their house?"

"Rumor has it that Anthony Bliss had ulterior motives for relocating his family." I leaned closer and dropped my voice. "It's believed that he was trying to outrun a curse."

"A curse?" Elijah asked skeptically.

"There are different versions of who placed the curse on the family from gypsies to Native Americans, but it seems to have started with Anthony's father, John. He was reported to be a ruthless businessman who lied and manipulated to get his way. The curse was placed on him and his heirs because the sins of the father are passed along to their offspring."

"That's bullshit," Elijah said.

"Which part?"

"The sins of the father thing. I mean, I've heard that before, of course, but I think it's bullshit." I could tell he was enthralled by my story though.

"Anyway, John Bliss died of a heart attack in his mistress's bed in upstate New York supposedly a week after he was cursed. He left behind a wife and four sons. Anthony was the youngest."

"Let me guess, his three brothers all died from mysterious deaths."

"One of them died in war, one of them died after falling from a horse and breaking his neck, and the third brother drowned in a river. John was the last Bliss standing and decided to try and outrun the curse."

"Kind of like out of sight, out of mind?" Elijah asked.

"That's how the story goes."

"Okay, so he moved here, named the town after himself, and brought the railroad through Blissville. Then what?"

"He disappeared without a trace in 1850."

"What?"

"Seriously, he just disappeared. He went for a horse ride like he normally did every day regardless of the weather and never returned."

"What happened to his family?" Elijah asked.

"Well, Melanie Bliss was distraught and was never seen in public again. Too many years had passed since his last brother died for her to believe that he was a victim of the curse. She was convinced he left her to start a new life, so she was too ashamed to show her face in town. Her sister came to live with them and assumed care for the children until Melanie died of a broken heart."

Elijah rolled his eyes like he doubted that was a legitimate cause of death. "Then what happened?"

"Melanie's sister packed up the children, sold the house to a prominent doctor in town, and moved back to New York. She shipped what she wanted to keep and left everything else behind. From what I've heard, Melanie held onto all of Anthony's things in case he returned, but her sister had no desire to drag his crap back to New York after he left his family high and dry. Dr. Martin's family moved in and reported that inexplicable things kept happening. Doors slamming in parts of the house where no one was or the smell of pipe tobacco floating through the air when no one in the family smoked."

"They thought it was haunted?" Elijah asked.

"Yes, but they didn't feel like the ghost was trying to hurt them, so they stayed there. The house remained in their family for many decades until the kids sold it to the Renzos after both their parents died. The caveat was that the Renzos took possession of the contents as well as the house. Which meant that they possibly inherited some of Anthony Bliss's possessions as well. I was hoping to find treasures from the early railroad days. I already have an original depot sign showing the destinations for various cities and the departure times. I won't part with that no matter how much someone offers me, but I had hoped to find something similar to sell."

"So, no fine china or jewelry?"

"There's a possibility that those things were present also. Anthony inherited a lot after his mother passed on and I don't think Melanie cared for her mother-in-law. Thom told me in his email that his mother had once found a vintage pearl necklace in a black velvet pouch. They were the kind that you tied behind your neck with satin or velvet ribbons. He said that they were too fragile to be worn and his mother planned to restring them. He wasn't sure if she ever did though because she never mentioned them again."

"Vintage pearls and railroad stuff. Anything else?"

"You could always talk to Homer Stillwater who runs the Blissville Historical Society and Museum."

"You have a historical society and museum?" Elijah asked incredulously.

"There's so much more to this tiny town than meets the eye," I told him. "They're only open a few days a week, but I can pull some strings to see if Homer will meet you today."

"What kind of strings?"

"His wife is my part-time employee, Elijah. I wasn't going to offer up sexual favors."

"Not this early in the morning anyway," Milo interjected, letting me know he'd been eavesdropping the entire time.

Elijah snorted. "Good to know," he said to my idiot brother.

I glanced at my watch and saw that we'd been talking longer than I realized. "Do you have any other questions for me? I should get back to helping Milo since our faithful customers will be showing up soon."

Elijah tucked his notebook and pen inside an interior pocket of his battered, black leather jacket. When he looked at me again, the smoldering heat had returned to his dark brown eyes. "Do you have plans tonight?"

"No."

"You do now." I should've been offended by his bold assumption and arrogance, but it would've been a lie. He wanted me; I wanted him. No games or pretense was wanted or needed. "What time do you get off?" His face turned a light shade of pink when I raised a brow at his question. "From work."

"I should be home by five thirty."

"I'd kill for a steak dinner," Elijah said. "Does that appeal to you?"

"It sounds great."

"Does six o'clock work for you, or do you need more time?"

"Six is fine." Neither of us made a move to get up until I heard Milo curse the espresso machine. It was a bit tricky at times and he had no patience with it. He sounded like he was a few seconds away from taking a hammer to the expensive piece of equipment. "I better go."

"See you tonight, Maegan." I expected him to walk away, but he placed his hand on the back of my neck and pulled me to him for a brief kiss. "I hope you have a good day."

"You too."

"I think I just came in my pants," Milo said breathlessly behind me after the door closed behind Elijah. I heard our machine hiss followed by Milo's yelp.

I stifled a giggle even though I thought he deserved it for being nosy. I took over prepping the espresso machine to save Milo from further pain. Two of our baristas, Joe and Sarah, showed up and the four of us fell into an easy routine that lasted until our doors opened to the public. The town had heard about what happened to Thom, of course, so we were even busier than a normal Saturday morning. Some people stopped by to check on us, but most attempted to get grisly details or speculate on who amongst us was the killer.

For the most part, I plastered a smile on my face while accepting well wishes and deflecting questions from inappropriate jerks, but it was mentally draining. Curious Things opened at ten and was packed with customers all day long until I closed. My customers' wild speculations spanned from a cult killing to Anthony's ghost getting vengeance for Thom attempting to sell his things to strangers.

I don't think I took an easy breath until I locked the door after my last customer left at five thirty. I shut off the lights and let myself out the back door, stepping into the alley. I was running behind and eager to get home and changed for my… What was going on between Elijah and me? Was it a date? Two people consuming red meat before they fucked like animals? I was down with either of those things, to be honest.

I had just turned my key in the deadbolt lock when I detected movement near our dumpsters. Fear danced up my spine making the hair on the back of my neck stand up. I turned my head in that direction, but didn't see anyone.

"Hello?" I asked loudly as I grabbed the canister of pepper spray on my keychain and aimed it in front of me. "Is there anyone there?" It was hard to get the words past the lump of terror lodged in my throat.

My options were to go back inside and exit the store through the front door or continue down the alleyway to get to my parked car. Smart people would've chosen option number one, but I went with option number two. My heart pounded harder and faster with every step I took toward the dumpster. If this were a movie, the audience would be yelling insults at me right before the psycho killer jumped out of the dumpster and attacked me.

My eyes kept shifting from the path in front of me to the closed lids as I walked by them, but I could tell the sound was coming from the other side of the bins, not inside them. Just as I stepped even with the far corner of the last dumpster, a black ball of hissing fur came flying around the corner.

I screamed and dropped my keys then clutched my heart while I tried to catch my breath. "Damn cat!" I hissed angrily.

I laughed nervously when I realized that I wasn't going to drop dead from a heart attack but then I saw what had drawn the cat's attention. Someone placed an oddly shaped item wrapped in bloody newspaper beside the dumpster. "This can't be good," I said, blindly fishing my phone out of my purse while I kept my eyes on my surroundings.

"Or a coincidence," I whispered.

Chapter Fourteen

Elijah

"THIS CAN'T BE A COINCIDENCE, WEN." THE SICK FEELING I got in the pit of my stomach when Maegan called me intensified as I stared down at the bloody evidence left behind her shop.

"I don't think so either, Markham."

The two of us had donned rubber gloves and blue booties before entering the alley to keep from further contaminating the scene. We squatted down next to the object wrapped in bloody newspaper and did the rock, paper, scissors game. The loser had to open the newspaper to see what was hidden inside. I went with paper and Wen chose scissors.

"Dammit," I muttered.

"I hope it's not a severed head, pal."

"It wouldn't be the first time," I said to my temporary partner. I'd seen the absolute worst the world had to offer in my roles as soldier and cop. I reached down and slowly peeled back the sides to reveal a bloody marble bust of a man's head. "Sort of like a severed head," I told Wen.

"I think we're looking at the weapon that was used to bash in

Thom Renzo's skull." Wen held open the evidence bag, and I gingerly placed the bust and newspaper inside it. Maybe there was something significant about the newspaper that would leave a clue. "I'll get this to the lab."

"Thanks, I'll be there soon," I told him, but I had already turned my attention to the opening of the alley where I knew a certain blonde bombshell was waiting for me.

A few other officers were still looking for evidence with flashlights since the sun was rapidly setting. Once out of the alley, Wen and I placed our booties in a paper evidence bag and our rubber gloves in a bag designated for the biohazard disposal. The lab could check the booties to see if any viable evidence was found. It wasn't likely since we were walking in an alley, but it paid to be vigilant.

I found Maegan sitting in her SUV. She was staring off in space and didn't know that I had approached until I lightly tapped on her window. She jerked in her seat and I felt terrible that I scared her even more than she'd already been that evening. She blew out a relieved breath and unlocked her door. I went around to the passenger side and got in beside her.

"I'm sorry that I scared you."

"You'd think that I would've been more alert after what happened this evening," she said. "Can you tell me what that was?"

"It was a marble bust of a man's head. I'm pretty sure it's my murder weapon."

"Someone killed Thom on the night I was supposed to meet him then placed the murder weapon in the alley behind my business the very next day. Is that what you're telling me?" She was struggling to remain calm, but I heard the panic creeping into her voice. "But why?"

"That's what I'm going to figure out." I reached over and covered her hands with mine. "I need to go to the station to look at the evidence we collected in a better light. Is there someone you can call to hang out with you until I'm done? Maybe whoever drives that

Cadillac I saw in your driveway."

"That's my mom's car," she told me. "I would like to say that I'm a big girl and don't need a sitter, but I honestly don't want to be alone tonight. I think I'll grab Lulu and go to my parents' house."

"Oh." I sounded as disappointed as I felt. It wasn't that I expected her to throw me down and fuck me stupid after the night she had, but I just wanted to know that she was okay.

"Unless you still want to go out later. I'm not sure that I'll be very good company."

"I wouldn't expect you to be either," I replied. "Why don't you go to your parents' house for a little bit and I'll call you when I'm done at the station. I shouldn't be long because most of our evidence will have to be sent to the state lab. I'll pick us up something to eat at the diner and we'll just stay in tonight."

"That sounds perfect." She was holding up remarkably well and I was so proud of her. I wanted to pull her into my arms, but it wouldn't look very professional in front of my fellow officers.

I cupped her face with my hand and brushed my thumb over her cheekbone. "I want to kiss you, Freckles."

Maegan wrapped her hand around my wrist and leaned her head into my touch before she turned her face and kissed the palm of my hand. "Please," was her simple reply.

I pulled Maegan toward me slowly, keeping my gaze locked on her mesmerizing green eyes the entire time. The kiss wasn't about sex, it was about comfort—hers and mine. I think she knocked ten years off my life when I answered her distress call, and I needed to know she was truly okay. She needed to know I was there for her and would do everything in my power to keep her safe. I pressed my lips softly against hers then went back for a second, lingering kiss.

Maegan released a shaky breath when we pulled apart and offered me a crooked smile. At least for the time being, I gave her something to think about other than a crazy killer on the loose planting bloody evidence outside her business. My brain wanted to remain focused on the case, but my body was getting other ideas.

"I'm going to go now." *While I still can.* "What do you feel like eating?"

"I think Emma's beef stew and homemade dinner rolls can fix just about anything," Maegan told me. That was one item on the menu I still hadn't tried, and I decided to rectify that immediately.

"I'll call you when I'm leaving the diner."

"Thank you, Elijah."

"You're welcome, Maegan."

Getting out of her car and into my truck was harder than it should've been. I hardly knew the lady, but she already had a hold on me. I could've continued lying to myself that I didn't want her, or I could take a chance that I might've found the girl for me. I knew which one I wanted to be true, but the question was: how badly did I want it?

Captain Roman-Wyatt was at the station when I arrived. He asked Wen and me to give him an update on what happened that evening.

"I'm sorry that you got called in, Captain."

"It's part of the job description, Detective. Luckily, it doesn't happen very often. Nothing says 'Welcome to Blissville' like a homicide. I worked here a few years before I had to investigate one, so you must be special," he teased.

"Adrian will be pissed he missed all the excitement," Wen told our captain.

"Oh, no he won't," Adrian said, entering the captain's office. "I go out of town for a few days and all hell breaks loose. Can't y'all protect and serve the people without me?"

"Oh good, Adrian's back," Wen said. "The rest of us can go on home. He'll take it from here."

"Was there really a severed head dumped in the alley behind the coffee shop?"

"It was a bloody marble bust," I told my new partner. Even though I hadn't worked in the field with him yet, we had clicked right away when I met him the day I interviewed with the captain.

"Bust? Like a breast?" Adrian asked

"Bust, as in a marble statue of someone's head and shoulders," our captain answered. "Of course, your mind went there."

"Who was the bust of and what the hell was it doing in Maegan's alley?"

"I have a pretty good idea of who the bust was created to honor, but I need to confirm it. I'm hoping the newspaper will provide a clue, but if not, the guy from the historical society should be able to help us."

"Who do you think it is?" the captain asked me.

"I think it's Blissville's founder, Anthony Bliss."

"Who's he?" the captain asked.

I told him everything that Maegan had shared with me that morning. I had called Homer Stillwater to make an appointment with him, but he was out of town for the day. "I'd much rather help you solve a homicide than go antiquing with my wife, but I'm already in the doghouse," he had told me. "Can this wait until tomorrow? I can meet you at the historical society after church."

I had agreed to meet him, but I would have to revise our meeting location since I couldn't take a key piece of evidence out of the station. In the meantime, I planned to use everyone's favorite research tool: Google.

"Let's suit up and see what we have before we send it off to the state lab," the captain said. "I hope they can get the results back to us fairly quickly so we can for sure say the bust was used to kill Renzo."

"I have a contact in the state lab. I don't mind making a phone call or two," I offered.

"Is she pretty?" Adrian teased, implying that I knew her outside the job. I did, but not in the way he thought.

"Kelsey is very pretty, but better yet, she's a brilliant scientist. Her wife wouldn't approve of me trying to charm her to get my evidence moved up the priority list though. I've seen Valeria swing a bat for our co-ed softball team, so I won't be crossing any lines."

"Fair enough," Adrian replied.

In our small lab, Officer Jayna Murkowsky was a step ahead of us. She was scanning the bust with a handheld device that looked like something they used at a store for items too big to put on the conveyor belt. Instead of reading a barcode, it recorded the angles of the face and compiled the data into her computer to form a photo. On another computer, she had a split screen showing Anthony Bliss's image from two different angles.

"Left was definitely his strongest side," Adrian said.

"That's the side most people choose for selfies," Wen added.

"It's true that most people photograph best from the left side," Murkowsky agreed.

"How do you know that about selfies, Wen?" Adrian asked incredulously."Do you take a lot?"

"Teen sister."

"Ahhh," we all said.

"Does that same logic apply to dick pics?" Adrian pondered out loud.

"Only if your dick smiles, Detective," Murkowsky replied good-naturedly.

"Can we get back to the evidence please?" the captain asked. "I don't even want to know why Adrian wants to know the best side to photograph his dick."

"Sorry, sir," Adrian said. "I apologize, Officer Murkowsky."

"I'm not offended, Adrian."

"Let's take a look at the newspaper," I told Adrian. "It was getting dark in the alleyway so I couldn't be sure, but the parts of the newspaper not covered in blood looked brownish from age."

I carefully straightened out the wrinkled paper with gloved hands while Adrian had the camera ready to photograph any clues.

The paper was stiff to work with since it had been saturated with blood. There was also a lot of hair and flesh stuck to the paper from where it transferred off the bust. I finally spread the paper on the sterile surface and saw that it was even older than I thought. It was an article dated May 1, 1850.

"Anthony Bliss, railroad magnate and Blissville founder disappeared on the morning of April 30, 1850," I read out loud. "Was it premeditated or was Mr. Bliss a victim of foul play or his family curse?"

"Can you imagine the headings today?" Adrian asked. "Alien abduction would certainly be included."

"I can't help but wonder what the hell happened to him," I replied. "I wonder if the man kept journals or anything. As creepy as that cellar is, I'm pretty sure I have to go back and do some digging. Now that you're back…"

"I'm suddenly not feeling that good. Must've been something I ate. Wen, will help you out."

"Thanks a lot," Wen replied dryly.

"Adrian loves dark, dank cellars," the captain teased. "That last murder we had in Blissville required us to dig around through one."

"The captain's house," Adrian said.

"Someone was murdered in your cellar?" I asked the captain. "Internal Affairs must love you."

His lips tipped up into a quirky, half-smile. "It wasn't my house at the time."

"You bought a house where a homicide was committed though?" I asked. I wasn't sure how I felt about that.

"Married the prime suspect too," Adrian added.

"Josh?" I asked in shock.

"It's a long story," the captain said to me before turning to his former partner. "No one believed Josh killed Georgia Beaumont."

"I'll tell you all about it over dinner, partner," Adrian said cheerfully.

As much as I wanted to hear the story, I had someplace I wanted to be more that night. "I have plans tonight, but perhaps you can tell me all about it while we dig through boxes looking for journals or some other type of evidence."

"Fine," Adrian reluctantly agreed.

Officer Murkowsky's computer program beeped, interrupting me before I could answer. "Aha! It's a one hundred percent match to Anthony Bliss." We looked over her shoulder at the side-by-side comparisons. "See these circles on the bridge of his nose, his eyebrows, and his chin?"

"Yeah," we all answered.

"It's a tool that points out the different angles in the profiles. Green circles mean that the angles match and red means they're different." In every instance, the bust was a positive match to the documented photos of Anthony Bliss.

"That's great work, Murkowsky," the captain said.

"Thank you, sir. There's not much else we can do with the evidence, so I'll bag it and send it to Columbus. I didn't see any obvious fingerprints in the blood on the bust, but that doesn't mean they're not there. Hopefully we can get a DNA match for Thom from either the blood, hair, or tissue transferred to the statue or paper. I don't know how long it was exposed to the elements though."

"Approximately thirty minutes," I told her. "That's the time lapse between the employees leaving Books and Brew and Maegan leaving Curious Things."

"Are there any clues, confessions, or anything that will help us solve this case in the newspaper? Any circled letters that spell our next clue out?" Adrian asked hopefully.

"Nothing that I can tell, but the blood has smeared most of the ink. I can't read much beyond the headline. I have a feeling the bust was deliberately placed that way."

"You think the choice of murder weapon and newspaper used to wrap it are clues?" Wen asked.

"It seems so, but why? What the hell does Thom Renzo have to do with a man that disappeared one hundred and sixty-seven years ago?" I asked.

"Thom was about to let strangers comb through Anthony's things and sell the home he loved," Adrian tossed out there.

"You think the ghost of Anthony Bliss killed Thom Renzo using a statue of himself, wrapped it up in a newspaper article about his disappearance, and left it behind Maegan's business?" the captain disbelievingly asked. "That's a stretch."

"No, but it sounds like you do, Cap." Adrian raised a brow so high it nearly disappeared. "I meant who would be angry that Thom was about to do that? Do we know what happened to the Bliss kids once they moved away? Is it possible that a great-great-grandkid is pissed about Thom capitalizing on their family's misfortune?"

"That sounds slightly more plausible than the captain's theory," I told Adrian.

"I didn't say that I believed that," Captain Roman-Wyatt interjected. "Is there anyone in town with a vested interest in that property who took exception to Thom making a buck on Bliss's belongings?"

"I guess we'll find out when we talk to Homer Stillwater from the historical society. I'm meeting him after church tomorrow. I'm thinking we can dig through the cellar in the morning before we meet with him in case we find anything else of importance."

"Okay, fine," Adrian grumbled. "Can I at least sleep in until eight on my last vacation day?"

"How can you sleep until eight with a newborn in the house?" the captain asked, sounding a little jealous. "Dylan and Destiny still aren't sleeping that late."

"Lucky, I guess," Adrian said with a shrug. "How does nine tomorrow morning work? I'll meet you at that haunted mansion."

"Sounds good to me. See you tomorrow, partner."

Adrian discarded his protective gear and patted me on the shoulder before he left the small lab. "I'm going to stop by the diner and pick up dinner for Maegan," I said, discarding my gloves, goggles, face mask, surgical cap, and sterile gown in the biohazard bin.

"How's she holding up?" Officer Murkowsky asked.

"She was pretty shook up when she called me, but she seemed calm by the time I arrived."

"She's a tough lady," Murkowsky replied.

I knew that was true, but my protective instincts were tripped big time. "I hate that it appears our killer is trying to involve Maegan. It feels like a threat to me, and I don't fucking like it."

"Maegan beat cancer, so she'll survive this bastard too."

I wasn't sure how to respond to the news. Did it surprise me that Maegan kicked cancer's ass? No, but I still hated that she went through it. A million questions went through my mind, but Murkowsky wasn't the one I should ask, and I sure as hell wouldn't pose them to Maegan after the night she had. The right time would come when I could ask Freckles.

"Thanks for your help tonight, Wen," I said, steering the conversation back to a less personal one for me. "If you're not busy tomorrow…"

"I'll be there."

"Goodnight, everyone," I said with a small wave. My mind had already moved on from the evidence we found to the fierce woman who was waiting for me.

Chapter Fifteen

"NO, MARILYN, IT WASN'T A SEVERED HEAD," MY MOM said into the phone. "Maegan is fine, by the way. Thank you for asking." She jabbed the button on the cordless phone to disconnect the call. "It's times like these you miss slamming the old-fashioned phones down to hang up on someone. Stabbing that button isn't nearly as satisfying."

"That makes how many calls since Maegan got here?" my dad asked.

"I lost count," my mom replied.

"At least fifteen," Milo said from beside me on the couch. "We've only been here for twenty minutes too. This must be a record for nosy calls."

"Not a single one of them asked about her well-being?" Dennis Miracle wasn't pleased that no one asked about his baby girl. "You remember that when these same people expect you to work ridiculous hours procuring some nineteen fifties vase or a British teapot that is rumored to have traveled over on the Mayflower. You need to start charging more for your time."

"I will, Daddy," I said, nodding my head. "I'm going to need a list of names, Mama."

My mom, thinking I was serious, pulled a pad of paper and pen out of the drawer in the side table and began writing names down. It was best to give her something else to focus on before she started knocking on doors and giving them a piece of her mind.

"You and Lulu should stay here with us tonight," Mom said.

"She has a date with the cop," Milo told her before I could respond.

"Really?" my mom asked, looking up from her Nosy List.

"It's not a date," I told her. "Elijah is just picking up dinner for me at the diner and making sure that I'm okay after tonight."

"You didn't tell me you had a boyfriend. When are we going to meet this fella?" Dad asked.

"He's not my boyfriend, Daddy, so there's no reason for you to meet him."

"If there's food involved then it's a date," Mom said, looking at me over the rim of her glasses. "Is that what you're going to wear?" I looked down at my outfit and didn't think there was anything wrong with my casual jeans and sweater. Saturdays were about comfort for me since they were my longest work day.

"Don't forget about sex," Milo tossed out there. "I saw the sparks flying between the two of you this morning, so don't tell me you're not planning to shimmy on up that sexy-as-fuck tree."

"I don't want to hear this," my dad said, plugging his ears and most likely praying he could unhear what Milo had just said.

"Milo, stop it," I hissed.

"What?" he asked innocently.

"Elijah and I aren't dating. We're just…"

"Fu—"

I covered his mouth before he could finish. Technically, Elijah and I were fuck buddies, or neighbors who fucked, but that wasn't something I wanted my parents to know. Not only that, I didn't like reducing what I shared with Elijah to something that sounded so crude. I didn't have expectations of a happily ever after with the man, but a girl could hope. Right?

"Enough," I said firmly. One hand still covered Milo's mouth, and I used my index finger on my free hand to point at him as a warning. "Are you going to behave?"

"Mmm hmmm," Milo mumbled against my palm. He dramatically gasped for air when I lifted my hand. "You don't let me have any fun, Maegan. It's like you go out of your way to steal the spotlight."

"What are you talking about?"

"I was born first and our parents were overjoyed with their dark-haired angel, but then you had to come kicking and screaming into the world with your gleaming blonde hair."

"Oh, whatever," I replied. "I had zero control of our birth order or the color of my hair."

"Let's talk about my coming out confession over pot roast, carrots, and potatoes," Milo countered.

"You remember what we had for dinner?" my dad asked.

"It was a momentous occasion in a young lad's life," Milo replied huffily.

"My pot roast *is* pretty spectacular," my mom teased.

"There I sat," Milo said theatrically, "my heart pounding in my chest just knowing that it could be my last meal in the house."

"Did he think we were moving out of Blissville because he was gay?" my dad asked my mom.

"Dennis, I think he's trying to imply that he worried we would toss him out on the street because he liked to kiss boys."

"Oh," my father replied then looked at Milo. "Dude, there was glitter in your afterbirth. We knew from day one that you would be fabulous. There was never a chance that we would toss you out."

"Good to know, Father, but that doesn't detract from how Maegan stole the show."

"I did not," I said between loud guffaws of laughter. "You're insane."

"Shall we recap what happened? Mom and Dad were sitting at the dinner table staring at me with their mouths hanging open after I poured my heart and soul into my big announcement. You—"

"Wait a minute! They couldn't understand a word you were saying because you were sobbing the whole time. I just clarified things for you."

"I had no idea what you said," Dad agreed. "I could only make out every fourth word you said and those weren't real clear."

"It was an emotional night for me," Milo declared defensively.

"I was too busy staring at the herbs stuck in your braces," Mom confessed. "Like your father said, we already knew that you were into boys. I knew it was no coincidence that your GI Joes and Maegan's Ken dolls shared a bed in Barbie's playhouse."

"Do you think Barbie knew?" my father asked.

"How could she not? The evidence was right in front of her."

"I always thought that Barbie was too self-absorbed," Dad replied. "How much time could she spend paying attention to her man if she was always putting on lipstick? No one looks that plastic all the time."

"She *is* plastic, love. Looking pretty and being aware of the people around you aren't mutually exclusive. There's nothing wrong with putting your best foot forward."

"Says the former beauty queen," Milo muttered under his breath.

My mom narrowed her eyes at my brother, letting him know that she caught his little remark. "A woman can put on lipstick and pay attention to her family. I wear lipstick and… wait! Are you saying that I'm self-absorbed or don't have my priorities straight?" she asked my father.

He stared at her through wide eyes, his mouth opening and shutting as he tried to find the right words to say. "I would never—"

"Can we *please* get back to how Maegan ruined my coming out?" Milo asked with a pout.

"Sure," Dad said, sounding relieved to shift the spotlight on someone else.

"We're very sorry to have interrupted your hallucinations," Mom added.

"As I was saying," Milo continued, "I was sitting there with my heart in my throat and Maegan just blurts out that she has an announcement too. She paused for dramatic effect to ensure she had your full attention, which *I* taught her, then said 'I like boys too.' You guys were like 'oh, okay' then started talking about how you hope Maegan and I don't get crushes on the same boy."

"It's still a concern," my mom said. "We'd hate for you two to fight over the same guy."

"Our tastes are completely different," Milo said, sniffing the air snobbishly.

I thought that my heartthrob and his weren't all that different. Both Andy and Elijah had similar builds and physical appearances, but that's as far as I could compare since I didn't know much about Elijah's personality. Of course, Andy seemed to have changed a lot since he moved back to Blissville, so I couldn't say that I really knew him anymore either.

"Let's not forget Maegan's theatrics our junior year in high school," Milo continued. The gleam in his eyes told me that he was enjoying himself immensely. "I finally got my first boyfriend and Maegan had to go and get cancer."

I snorted and rolled my eyes. "I'm so sorry that my battle with leukemia was a hardship for *you*." What I loved most about my brother was that he *never* looked at me different or changed the way he treated me. Many of the kids at school treated me like a pariah, almost like they worried they would catch it if they breathed the same air as me.

"You just had to show off your perfectly round head and impeccable bone structure when you lost your hair," Milo teased, but he threw his arm around my shoulders and pulled me until my head rested on his shoulder. He wasn't taking a chance that I mistook his teasing as genuine hurt or criticism.

I hoped my laughter dispelled any doubts. "I'm sorry, I think. That almost sounded like an offhanded compliment."

"You should be sorry, so don't you dare get cancer again," he said haughtily. "You've had your fair share of attention, which is why you should've let *me* discover the severed head in the alleyway."

"Oh, you!" I elbowed him in the stomach and sat up. "It wasn't a severed head."

"Finger?"

"Nope."

"Foot?"

I shook my head. "I told you already. It was a marble bust."

"That's much too boring for your typical theatrics. Last night it was a dead body and tonight it was the potential murder weapon. Does that mean you can expect the killer to come knocking tomorrow, or do you think he'll toy with you some more?"

Okay, sometimes Milo's sense of humor runs a little on the macabre side, but I knew he didn't really want the killer to come knocking on my door. He had the twisted mind of Stephen King but sometimes his attention span resembled that of a five-year-old.

The killer entered the back door and silently crept up the back staircase, careful to avoid the creaks in the steps he had discovered the last time he was in her house. He was only a few feet away from the top when… Squirrel!

I giggled at my inner musings, but shook my head when Milo raised a brow in question. He wouldn't find it nearly as funny as I did.

"You think a crazed killer on the loose is funny?" he asked.

"No, I think the idea that the killer has a personal vendetta against me is funny."

"I think you need to consider moving in here until he's captured just to be safe," Mom said.

"Yeah, Mae. Your bedroom is in the exact same shape that you left it," Milo said. "Same posters and pictures on the wall and all your trophies still lining the shelves. I bet Mom goes in there every week to dust them just in case you ever need to move back home."

"I do not," Mom rebutted.

"More like once a month," Dad countered. "She does your old room too."

"Well, it isn't because I'm expecting my kids to move back home, Dennis. You know damned well I can't sleep if there's dust in the house."

"Of course, I know it," my dad replied. "That doesn't make it sane."

"Sane? Are you saying I'm insane?"

"Just when it comes to dust," my father answered calmly.

I could sense that my mom was working up to a good snit. I might rather tango with a killer than watch my parents argue on a Saturday night. As if I emitted a distress signal, Elijah chose that exact minute to call me.

"Hello?"

"I got extra rolls, Freckles. Emma put in some cinnamon butter for you. She said you love it."

"Aww, I do."

"I think they just got engaged," Milo said to my parents.

"What?" my parents asked at the same time. I shook my head and elbowed my brother again.

"Your house or mine?" I asked Elijah.

"I imagine you'll feel more comfortable in your own bed, so we'll hang at your house tonight." *Bed?* I wanted to tease him about his assumption, but let it go, especially with my family hanging onto my every word.

"Sounds good."

"Maegan, I didn't mean to imply that…"

"I know," I assured Elijah. "I'll see you in fifteen minutes or less."

"Bye, Freckles."

I stood up and smiled. "Well, this has been an entertaining night to say the least, but I must be going. There's a guy across town that's delivering Emma's beef stew and extra dinner rolls to my front door. I don't want to be late."

"It *is* a date," my mom said hopefully.

"Mom, its… I don't know what's going on with Elijah and me, but it's exactly what I need right now."

"That's good enough for us, darling," she said with a sweet smile.

My parents hugged me a little harder and held on a little longer than normal. "I'm going to be okay," I told them.

"Of course, you are," Dad said. "You're a badass, Maegan. That's why those people didn't ask how you were holding up. They know that you're a warrior."

"Thanks, Daddy."

"I'll walk you out, Mae," Milo offered.

When we reached my SUV, Milo pulled me into the circle of his arms. He couldn't hug me as tight as normal with Lulu tucked between us, but I understood the sentiment. His teasing was to cover up the fear he felt for me.

"I'm going to be okay, Milo. No one has a reason to hurt me."

"I want to believe that, Maegan. You're my sister and best friend; I can't lose you."

"No one is losing me. Elijah will keep me safe and catch the killer."

"Don't let *all* the air out of his muscles with sex then," Milo said then pinched the tip of my nose. "He needs to save up some strength and stamina in case he wants to use that body for something other than pleasing you."

I thought back to the glimpse of strength and stamina that I witnessed already. I had a feeling it was just the tip of the iceberg too. "Somehow I don't think Elijah has to worry about that."

"Now you're just bragging. Take your lucky ass on out of here and go get you some."

"Want to grab breakfast in the morning before we open?" I asked once I put Lulu in the car.

"I'll call you once I'm up and moving. Let's cross our fingers that nothing goes wrong at Books and Brew because we could both use an easy day."

"I hear you. Night, Milo." I pulled the door shut and fired the engine to life. Milo waved when I backed out of the driveway. I glanced in the rearview mirror when I reached the intersection at the end of the street and saw that he was still watching me. I felt his fear as strong as I felt my own earlier in the evening.

I'm going to be okay. I wasn't sure if I was trying to convince Milo or myself, maybe both. I wanted it to be true and decided that's how it would be. Whoever killed Thom was going to screw up and get caught. I just needed to stay out of his way until that happened.

Elijah was waiting on my front porch with a huge paper bag filled with food. "Aren't you cold?" I asked when I joined him.

"Focused," he said, scanning the street. "Take the bag and hand me your keys, Freckles."

"Why?"

"I'm going in first to make sure things are okay."

"What if he attacks me on the front porch while you're checking out my house?'

"You're going inside with me, but you'll stay by the front door while I check things out."

"This is silly," I said, marching around him and sliding my key in the front door. "I was just here earlier and nothing was disturbed." I pushed open the door and a blur of black fur darted out the door, scaring the fuck out of me. I cried out in surprise and Lulu barked at the escaping intruder.

"Since when did you have a cat?" Elijah asked.

"I don't have a cat, and it wasn't here when I picked Lulu up." I covered my racing heart with my hand and looked up into Elijah's eyes. "I can't be sure, but I think that is the same cat from the alley when I discovered the bloody object."

"Fuck me!" Elijah said, pulling out his cell phone.

"I had planned on it," I mumbled.

Chapter Sixteen

Elijah

S O MUCH FOR A QUIET SATURDAY NIGHT WITH MAEGAN. RED and blue lights bounced off all the houses on our street from the three patrol cars that responded to my call while our neighbors watched the flutter of activity in and out of Maegan's home from their lawns, porches, or big picture windows.

Adrian pulled up in front of the house and shook his head when he got out of his car. "We gotta stop meeting like this," he said when he joined Jones, Wen, and me on the sidewalk. "Where's Maegan? Is she okay?" he asked Jones. Why'd he ask him? Did they have a history, Jones and Maegan?

"She's at my house with Officer Kasey," I replied, trying to keep the possessiveness I felt out of my voice. "She's okay; just a little shocked from everything that's happened in the last thirty hours." I thought Maegan was taking it better than most people would, but I couldn't tell if that was a front for me, or just the way she handled things.

"Did you find any prints or evidence to nail this bastard?" Adrian asked me.

"There were no signs of forced entry, and we didn't find any traces of an intruder in that house. In fact, if the cat hadn't darted out the front door, we wouldn't have known that our killer had paid her a visit."

"Do we really know for sure he was here? Maybe the cat darted in the house when Maegan was letting her dog out before she headed to her parents' house," Jones suggested.

"The very same cat that startled her in the alley where the killer left the murder weapon?" I asked him.

"Do we really know it's the same cat? There are a lot of black cats in the world," he countered.

"Sure, both things are true, Jones, but my gut tells me that isn't the case," I said. "My instincts tell me that the killer lay in wait to observe Maegan's reaction when she found the evidence. He was close enough to snatch the cat when it ran out of the alley. Then he waited for Maegan to leave, found a way inside her home, and put the cat inside to let her know he was there."

"I don't know, man," Jones hedged. "That seems farfetched to me."

I blew out a frustrated breath and willed myself not to snap. I was new to the department and making enemies of veteran cops on the force during my first week wasn't a good idea. "Look—"

"Too much of a coincidence, Jones," Adrian interrupted, winking to let me know he had my back. I took a few more calming breaths to get my shit under control. "There's nothing neat and tidy about someone clearly unstable enough to kill. Don't try to rationalize the irrational. The facts are that someone killed Thom Renzo not long before Maegan arrived at the house. We don't know if the killer knew Maegan was due to arrive or not. Approximately twenty-four hours later, Maegan finds what we believe is the bloody murder weapon behind her business. Fast forward a few more hours and Maegan returns home to find a strange cat in her house that is either the same cat or similar to the one behind the alley. If we could find the cat, we could check its paws for blood. Did anyone see which way the cat went?"

"Up there," I replied, pointing to a bare tree in Maegan's front yard. Of course, the cat was perched close to the top of the huge oak.

"Meow."

"I'm afraid of heights," Adrian said.

"I pulled a muscle playing basketball," Jones added.

"That means you need to shimmy up the tree, Romeo, and grab that cat," Adrian told me. "Unless you want us to call the fire department. They'll be happy to flex their muscles for Maegan."

"Hey, I'm starting to feel better now," Jones said, moving toward the tree. He suddenly sounded eager to impress Maegan or prevent the firemen from impressing her. I wasn't happy either way.

I wondered if I was the only one who heard the low growl in my throat. "I can handle this," I said calmly. I grew up climbing trees and playing rough. I didn't need some damn do-gooder with a ladder trying to impress my girl. I… *My girl?* I tabled that thought for later as I made my way to the tree.

I leaped up and grabbed a sturdy branch above my head and pulled myself up until my head and shoulders rose above the limb. I repositioned my hands over the top of the branch, grateful that there wasn't a layer of ice making my task more difficult, and continued to use my upper body strength to push up until the limb was even with my waist. Then I swung my left leg up and over like a gymnast until I straddled the thick branch.

I carefully got to my feet and reached above me for the next branch and repeated the process. Luckily, the limbs were denser the further I climbed, and I could just step between them like stairs as I got closer to the ball of black fur huddled at the top. The downside to the denser limbs was that they also became thinner. I had to test each limb before I moved onto the next. The cold made them brittle and likelier to break, so I tuned out the pseudo-encouraging words like "don't fall and break your neck" and "only fifteen more feet to go" from down below.

"Elijah!" Maegan yelled. "What the hell are you doing up there?"

I made sure I had a good grip on the limbs above my head before I looked down at her. She stood on my front porch with her arms crossed over her chest. "I'm trying to interview a witness. What does it look like I'm doing?"

"It looks like you're taking unnecessary risks with your life," Maegan fired back. "There's a much easier way to get that cat out of the tree."

"How? Ask it nicely?"

"No, smartass." Even from the distance I could clearly see her eye roll. "Watch and learn." Maegan marched across both our yards and into her house. She returned less than a minute later with a can of something in her hand. "Watch yourself," she warned as she popped the top. "Here, kitty kitty kitty."

The black cat scrambled down the tree, using my shoulder as a launch pad to leap to the lower limbs. Maegan knelt and placed the can on the porch. The cat had devoured half the contents before I made it back to solid ground.

"Tuna," I said once I reached the porch and could smell what the cat was wolfing down as fast as it could.

"Works every time." Maegan stroked the cat's back and it began to purr, but who could blame it? I'd had those lovely hands on my body and I reacted similarly. "I can feel every rib and vertebra of his spine."

"How do you know it's a he?" I asked her.

She looked at me like I was an idiot. The purring got louder the longer she petted him. "He's been through a traumatic experience."

"After he's done eating, I'd like to look at his paws to see if I can prove this was the cat in the alley."

"You doubt me?" Maegan asked.

"Not me, no."

"Who doubts me then?"

"Officer Jones," I said, not caring that I threw his ass under the bus. "Don't spit in his coffee or anything though."

Maegan snorted. "I wouldn't dream of it." She leaned toward me and lowered her voice. "I'm going to stop giving him the biggest apple fritter though."

"That's my girl." I hadn't realized what I said until a soft blush crept up Maegan's neck. I wasn't sure what to say. I didn't want to take it back and hurt her feelings, but I didn't want to give her false hope. The words just flowed out of my mouth naturally, and I wasn't sure how I felt about that. I lifted the cat and handed him to Maegan. I motioned for Jones to come over. "Let's check this fella out."

Jones stood beside me and aimed a flashlight on the cat's front paws. Unfortunately, Maegan's rack beneath her super soft-looking sweater was just as illuminated as the cat. I knew damn well what Jones was looking at, because I had a hard time concentrating on the task at hand too. I very well couldn't tell Maegan to cover her tits with a coat like I wanted to, so I decided to get the job done quickly and send Jones on his merry way.

"Looks like dried blood to me, Jones."

"I'm not crazy, Jones," Maegan said.

"No one said you're crazy, Maegan," I said in a soothing voice. "Jones just pointed out that black cats are common."

"You told her that I said she was crazy?" Jones asked incredulously.

"I told her that you had your doubts that it was the same cat." I gestured to the feline who had started squirming in Maegan's arms. It probably felt the rising tension and wanted to get the fuck away. There was no telling how the killer treated the animal while it was in his custody. "Let's swab his feet to see if we can match the blood."

"It's okay, sweet boy," Maegan cooed to the frightened cat, but her soft voice also soothed the beast stirring inside me. "I won't let anyone hurt you." Lulu barked from my front porch sounding like she was giving her mistress hell. "Don't you worry about Lulu; she'll come around."

The cat growled low in his throat when Jones swabbed his paws, but he didn't attempt to claw him or get away. Once we finished, Maegan rewarded the cat with extra cuddles as she carried him across the yard and inside my house.

"Looks like you're getting a cat, partner," Adrian said.

"No, Maegan is getting a cat," I corrected him. "She doesn't live with me."

"Yet," Adrian said. "See you in the morning, Elijah."

"Goodnight, Adrian."

The rest of the officers packed their stuff up and took off also. A few of them gave me curious looks and I knew they were speculating about my relationship with Maegan. Instead of dwelling on it, I locked Maegan's house and jogged over to mine.

I saw that Maegan's new friend was fast at home on her lap when I walked through the door. "He looks to be in relatively good health. I don't see any mange or fleas on him. He's just skinny."

"You'll have him right in no time," I told her. "Hey, the previous owner left behind a cat litter pan, liners, and litter in the closet in the laundry room. I think there might even be some food. Hopefully it's enough to tide the little guy over until you can get to the pet store to pick up more supplies."

"Oh! I'm not sure I'm keeping him. I bet someone would love to adopt a handsome boy like him from the county animal shelter."

The cat purred loud enough to be heard over Lulu's snoring, which was pretty impressive. "Maegan, you might as well accept that the little rascal is all yours now."

"Rascal," Maegan repeated like she was trying to see if the name fit her new pet. "I think that's a perfect name for him."

Maegan's cell phone rang and she pulled it out of her pocket. "Everything is fine, Mama," she said in way of greeting. "There's no need to come over. Besides, I'm at Elijah's house."

I went into the kitchen to grab us some drinks and noticed the bag of food that I'd forgot about when the cat darted out Maegan's door. My stomach chose that moment to make its displeasure known. Luckily, the stew and dinner rolls would reheat nicely. I popped the containers in the microwave for a few minutes and looked in the refrigerator for something to drink. The options were pretty slim— Coke, beer, water, or milk. I had no idea what Maegan wanted, but I cracked a beer open for myself and took a long sip. What. A. Day.

"I'll take one of those too," Maegan softly said when she entered the kitchen. "I hoped Miss Emma included a lot of cinnamon butter because it's a two-roll kind of night." Maegan pulled the box holding the bread out of the bag and flipped open the top. "Oh yeah, this will help."

I handed Maegan a beer and opened the microwave to give the stew a good stir before starting it back up again. "This smells like heaven."

"Tastes even better," Maegan said. She wasn't trying to be coy or sexy, but I couldn't help but equate her words with the way I felt about her pussy.

Down, boy! My dick had its own agenda, but I was mature enough to ignore it. The last thing Maegan probably wanted, or needed, was to be mauled by me. She needed comfort and care, not a douche bag who couldn't wait to part her legs and slide into her hot, wet….

"Do you mind if I take a shower?" she asked.

I nearly moaned out loud just thinking about her standing naked in my shower, water streaming down her luscious body. "Of course not," I managed to say even though my mouth suddenly felt as dry as the Sahara Desert.

"Care to join me?"

"I… uh…"

Maegan smiled because she knew she had me by the balls. The lady was no shrinking violet. She knew what she wanted and went after it. She walked around me and turned off the microwave before she circled back around to hook my belt loop with her index finger. Maegan started walking backwards, but she didn't have to pull me. In fact, I scooped her up in my arms and took the stairs two at a time.

Maegan laughed gleefully over my exuberance until I flipped on the bathroom light. She gasped and covered her mouth in surprise. I looked around the room to see what caused her reaction and caught her staring at the huge clawfoot bathtub in the corner.

"Oh, Elijah! It's magnificent."

"I've been told that a time or two," I told her.

"Yes, your cock is amazing, but that bathtub is… just wow."

"Would you like to take a bath instead of a shower? I can go downstairs and wait for you."

"Or you can get in that tub with me," she suggested.

"I'm not much of a bath guy."

"Do you have any idea of the things I could do to you in that tub?"

"Let me grab some clean towels," I said, setting her feet on the bathroom tile.

"And condoms!"

"Oh, hell yeah."

Maegan had already stripped her clothes off and was running water in the tub when I returned from my bedroom. I stood in the doorway and raked my eyes over her toned legs and perky ass. My dick throbbed, demanding attention, but all I could do was stare. She looked over her shoulder and winked at me, and damn, it was all I could do to keep from mounting her right then.

"You're about to become a bath guy, Elijah. A big fan."

"Okay."

"Take off your clothes and bring that box of condoms with you. I like your preparedness. Let me guess; you were a Boy Scout."

I laid the towels on the closed toilet lid and brought my right hand up to salute her. I confess my eyes didn't stay locked on hers, but how could they with her beautiful body on display. I whipped my shirt off at the same time I toed out of my shoes.

"Let me help," she said when I reached for my belt. Maegan

closed the distance between us and knocked my hands out of the way. She sank down to her knees, unfastened my jeans, and pulled them down to midthigh along with my underwear. "You are magnificent," she said when my cock sprang forward.

"I just want you to know that I wasn't expecting sex when I invited you to stay here tonight."

"I know." Maegan slowly licked her lips like my cock was a treat she couldn't wait to devour.

"Just because I have a dick doesn't mean I am one," I said, trying not to push said appendage toward her parted lips. "We don't need sex tonight."

"Your cock doesn't agree." She wrapped her fist around the base of my dick and pumped it a few times.

I groaned in ecstasy then said, "You're naked, Maegan. Of course, he's hard and eager to have you. If this doesn't feel right then we won't do it."

"I'm eager for him to have me." She looked up into my eyes and I saw certainty in her green irises. "Nothing has ever felt so right."

I cupped the back of her head in my head and said, "Then let me love you."

Chapter Seventeen

Maegan

I KNEW BETTER THAN TO READ TOO MUCH INTO ELIJAH'S WORDS. He wanted to physically love me, not emotionally. There was a big difference, but not enough that I gave a fuck at that precise moment. My breasts were swollen and my clit throbbed hard enough to tip the balance in favor of pain over pleasure. I was every cliché I'd ever read in a romance novel from my aching nipples to my wet pussy, and I wasn't about to let my brain ruin this for me.

As badly as I wanted to ride Elijah's cock, I didn't want to waste the opportunity my current position afforded me. I felt his gaze on my mouth and the way his grip tightened on my skull when I licked my lips in anticipation of sliding them down the length of his erection. Elijah's eagerness radiated off his body as I leaned forward and captured the bead of pre-cum gathering at his slit with my tongue, swirling it around the velvety head, then retracting it back inside my mouth.

Elijah's eyes snapped up to meet mine as a moan rumbled low in his throat. His cupped my chin with his free hand, applying enough pressure to open my jaw, but not enough to hurt me. I released his cock and placed both of my hands on the back of his thighs. Elijah stepped forward until his cock jutted against my parted lips, painting them with his essence. His upper body looked like cut marble and the muscles in his legs tensed beneath my hands from the restraint he exuded over himself.

He removed his hand from the back of my head and firmly gripped his shaft, feeding his cock to me slowly. I curled my tongue up slightly at the tip to tease that vein that ran from base to crown.

"Maegan," Elijah said huskily. "You feel so good." He hadn't seen anything yet. I channeled every gay porn video I'd ever watched and worked his cock like a champ, savoring every grunt and groan I elicited from him. Looking at us, one would think that Elijah was the powerful one in our dynamic, but I ruled him from my knees and had the power to bring him to his. That knowledge was a heady thing and I laved, licked, sucked, and savored every second that he was in my mouth and every response I garnered from him spurred me on.

It was easy to lose myself in him because every single thing about the man, from the natural, masculine scent of his skin to his ripped body, drove me wild. It felt like our bodies communicated in their own special language when he was inside me. It was thrilling in both beautiful and terrifying ways; like he could either heal or destroy me if I let him.

Lust and need glittered in his dark gaze as Elijah approached the point of no return. He pulled his cock from my mouth and pushed his jeans down to his knees and gravity took it from there. He stepped out of his jeans and kicked them out of the way leaving him in nothing but a pair of black socks. Not even Elijah could pull off that look, so I slid my hands down his legs and removed his socks so that we were both naked.

I turned off the water and said, "Our bath is ready."

"Ladies first," Elijah said.

"Huh uh," I replied. "You sink down in there and I'm going to sink down on your cock."

"Jesus, Freckles." Elijah reached for a condom and quickly suited up before he eased into the water.

I sounded confident, but the truth was I had never attempted bathtub sex before and wasn't one hundred percent sure it would work. I'd be damned if I showed Elijah that though. Luckily the tub was deep enough so that it came up to his mid-torso, leaving his carved upper chest on display. I couldn't wait to run my hands over his pecs, tease his nipples, and grip those massive shoulders while I… *Stop daydreaming and get to living.*

Elijah held out his hand, and I accepted it as I stepped into the tub. Not only was the tub deep, it was wide enough to accommodate me comfortably when I straddled his thick thighs. It wasn't exactly where I wanted to be, but I felt the need to draw out our pleasure even more. I took the hand that held mine and placed it against my upper chest near my collarbone.

"Touch me, Elijah."

I expected him to go straight for one of my breasts since he was so fond of them, but he surprised me by gliding it slowly down the center of my body beneath the water line until he reached my bare pussy. He turned his wrists and slid two fingers inside me, hooking them while covering my mound with his palm. He pulled his arm back slightly, tugging me toward him playfully.

"You're too far away, Freckles. Come a little closer."

"Says the Big Bad Wolf," I replied coyly, but slid up his legs until I felt his hard-on brush my inner thigh.

"Let's not pretend it isn't exactly where your greedy cunt wants to be," Elijah told me. "Fuck me like you mean it." Elijah released my pussy and leaned back against the tub, propping his arms on the sides. "Take what you want, baby."

I gripped his cock at the base and lowered myself on his turgid rod. My head felt too heavy to hold up so I let it fall back, closing my eyes and just savoring the way he made me feel. I braced my hands on his shoulders and began to move, slowly at first because it was too amazing to rush. The water lapped against the sides from the waves my undulating hips made, going higher and coming faster as I gave in to the passion rising through me.

"You are so beautiful." Elijah's words snapped me out of my sensual trance and I opened my eyes to meet his hot gaze. He touched me then, and not just with his hands. I felt him in my soul. I was in so much trouble, but it had never sounded or felt so fucking good. Elijah took a breast in each of his hands, flicking his thumbs over the tips of my nipples. His jaw tightened as arousal threatened to pull him beneath the current with me. God, I wanted to make him lose control with me. I placed my hand over his and moved them down to hold my hips beneath the water line. I pressed my breasts against his chest and rocked up and down his length faster. Elijah captured my mouth in a hot, hungry kiss, catching my gasps of pleasure on his tongue. The friction created by rubbing my sensitive nipples against his chest hair and grinding my swollen clit against his washboard abs sent me spiraling into a hard orgasm. My pussy contracted around his cock, milking his orgasm from him at the same time.

My body shook and trembled as pleasure rippled through me. Elijah kissed me through it, never taking his mouth from mine until I collapsed against his chest in exhaustion. He rubbed his hand up and down my back, and maybe it was wishful thinking, but he seemed content to hold me tight against him. All the emotions from earlier in the evening, the ones I could ignore while my body demanded satisfaction, flooded my brain causing me to shiver hard. I wasn't cold, in fact, I was the furthest thing from it; I was frightened.

"I got you, Freckles. Please believe me." I lifted my head and looked into his eyes. "Let me feed you and tuck you into a warm bed so we can say goodbye to this day. Tomorrow is a new day, and I'll move heaven and earth to solve this case and eliminate the danger to you. Say you believe me."

I could tell how much he wanted me to trust him, and I suspected there was a clue somewhere in his words that explained the aloofness I saw in his eyes at times. I hoped to unravel all his mysteries, but it would need to happen another day because it would require more energy than I had to give after a trying day and an earth-shattering climax.

"I believe you, Elijah."

"Atta girl, Freckles."

"What do you feel like watching?" Elijah asked as he scrolled through the cable guide on his screen.

"I'm not picky." I blew softly on the spoonful of savory stew in front of my lips. "I'm mostly interested in the food."

"Since you already had your way with me," Elijah teased. "How about this?"

I glanced up and saw *The Notebook* highlighted. I set my spoon back in the carton, placed it on the coffee table, and pinned him with a menacing glare. "Are you asking because I'm a woman?"

"Um…"

"Are you assuming because I have tits that I want to watch a chick flick?" I asked.

"Uh, no…"

"What did you base your decision on then?"

"Well, my mom and my ex loved this movie. They talked about it all the time," Elijah said, managing to sound both defensive *and* fearful.

"Don't lump me in the category with any of your exes," I warned him. "I'm sure your mom is really sweet, but chick flicks aren't for me. I had to suffer through hours of them with my mom last night to make *her* feel better about *me* nearly discovering a dead body last night. Just be glad I talked her down from coming over here tonight."

"I'm sure your mom is a lovely person," Elijah countered.

"She is, but she would've crimped our style." I tipped my head toward the second story where the magic had happened.

"So, what would you like to watch?" Elijah asked, holding the remote toward me. He picked up his stew and started eating it while I took over surfing duties.

"This!" I announced when I came to one of the movies I had loved watching with my dad.

"*Lethal Weapon*?"

"What's wrong with it?" I asked him.

"Nothing; it's a great movie. I'm just surprised you think so."

"Because I'm a woman?"

"No, not really. Well, maybe. I guess I'm basing it on my universe where women don't care for action movies."

"Perhaps you need to expand your universe." I thought about what I said and how awkward it sounded. I basically encouraged Elijah to go out and meet more women.

"Nah," Elijah said, hooking his free arm around my shoulders and pulling me to him. He kissed my temple then dropped his arm from my shoulders. "I like my *universe* the way it is right now."

I wasn't convinced that he truly meant what his words implied. Elijah owed me nothing, but I hoped I wouldn't have to see a parade of women coming and going from his house anytime soon. In fact, my churning stomach at the mere thought of another woman curling up next to him on the couch told me that I was more invested than I had realized. I tried to mentally put some distance between us when I straightened away from him, but it didn't work. I felt his pull like a huge invisible magnet.

We settled into comfortable silence while we ate our savory stew and watched the shenanigans of Riggs and Murtaugh. I expected Elijah to interject and tell me which parts were not how real cops did things, but he just laughed along with me.

"Ready for dessert?" Elijah asked halfway through the movie.

"Dessert?" Hell, I thought we already had dessert before dinner.

"Miss Emma said that you love pecan pie and added two pieces in the bag. She said it won't make up for the rough couple of days you've had, but she hoped to put a smile on your face."

"That was so sweet of her," I said, rubbing my hands together gleefully. "Emma makes the best pies."

"This is a very nice town," Elijah said. "You look out for one another here."

"You mean when we're not killing each other?"

"Thom Renzo hasn't lived here in several years, Maegan. Maybe his trouble followed him here from Kentucky."

I wanted it to be true, but I wasn't holding my breath. Wouldn't the killer flee back to where they came from instead of hanging around and risk getting caught? I hated wondering if the person that stood across me at the counter or was on the other end of the phone line was the person who ended Thom's life. That person apparently wanted to pull me into the murder investigation by dropping off evidence behind my building and putting the only witness inside my house. It wouldn't be the first time that our town was shocked when one of our citizens turned out to be a killer, which meant my negligence was unacceptable.

"I know why there was no forced entry at my house tonight," I said guiltily.

"Let me guess," Elijah said dryly, "you had a key hidden beneath the doormat."

"No, but just as stupid. It was under the planter on my porch."

"Stay here," Elijah said, jumping to his feet. He ran out the front door without even stopping to put shoes on.

I turned off the television and cuddled my pets closer to me. Surprisingly, Lulu took to Rascal right away. Maybe she sensed his loneliness or smelled his terror, either way, I was just grateful that they got along and hoped that Rascal's difficult days would soon become a distant memory.

Elijah wasn't gone long, and when he returned, he was wearing black latex gloves and holding a folded piece of paper in one hand and an evidence bag in another.

"What's that?" I asked with a pounding heart.

"It looks like evidence," he said. "I stopped by my truck to grab a few things in case. Will you put on the extra pair of gloves in my pocket and open the evidence bag for me?"

"Sure." I set the pets on the couch and walked to him.

"I don't know what's inside this folded piece of paper, but I don't want you to look until I know it's not too graphic."

"I won't faint," I said dryly.

"I know you're a badass, Freckles. Just do this for me. Some things can't be unseen if you know what I mean. Just let me protect you from the ugliness the best I can, okay?" I knew he referred to Thom's dead body.

"Okay." Being an independent woman didn't equal being silly. Did I want to see graphic images of dead bodies or read something creepy that was written about me? No, and those were the two most likely scenarios. So, I let Elijah don the figurative cape and shelter me from the ugliness.

"Hold open the bag in case something falls out," Elijah said then slowly opened the paper. My spare key fell into the bag. "Huh, not what I expected," he said once he examined it. "Abandoned barn on Willow-Jasper Road about a quarter mile past New Albany Road," Elijah read out loud.

"That's what it says?" I asked. "What's he referring to?"

He carefully slid the letter inside the evidence bag then sealed it. He crossed the room to the coffee table and picked up his phone. "There's only one way to find out," Elijah responded.

Chapter Eighteen

Elijah

"Hey, partner," I said when Adrian answered his phone. "What are you doing right now?"

"I know what I want to be doing right now, and it sure as hell doesn't involve talking to you. What's up?"

"Maegan just realized how our guy got inside her house without forcing his way in. She had a spare key hidden beneath a flower pot on her front porch." I tried to keep any trace of scorn from my voice, but her raised brow said that I had failed to do so. "On a whim, I decided to grab it just in case there was a usable print left behind."

"Any luck?"

"Our killer left a note." I recited the message to Adrian.

"We need to get out there," my partner said. "I'd prefer to wait until daylight, but we can't take that chance."

"I agree," I said. "I want to have someone stay with Maegan while we go check it out."

"Bring her over here, Elijah. She can hang out with Sally Ann and the kids. Or, I bet Jones wouldn't mind…"

"We'll be over in a few minutes," I snapped before I hung up.

"Where are we going?" Maegan asked slowly. "I gotta tell you,

Big Guns, that I'm not crazy about you finding a babysitter for me."

There was nothing infantile about Maegan or the feelings she stirred inside me. I didn't want to go caveman on her, but I'd do it if it meant she stayed safe. I thought I would give reason and logic a shot first, but if that failed, I would throw her over my shoulder and carry her away to safety.

"I know that you don't need a babysitter, Maegan. This isn't about your capabilities; this is about his. This person is determined to involve you in this case. Why? I have no clue. You have no clue. Until we know, I'm not taking a chance with your safety. He could be luring me away so that he can get to you. I will not make it easy for him, Freckles. I want you safe, and frankly, I don't care if you get pissed off about it. So, it's either Officer Kasey comes back to spend time with you"—ain't no fucking way Jones was coming into my home to flex his muscles and try to steal my girl—"or, you hang out with Sally Ann while Adrian and I investigate."

"That's not really much of a choice," Maegan said. "I'll take Sally Ann since Officer Jones isn't an option." Her wicked smile told me that she'd overheard Adrian's dig, or maybe she knew Jones had a thing for her. Either way, she seemed to enjoy winding me up.

"You think you're funny?" I asked, suddenly forgetting about everything but marking my territory like the animal I was. "You think I'd let Jones come in here and get close to you, Freckles. No. Fucking Way."

"Are you going to piss on my leg? I'm not into that, Elijah."

"I have better ways of marking you as mine, but it will have to wait until we get back. I have a potential crime scene to investigate." Those last few words had the same effect as dumping a gallon of ice water on my head. My focus shifted away from thumping my chest to getting out to Willow-Jasper Road to see what our guy left behind.

"Can we stop by my house so I can change clothes?" She gestured to her body that was bare except for my T-shirt that she had borrowed. Her toned legs looked like they stretched for miles beneath the hem.

"Sure, but only if you promise to change back into that shirt when we get back ho... here." I had almost screwed up and said home. There was no denying that I liked Maegan a lot, and I was pretty sure that the like could develop into something stronger and really special if I wasn't so fucked up in the head. But I was a mess, and our relationship was nowhere near the moving-in-together phase.

Maegan smiled crookedly at my swift recovery. "You have yourself a deal."

"Okay, team, we have no idea what's inside that barn. It could be a piece of evidence for our case, or it could be a trap. I want every single one of us to return home to our families or significant others," Captain Roman-Wyatt said firmly.

He had arrived on the scene at the same time as Adrian and me. A few squad cars from our department were already there prepared to secure the area, as were a few deputies from the Carter County Sheriff's Department since this barn was in their jurisdiction. The captain held them off until the fire department showed up with equipment to make our jobs safer and easier.

"That's right," Lieutenant Dorchester from the CCSD said. "Be diligent, ladies and gentlemen."

Adrian had told me briefly about John Dorchester's time working with our department on special assignments when he arrived. Due to the seriousness of the situation, I wasn't getting to see his jokester side, but I hoped to remedy that at some point.

The fire tanker that arrived on the scene was equipped with the portable lights they attached to the top of the fire truck to illuminate nighttime fires or emergency scenes. The poles rose several feet from the truck and looked like miniature stadium lights you saw at football fields and baseball diamonds.

"The township invested in LED bulbs too. No one look directly at the lights," the fire chief said loudly. "Light 'em up, Dallas."

The firefighter flipped a switched and flooded our scene with brilliant, blinding light. The fire chief hadn't been joking when he said not to look directly at the bulbs. Jesus!

Both the captain and lieutenant were dressed in bulletproof vests and helmets like the rest of us. The captain had said to me once that he'd never ask his men or women to do something he wasn't willing to do himself. It was obvious the lieutenant felt the same way. We spread out in formation and creeped along the deeply pitted gravel driveway and grassy areas until we had the structure surrounded.

From the road, the barn looked like it was intact, but once you rounded the curve in the driveway, you saw that one side of the barn had rotted from disuse and abandonment.

"Fuck! I bet that's Renzo's car," Adrian said beside me as we cautiously approached, keeping our guns aimed in front of us.

"What's it doing out here? Who drove it? His killer?" I asked. "Then why tip us off about where he dumped the car? God knows how long it would've taken someone to see this car abandoned here."

"We'll have to check into the landowner's identity," Adrian said, his voice lowering as we crept closer to the dilapidated barn. "See if there's a connection to the Renzo family."

"Thom's killer has to be familiar with this area," I told my partner. "How else did he know about this barn?"

"We'll find out when we catch him," Adrian replied.

"Hold up, everyone," I called out. "The trunk is slightly ajar." I circled around to the back of the vehicle and verified that the license plates and description of the car matched the information we pulled from Kentucky's Department of Motor Vehicles. "This is definitely Renzo's car." A few officers approached the car and aimed their guns at the trunk while others checked the front and interior of the car to look for anything that could put our lives in jeopardy.

"Count of three, I want you to open the trunk," Adrian said. I cracked a smile when I recalled the well-known banter between

Riggs and Murtaugh when it came to counting down.

"On three or after three?" I asked Adrian.

His lips curled into a half-smile. "One, two, three, then open it. Otherwise, it's really only a count of two." I heard the captain snort from his position.

"Got it. Ready." I kept my gun aimed at the vehicle with my right hand as I reached for the trunk lid with my left.

"Three, two…."

"Hold up! I thought you were counting to three," Dorchester said. "That's counting down from three. Which is it?"

"Counting down I guess, *Lieutenant*."

"So, does he open on one or after one?"

"Three, two, one, then he opens the lid."

"It's a good damned thing there's not someone waiting to jump out at us or," Jones said.

"They would've fallen asleep from boredom," Kasey added.

"Oh, fuck it!" I reached for the lid and jerked it open. Luckily, nothing exploded and no one opened fire on us. That was the end of the good news, because I knew whatever was in the black duffle bag was going to be really bad. I unzipped the bag and opened it.

Adrian whistled between his teeth as he returned his gun to his harness. "Whoa, partner. What the hell do we have here?"

"Nothing good," I replied, looking at the rope, duct tape, a wicked-looking knife, chloroform, and a roll of black trash bags inside the trunk. My stomach pitched and rolled, threatening to reject the dinner I had shared with Maegan. Those were items I would associate with someone who planned to kidnap someone and do God knows what to them. Who were they intended for? Fuck! I didn't want to evaluate *that* possibility. "The question is: do they belong to Renzo or his killer?"

"We'll have to see if we can lift some prints for testing. It's a good thing you know someone in the state lab that can help us process them quicker."

"I didn't promise that," I clarified. "I said I would try."

"I think you insinuated that you'd get it done."

"I don't think we're recalling the same conversation," I told Adrian as we moved out of the way so the lab guys could move in to do their thing. "We're going to want to haul that car back to a secure location so we can check out the interior thoroughly."

"If that stuff belonged to Renzo, do you suppose he intended to use it on Maegan?"

"Jesus, I hope not," I said, but the sickening feeling from earlier had only intensified. "I can't help but think that it was though. Damn, Adrian, I'm starting to think the person who killed Thom did us a big favor." I'm not embarrassed to admit that my hands shook when I pulled my phone out of my pocket.

I tapped out a quick message to Maegan to let her know I was okay. I saw the worry in her eyes when she stood on her tiptoes and kissed me goodbye in Adrian and Sally Ann's living room. Sally Ann had wrapped her arm around Maegan's shoulder and guided her to the couch. I realized then that she was in the best possible company under the circumstances.

Thank you for telling me. I hope to see you soon. Maegan's response came back fast, making me think she was watching her phone for word from me. The idea warmed the terror that had gripped my heart with its icy fingers, but it didn't thaw it entirely. I had no idea who those tools of terror belonged to and zero confidence that Maegan was completely out of the woods.

"Let's get this scene processed so we can get back to the girls," I said.

"Sally Ann knows how to defend herself and Maegan," Adrian told me. While I was glad to hear that, I hated that it was necessary.

The initial search of the interior didn't turn up much, but there was a bloody stain on the passenger seat of the car. It wasn't enough blood to signal a crime had been committed in the car; it appeared to be more from a transfer off a bloody object.

"I bet that's from the marble bust. I bet we'll match that blood to Renzo's."

"That's what I was thinking too."

"All right, so this person bashes Renzo's skull, gets in his victim's car and drives it here with the bloody weapon riding shotgun. Why dump it here then?"

"Why stash the evidence behind Maegan's shop and slip the note beneath a planter to tip us off to its location. Why not just leave the car at the original crime scene if he wanted us to find it?"

"It must have something to do with Maegan?"

"You think she's in trouble?" Adrian asked me.

"Even if this guy saved Maegan from a horrible fate at Renzo's hands, he's still a killer. As you pointed out, he's included Maegan in every step. It's more imperative than ever to find out who all knew that Thom was coming to town to meet Maegan that night. She said it was spur of the moment. An email she received directly from Thom when he'd communicated with her through a local realtor the previous times."

"We'll track Becker down first thing tomorrow before we pay a visit to the historical society."

It was another hour before we returned to the Goode's home. Maegan was sound asleep in the recliner with Adrian and Sally Ann's infant son sleeping against her chest. She didn't wake up until Sally Ann took the baby from her arms.

"What time is it?" she asked, rubbing her tired eyes.

"Late," I answered. "Past your bedtime it would seem."

Maegan smiled ruefully. "Babies always make me sleepy." She stood up from the recliner and slid her arms into her coat that I held open for her.

"Sure, that's it," I teased.

Maegan was unusually quiet on the short ride home. I glanced over and saw her chewing her bottom lip like she was worrying about something. I squeezed her knee to reassure her, but was uncertain what to say. It had to be a terribly frightening experience to know that someone could want to hurt her. Hell, I'd been in terrifying situations before, but at least I knew who my enemy was and had a good idea when I could expect their attack. For Maegan, she probably felt like a sitting duck.

"We're going to catch him," I told her once we were back at my warm house.

"I know you will, Elijah," she said, but the tone of her voice didn't sound as confident as her words. "That's not what's on my mind." Her voice cracked and she started nibbling on her lower lip again. I realized then that she'd been biting her lip to stop herself from crying.

I'm just as nervous and helpless around a crying woman as the next guy, but I had a feeling that Maegan wasn't one who cried very often. I knew firsthand how dangerous bottling up emotions could be. They often exploded in the worst ways and at the least convenient times. I somehow doubted that Maegan was going to start a bar fight to alleviate the tension rising inside her, but I didn't want her to feel miserable if having a good cry would help.

I pulled her into my arms and tucked her head beneath my chin. "It's okay to cry, Maegan. Let it out." And she did. I held onto her, absorbing her tears and anguish with my shirt and wishing I could somehow erase her fears. "I won't let anyone hurt you, Freckles."

"I'm not crying about that," she mumbled against my throat.

"What has you so heartbroken tonight then?"

Maegan pulled out of my arms and raised her chin so she could look into my eyes. "It's more than my heart that's broken."

"What do you mean?"

"I can't have children, Elijah. I've known it since I was seventeen, and I'm okay with it most of the time, but it sneaks up and sucker punches me when I'm vulnerable. Holding Avery was both amazing and heartbreaking because I'll never have that for myself. I'll never feel my child growing inside me. I've wanted kids for as long as I can remember, but it won't happen."

I wiped her tears and pressed my lips to her forehead. Damn, my heart broke for her. "There's more than one way to be a mom, Freckles. There are so many kids in the world who need love. One day, when the time is right, you're going to be one hell of a fierce mama. I just know it."

"Thank you, Elijah," she said tearfully. "I'm so sorry for blubbering all over you when you have more important things to deal with."

"You don't need to apologize, Maegan. I meant what I said." I tipped her head up and aimed my best lecherous look at her. "Damn, you're going to be the hottest MILF the world has ever seen."

"Oh you!" She swatted at me, but at least the sadness was replaced with mirth. "Enough yapping; take me to bed. I'm suddenly feeling more alert."

"Yes, ma'am."

Chapter Nineteen

Maegan

BOOKS AND BREW WAS MUCH BUSIER THAN A TYPICAL SUNDAY morning. Most of the residents attended one of the four churches in our small town and usually only the "sinners" stopped by for a hot beverage and a pastry before noon. Not that morning though.

"I'm worried we might run out of doughnuts," Milo whispered in my ear.

"Then we'll have to put the cookies and cupcakes out early," I told him, sounding much calmer than I felt. My life had suddenly turned from an orderly existence to one of constant upheaval with me starring in a role I did not audition for. I was beyond ready for the curtain call so I could exit the stage.

Some good things have come from the chaos, the little voice inside my head whispered. *Elijah.* I had no idea how long he would be a part of my life and refused to give it much thought. Why borrow heartache? It would only ruin the moments that I shared with him. Take that morning for instance. I could've bemoaned that waking up in his arms was temporary, *or* I could've moaned for delicious reasons when we greeted the dawn tangled up with each other, feeling him in the deepest parts of me. When viewed in that light, there really wasn't much need to debate the merits of guarding my heart versus embracing the way Elijah made it race.

"Earth to Maegan!" I snapped back to reality when Milo snapped his fingers. "Where'd you go?" Then he shook his head and smiled ruefully. "Never mind. Your brat pack has turned out in full force to support you."

I looked over to where he pointed and saw that my best friends had indeed showed up that morning. Vanessa, April, Candace, and Violet were the best friends any girl could ask for, and I had loved them since I was a little girl. I walked from behind the counter and accepted the group hug I needed and deserved. I knew they were worried about me if they were dressed and in my shop before nine in the morning. My best friends fell into the "sinners" category and didn't do early Sunday mornings. I pulled back from the hug and braced myself for the backlash.

"Why haven't you returned our calls," Candace asked me.

"I'm sorry, Candy Apple," I told her, using the nickname my brother tagged her with when we were little. He said her bright red hair resembled the candy coating he was so fond of when we were kids.

"Seriously!" Vanessa said. "I called *and* texted you last night and the one before, but you didn't answer or reply. I was worried sick. I even drove to your house. Your car was home, but you weren't."

"I called your mom and she said that you were safe and sound with Elijah," Violet said. "Um, who's Elijah, Maegan?"

"You better have a really good excuse, young lady," April said hotly.

"Excuse me, ladies," a delicious, deep voice said, interrupting my interrogation. "It's all my fault."

I saw four sets of eyes widen in surprise before they checked Elijah out from the toes of his badass boots to the top of his shiny dark head.

"I understand now," Candace said while the others were still trying to form words. She looked at our friends and said, "Close your mouths, ladies. If we want to be rude we can do it by asking a ton of questions." She clapped her hands happily. "I'll go first. Um, who the hell are you, Big Sexy?"

Elijah smirked and extended his hand to Candace. "That's Detective Big Sexy to you," he teased. "Elijah Markham at your service."

April giggled and blushed when she shook his hand. "I'm sorry, Maegan. You're forgiven."

"It's nice to meet you, Elijah, Detective Big Sexy, sir," Violet rambled. "Maegan, I didn't know that Blissville's Finest started offering police protection these days."

"They're not," Elijah clarified. "I'm offering personal protection."

"For hire?" Candace inquired, batting her eyelashes flirtatiously.

"No," Elijah and I answered at the same time.

My face flushed pink with embarrassment. Hadn't I told the man that I wasn't laying claim to him, but there I was ready to claw Candace's stunning, whiskey-hued eyes out of her head. "Stop making him sound like a male prostitute," I added to try to cover my faux pas.

"I provide protective duties to Maegan only," Elijah clarified. He put his arm around me and pulled me into his side. *What's this? What's happening here? A declaration?*

"How interesting," Vanessa observed shrewdly. "If I didn't know Maegan, I would think she orchestrated the entire thing to snag the hunky new detective in town." Her lips quivered telling me how hard she struggled to keep a suspicious, sour look on her pretty face.

"We had already met," I told Van, rolling my eyes.

"We're neighbors," Elijah said.

"Oh! He's the one that drives that obnoxious hunk of metal?" Violet exclaimed. I wanted the ground to open up and swallow me when she repeated the words I'd used to describe the truck that rumbled into the driveway and woke me each morning before my alarm clock went off.

"Hey!" Elijah said in a wounded voice. "That hunk of metal used to belong to my grandfather. It has rich history and character, things I'm sure Maegan appreciates."

Don't throw me under the bus, girls. Don't throw me under the bus, girls. Don't…

"Maegan?" Elijah asked suspiciously.

"Um, it might have annoyed me when you first moved in because I wasn't used to it. Now, I find it charming with loads of character."

Elijah's raised brow told me he wasn't buying it for a second. It was the truth though. The truck and the man went together. Big, sturdy, strong, rusty around the edges, but completely charming. I reminded myself to tell him that when we were alone. *If,* I corrected.

"Uh huh," he finally replied. "The investigation will take me out of town for parts of the day, so call nine-one-one if you have an emergency. I'll try to be back before you close for the day. If not, call Officer Kasey. She'll hang out with you at my house until I can return. You put my spare key on your ring, right?"

I nodded. It had been a complete shock when he slid it across the table to me while I was sipping coffee that morning. I knew his true intention behind the gesture, but that didn't stop my heart from racing with excitement. "Be careful," I told Elijah.

"You too." He started to walk away but turned back and kissed my forehead. "Have a good day, Freckles."

I just stood there staring at him as he walked away.

"No further explanation is needed, honey," April said.

"We totally get it, love," Vanessa added.

"Girl, I'd ignore my phone too," Candace said with a snort.

I turned to look back at my friends and found them all looking at me with goofy grins. "What?"

"We're just happy that you're okay," Vanessa said.

"Happy and healthy," Violet supplied.

"I think it's safe to add horny into that mix," April interjected.

"Uh huh," they all said at once.

"Maegan, I could use some help here if it's not too much trouble," Milo said dramatically.

"I better get back to Milo. Girls, we have so much catching up to do though. We need a girl's night. How does Margarita Monday sound?"

"Perfect," Vanessa answered. "Let's do it at my place since your house seems to be a crime scene these days."

"Oh, stop!" I replied. "No crimes have been committed at my house."

"Let's just play it safe. We don't want any uninvited guests."

"Sounds good to me. How does six work?"

We all agreed that six o'clock worked for each of us, so we hugged and said our goodbyes so I could return to work behind the counter.

"I'm thinking champagne," Milo said to me before I could greet the next customer in line.

"To drink? Have you already started?" I asked because his comment made no sense to me.

"As in the color of the bridesmaid's dresses at your wedding. That hue compliments each of their skin tones *and* mine as your Man of Honor."

"Whoa!" I exclaimed. "You got that from a forehead kiss?"

"His lips lingered for a few seconds beyond the norm for a simple forehead kiss. That, my sweet girl, was a declaration."

"You're so dramatic, Milo."

"Maybe so, but when am I wrong about these things?"

I wanted to argue with him, but I couldn't. He had been the voice of reason when it came to Clayton; I just didn't want to listen. I had seen him make predictions with other people that I didn't see coming either. I wished I could point out one instance where he'd been wrong to knock his ego down a peg, but couldn't find one until I looked into Andy Mason's eyes fifteen minutes later when he stepped up to the counter to place his order. Andy didn't know I existed though because he couldn't tear his eyes off my brother, who kept his back toward the counter. Milo always conversed with the customers rather than keep his back turned to them, but Andy was the exception to that rule. I knew damned well there was so much more going on between my brother and Beefcake, Handy, or Just Andy.

The phone rang just as Andy's latte was finished, giving me an excuse to walk away for a second so that Milo would be forced to face him. I imagined their hands touching briefly as Milo handed him his cup. Then their eyes would meet and Milo would finally see what the rest of us did. Andy Mason had never gotten over him, just as surely as Milo still carried a torch for him.

The moment I anticipated turned out to be a huge let down because Milo set Andy's cup on the counter instead of handing it to him and his "have a *great* day" was filled with enough sass to make me think he wished the opposite for his high school sweetheart.

"It's not looking so hot right about now," Andy said before he walked away.

"Hello, Maegan, are you there?" the voice on the other end of the phone asked.

It was then that I realized how odd the caller's voice sounded. It was distorted and metallic sounding. Fear and unease washed over me.

"Who is this?" I asked sharply. "What do you want with me?"

"I saved you, Maegan. Did your boyfriend tell you?"

"I don't know what you're talking about," I told the person. "How did you save me? You left evidence behind my shop and at my home."

"Thom Renzo was a sick fuck who had evil plans for you." Fear clawed at my throat and made my stomach churn. Bile rose in my throat and I feared that I was about to vomit in front of our customers. I ran into the back room for privacy, knowing that Milo was following behind. I heard him talking on his cell phone and suspected he was calling the police.

"I gotta go, Maegan. I just wanted you to know that I'm not trying to hurt you. I wanted to help you and expose Thom for the sick animal he was. I tried legal channels but no one listened to me. The only thing to do with a sick animal is to put it down."

"You didn't hurt Rascal," I added.

"The cat? He's not sick, he's just lonely. Take good care of him and yourself. I'm sorry that I scared you."

"Wait!" I yelled, but I heard the audible click from the call getting disconnected. "Damn it!"

"Write down everything that person just told you," Milo said. I looked over at him and saw that he was still on the phone. "Officer Kasey said to do it now while it's still fresh in your mind. She's on her way over."

"Milo, I can't believe this is happening to me," I told him, sounding as dazed and confused as I truly felt.

Milo hugged me tight then said, "Sis, write it down." He slid a piece of paper and a pen to me. "Take as much time as you need. I'll take care of the shop."

Officer Kasey must've practically been in earshot because she arrived on the scene fast. Had she been assigned to keep an eye on me or was it coincidence? I couldn't help but crack a small smile when I realized he didn't ask Jones to watch over me. I wanted to claim it as a victory for women's lib, but I thought it had more to do with Elijah not wanting Jones near me.

"Keep writing," she said when I started to put my pencil down, thinking she would want to question me. "I don't want my questions to influence your perceptions. We'll go over it once you're done."

Her cell phone rang and she moved over to the far end of the room to answer it. Even so, I would've known who she was talking to even if I hadn't overheard her say, "Yes, Detective. I'm with her now. She's okay." Officer Kasey listened to whatever Elijah had to say then replied, "Yes, sir."

After she hung up the phone, I said, "I'm finished now, Officer Kasey."

"You've known me since fifth grade. It's okay to call me Marley when I'm in uniform," she said with a rueful smile.

"I'm just trying to be respectful."

"And I appreciate it," she replied as she took the sheet of paper from my hands. "Let's see what you have here." She set the paper on the counter and pulled a pen out of her pocket. "I'm going to read each thing back to you and I want you to tell me anything that stands out, emphasis on certain words or changes in tone."

"The voice was distorted by something," I told Marley, "but I can tell you which words he or she emphasized."

"You don't think we're dealing with a guy?"

I shook my head. "You'll see what I mean when we discuss each comment."

"All right."

We went through my note line by line, discussing every nuance of every word said to me. I understood why Marley wanted me to write everything down before we discussed it. My first impression was crucial, and it would've been easy to influence my reactions or forget a key remark during the thorough interview that lasted at least twenty minutes.

"So this killer feels like she saved you," Marley said out loud.

"You agree it's a woman?" I asked. "Thom did something horrible to her and she's trying to get justice when she feels the system failed her."

"It could also be a man who's trying to punish Renzo for something he did to his sister, or someone else he loved," Marley countered. "But a woman could've easily pulled off Renzo's murder. It didn't require a lot of strength." She was talking more to herself by that point.

"What did Elijah find last night?"

"I can't tell you that, Maegan. It's evidence in an ongoing

investigation. I'm certain that Elijah will tell you when he can. He's not deliberately keeping you in the dark. To be honest, the evidence in the trunk could've been planted there by Renzo's killer. Telling you about those items before we know where they came from could cause undue panic."

In my heart, I knew what she said made sense. I also knew that if Officer Jones had been standing there, he'd have told me every damn thing they found in that trunk. *Double damn you, Elijah.*

Chapter Twenty

Elijah

T ALKING TO THE REALTOR DIDN'T TURN UP ANY NEW LEADS. Becker Philips didn't know anything other than Thom Renzo had agreed to give Maegan first crack at the items in the house. He had set up an appointment through Becker then canceled suddenly the night they were to meet. He did agree that it was odd that Thom contacted Maegan directly by email instead of going through him again. I thought it was odd that Thom had Maegan's email until I saw it listed on her website beneath the contact information. Becker didn't know anything about the meeting Thom had set up last minute on Friday, which made me think that those items in the trunk belonged to our *victim* and he planned to use them on Maegan.

My body went hot and cold and I felt physically ill. I was cold from fear and hot with the flush of someone who was about to lose their breakfast. I closed my eyes and focused on the smile on Maegan's face that morning when she woke up and found me watching her sleep like a creeper. I held onto the look of surprise on her face after I kissed her forehead in front of her friends, brother, and everyone else inside Books and Brew. Maegan was okay, she was safe, and she would remain that way.

I went through the motions of shaking Becker's hand and thanking him for his assistance before I headed for the door. I heard Adrian ask the man to call either of us if he thought of something new that might help.

I stood out on the sidewalk in front of the man's business to wait for Adrian. Usually, I would've hauled ass to get out of the cold, but it actually felt good against my flushed face. I tilted my head up and embraced the chilly air that matched the icy tentacles of fear wrapped around my heart.

"We have a lot of time to kill before we meet with Homer Stillwater. Let's say we get back to the station and make some calls to the Kentucky State Police and make arrangements to search Thom Renzo's residence and speak with his co-workers at his place of employment tomorrow," I told my partner.

"Working with other jurisdictions can be tough, but we've been really lucky in the past. Let's hope for the best and see what happens," Adrian replied.

We were still twenty minutes outside of town when dispatch called and told me that Maegan had been contacted by our prime suspect. They told me that Officer Kasey responded to the call and would contact me when she had additional information.

"Fuck that," I had said after disconnecting the call. "I'm not waiting."

I had dialed Kasey's phone and she answered right away. She assured me that Maegan was fine and explained that she was currently writing down everything our suspect said while it was fresh in her mind.

Even though I didn't know Officer Kasey well, I trusted her. She was smart, capable, and dedicated to her job. She told me she had it under control and I believed her. Therefore, I didn't ask Adrian to flip on the lights and sirens.

By the time we reached Books and Brew, Kasey was wrapping

up her interview and deflecting questions that Maegan had about the evidence we found inside Renzo's trunk. How the hell did she even know to ask that? Kasey fielded that like a pro, but I bet Jones would've told her everything her pretty heart desired.

"Ah, Detective," Kasey said. "Perfect timing."

"Yes," Maegan said agreeably. "Marley didn't want to tell me about the evidence you found in Renzo's trunk. My caller said that she saved me. What did she mean by that, Elijah?"

"She?" I asked. "Our killer is a woman?"

"It's a theory," Kasey said. "Hear her out and tell us what you think."

I listened as Maegan recounted the conversation word for word. She closed her eyes and concentrated on the highs and lows of the caller's voice, which probably wasn't easy since it was distorted.

"Elijah, I know killing someone is typically considered a personal thing, but this seems… more. She feels like she did the world a favor. I'm afraid what you're going to find when you dig deeper into Thom's background. I'm scared about how close I came to being a victim of something horrible. It was really bad, wasn't it?"

"Yes," I said tersely. "I can't divulge the contents of the trunk, but I will confirm that there's a high probability that Thom Renzo had no intentions of letting you sort through the junk in the cellar."

"It's not junk," Maegan said, hands on her hips in irritation. I just confirmed her fears and she chose to get mad about my junk reference. Or was she using that as an outlet for the riotous emotions coursing through her body? She grabbed onto any emotion that alleviated the fear; that's what I would've done in her place.

"You're right, Freckles. I'm sorry." I wasn't about to argue with her when I had healthier ways to help her work through her frustration and fear.

"I agree that the killer's statement indicates a passionate dislike of Thom Renzo and doesn't appear to have anything to do with the Bliss property. I'm still not sure why you think you were talking to a woman. I'm fully aware that women are capable of committing murder, but statistics are still in favor of men committing violent crimes."

"Nothing about the crime rules out a woman," Kasey pointed out. "Nothing about the murder required brute force or extraordinary strength. It seems like a well-planned, clean execution."

"Except it wasn't well-planned because Renzo's call to Maegan was out of the blue," I challenged.

"It was out of the blue for Maegan, but that doesn't mean it was that way for Renzo," Kasey countered. "He could've planned it all along."

"You make a very valid point," I told Kasey. My gears started grinding again, and I knew the rest of our conversation needed to occur in the privacy of the police station. "Can you guys give me a few minutes alone with Maegan?" I asked Adrian and Kasey.

"Sure," they both said.

I leaned my back against the counter, placed my hands on Maegan's hips, and pulled her toward me. "Listen, Freckles, I'm not deliberately keeping you in the dark. Please tell me you know that."

"I do, Elijah. I don't like it, but I respect it." She smiled at me, but I noticed that it didn't quite reach her eyes.

I raised a hand and cupped her face. I breathed easier when she leaned into my touch, but refused to think about why it mattered so much to me. It just did. I would make time to evaluate what the hell I wanted to happen between us later when I knew that all threats to her were eliminated.

"I need to head back to the station to make some calls, but I still plan on being here after you close. Maybe you are out of the woods, but I'm not willing to take that chance."

Maegan placed her hands on my chest and slid them up until they met behind my neck. "I don't want to be a burden to you. Lulu, Rascal, and I can stay with my parents or one of my friends can stay with me. I don't want you to feel obligated to—"

I covered her mouth with my index finger. "I'm right where I want to be, Freckles. I think you know it too." *Okay, maybe there wasn't much evaluating required.*

She gave me a genuine smile then. "A girl can hope."

I kissed her then. My lips lingered longer than a quick peck but didn't part hers to delve deeper inside her mouth. I needed assurance that she was fine; the rest could come later when we were alone and had more time to explore.

"What do you think, partner?" Adrian asked once we were back at the police station. Kasey and Captain Roman-Wyatt joined us in an interview room so we could have privacy.

"Kasey and Maegan both make excellent points. Maegan is the only one who's talked with the killer and is going off instincts."

"Women's intuition isn't something we want to discount," Kasey said with a wry smile. "Not to mention another certain case where the captain and Adrian had a run-in with a diabolical female. A certain seventy-year-old woman who snuck up on them and got the upper hand by hitting them over the head with something heavy. Maegan could be drawing on that knowledge just as much as intuition."

"What case is this?" I asked, looking between Adrian and our captain.

"Never you mind," Adrian said haughtily. "We still got our gal in the end. Well, I did anyway. The captain was in the hospital recovering from his injuries. See, he took his bad cop act too far and incurred a bigger wrath than my good ole boy routine."

"Are you finished?" the captain asked his former partner with an incredulous expression on his face before he shifted his attention back to me. "I'm still waiting for a return call from Lieutenant Snyder with the Kentucky State Police informing me what time you guys should arrive. Plan on it being an early morning tomorrow, fellas. It's at least a four-hour drive." He rose to his feet. "I'll be in touch with more specifics as soon as they become available."

"Have a good night, Captain," I said as he headed for the door.

"Same to all of you. Call right away if something breaks."

Once the captain left, we resumed talking about our case. Adrian and I told Kasey what the realtor said. She had made a good point at Books and Brew that maybe delaying Maegan's meeting had been intentional on his part. Did he need more time to work out a sick, twisted plan for her? If so, how would his killer have known that though?

"What if this person had been watching Renzo and waited for the opportunity. Was the killer privy to Renzo's intentions toward Maegan? If so, why not tell the police?"

"Because they failed him or her," I said softly.

"Or someone they love," Adrian added.

"Sometimes you can see why people snap," Kasey said. "But we still have to pursue this case like we would anyone else, even if Renzo turns out to be as vile as we suspect."

"Agreed," I told her. "If we turn a blind eye then we're no better than the criminals we try to put behind bars." I blew out a frustrated breath. "Let's start with what we know. Thom wasn't in contact with anyone local on a personal level, including his uncle who resides outside of town. According to his uncle, Thom didn't have anything to do with him beyond making final arrangements for his parents. Besides the auction house, Becker and Maegan were the only ones who recently talked to him. In all three cases, Renzo used email instead of the phone."

"I sure wish we could find his cell phone. Perhaps we'll get lucky and find his number when we search his residence tomorrow. A laptop with some clues would be greatly appreciated too." Adrian looked up toward the heavens like he was asking for some divine intervention.

"So, are you saying that the killer followed Renzo from Kentucky to Ohio, but didn't bring a murder weapon?" Kasey asked.

"Maybe our person has been watching Renzo for a long time.

Saw an opportunity. Maybe they did know that Maegan was in danger. Could be they showed up to warn Maegan and snapped, using the first thing they found to take Renzo out."

"Okay, let's continue with that theory for a minute and see where it leads us," I told them. "Our killer followed Renzo for four hours to Ohio and killed him at the first opportunity. Renzo didn't see or hear them pull in?"

"Maybe he was too busy lying in wait for Maegan. He wouldn't have known that she was bringing two men with her," Kasey said. Damn it. I knew she was just stating a likely possibility, but it made me sick to my stomach all over again. "Sorry," Kasey said when she saw my expression.

I waved her off. "Our killer must've stashed their car someplace close by then while they hid Renzo's car at that old barn."

"How'd they know about the place if they weren't from around here?" Adrian asked.

"They passed the place on their way to Renzo's house since they traveled down that road when they exited the interstate," Kasey pointed out.

"Then they traveled back on foot to pick up their car. It's possible," I said. It would've been a very cold two-mile walk, but it was doable.

"Or we're not talking about one killer."

My head snapped up from where I'd been studying my boots while I worked the case out in my head. "What makes you think that, Kasey?"

"It's just a possibility. Maybe they only planned to confront Renzo and things escalated. One driver took Renzo's car to the abandoned property and the other drove behind and picked them up."

"They stuck around at least twenty-four hours to drop off the evidence behind Maegan's shop and leave the clue at her house. Then they left town," I theorized.

"Yeah, that works," Adrian said. "The nearest hotel is in

Goodville. Let me make a call to see if they had any out of town guests, specifically Kentucky."

"I think we're onto something here," I said. "Sure, anger and intense emotions could propel someone to ignore the cold and other extreme conditions to focus on their goal"—I knew this from firsthand experience—"but, it also makes sense that they had help."

Adrian returned after a few minutes, shaking his head in disgust. "Well, there was a room rented to a Patsy Walker and Carol Danvers, who the clerk said were hot chicks from Kentucky. They slipped him some extra cash to *forget* to obtain their driver's license information."

"You've got to be kidding me," Kasey said.

"The kid admitted it. He said they were tall, blonde, and sexy as fuck. He tried to say that they glamorized him or some shit."

"Glamored," Kasey said. "It's a term associated with vampire lore," she explained when she saw my confused expression. "They can look into your eyes and get you to do whatever they want."

"Huh," Adrian said. "I doubt that flies with his manager though. She didn't seem very happy that he possibly let two murder suspects stay in their hotel."

"It's them," Kasey said confidently.

"How do you know?" I asked.

"Patsy Walker and Carol Danvers are also known as Hellcat and Captain Marvel. They're female superheroes," Kasey told us.

"Fuck!" Adrian said. "There's no way that's a coincidence. They called Maegan on their way out of town to let her know she was safe from them."

"So, we're looking for two smoking hot blondes that are somehow connected to Thom Renzo in Kentucky," I said. "It's not much, but I guess it's something."

"This case just took an interesting turn. I wish I could go with you guys," Kasey said. Then she threw her head back and had a good laugh at the raised-brow looks we aimed at her. "I've always been partial to blonde chicks. And you thought Jones was the one you had to worry about around your girl." Kasey slapped me on the arm as she walked past me. "Have a good night, fellas."

Adrian chuckled beside me. "I like Officer Kasey's style. See you in the morning, partner."

I looked down at my watch and saw that I had hours to kill before Maegan's shop closed, which meant I had time to plan a surprise for my girl. *Yeah, it was past time, I admit it.*

Chapter Twenty-One

Maegan

I THINK EVERYONE ON THE PLANET IS FAMILIAR WITH THE concept that news travels fast, bad news travels faster. Knowing it and living it are two completely different animals though. I'd experienced this plenty of times growing up in a small town. My mother was made aware of any transgression Milo and I committed long before we arrived home from school or anywhere else we might've caused mischief. That was before email and text messages were a thing, so you can imagine how much quicker gossip spread with modern technology. I was amazed that it took my mother until one o'clock to show up at Curious Things. She either found out about the phone call late or was biding her time. Either way, she was the first person through the door when I flipped the sign over to show that I was open for business.

"I'm surprised you're opening the shop today," she said, squeezing me tight enough to cut off my air supply. "Are you okay?"

"Fine," I wheezed.

Mom pulled back and looked at me then, grinning sheepishly. She looked like she had aged ten years overnight and that broke my heart. "What did he say to you on the phone?"

"Mom, I can't discuss it with anyone." Elijah hadn't said as much, but it seemed obvious to me that I needed to keep quiet about the call.

"I'm not just *anyone*, Maegan Miracle. I am your *mother*."

"Okay, but you have to look me in the eye and promise me that you won't speak to anyone about this."

"Of course," she replied, crossing her heart with her index finger.

"I won't repeat the specific words used, but the caller expressed that I had nothing to worry about. I guess they wanted me to know that his or her issue was with Thom, not me."

"Why did you say 'his or her'?" Mom asked.

"They used a voice distorter so I couldn't tell the gender of the caller." I didn't share my theories with her though. I knew I could trust her to keep my confidence, but I didn't want to betray Elijah or undermine his investigation.

"Why involve you then? What was the point of putting evidence at your place of business and home?"

I shrugged. There was no way I was going to tell her that the killer claimed to have saved me. "Maybe they were aware of my relationship with the lead detective?"

"So you're admitting there is a relationship between the two of you?" she asked.

"There's something going on between us, but I'm not sure what I'd label it."

"So don't. Labels are for clothes." She reached over and smoothed her hand over my wayward curls. "Just be happy, Maegan. That's all I want for you and Milo."

"I was happy before Elijah moved to town, Mom."

"You were content, my love, and that's not the same thing."

I couldn't argue with her because she was right. Well, I could have, but it would've been a waste of energy that I could expend in happier ways. "I can't believe my shop isn't overflowing with curious customers," I said, changing the subject.

"They've already been to the coffee shop this morning," she replied wryly. "They were practically lined up down the block when I attempted to see you earlier."

"You could've used the employee entrance in the back. You have a key," I reminded her.

"I could see that you were okay and that was enough to tide me over until I could give you a proper hug."

"Or squeeze the air out of my lungs," I teased. "I'm good, Mom." I looked over her shoulder and saw a tall brunette approach the door. I couldn't contain the soft growl that rumbled out of my chest.

My mother turned to see what had upset me. "Oh, that bitch," she said sassily right before the door opened. My mom positioned herself by my side and together we faced what was surely to be some kind of dig or insult.

"Oh my, Maegan," Amanda said breathlessly, batting her eyelashes and covering her mouth with a trembling hand. I noticed that the diamond engagement ring she supposedly threw at Clayton was back on her left hand. "I just had to make sure you were okay. I just heard about your troubles."

"My troubles?" I looked down at my whole, healthy body and around my pristine shop that was a huge source of pride for me. "I don't understand what you mean."

Amanda took a few steps closer to me, eyeing my mom warily like a person would a Rottweiler on guard. I couldn't blame my mom's protectiveness since this *woman*—and I used the word loosely—was the bane of my high school existence. She was downright evil before I had cancer because she saw me as competition. I missed most of my junior year while battling leukemia, but stayed on target to graduate with a private tutor. I was so self-conscious about my hair on my first day of school my senior year because the regrowth was little more than a buzz cut. I had hated wearing a wig. It didn't feel like me, and it seemed like people stared at me anyway when I wore it, so why not be comfortable? I put on my makeup and wore my favorite new outfit, determined to have a good day no matter what. I was a warrior who beat cancer dammit. *Rawr!*

My positive mood had lasted only until Amanda Jacobsen spotted me in the hallway and called me GI Jane loud enough for everyone around us to hear. Amanda's eyes glittered in delight when her comment garnered laughter from her little circle of followers, but I noticed the merriment didn't reach some of their eyes. They were nothing more than little bleating sheep who didn't think or act for themselves. I was determined not to let her see that her arrow had struck its target though.

"My mom said that you'll never be able to have kids. That sucks that you won't ever hold your own little *miracle* in your arms." She giggled over her witty play on words. "No man wants a wife who can't provide him children. Poor Maegan." That's what she started calling me, and it grated on my nerves far worse than GI Jane.

Yes, her sexist implication that women were only good for bringing children into the world sounded like something you'd expect to hear in the fifties, but it sliced me to the bone. I had overcome many hurdles the previous year, but I still hadn't come to terms with knowing that chemotherapy had saved my life while taking away my chance to give it. I had always wanted a large family and it would never happen. Everything else seemed very small in comparison.

"Well, look who it is. The Wicked Bitch of Blissville High," Milo had said when he walked up on the scene. "Take your flying twats and be gone before I borrow a bucket from the janitor and douse you with water."

"My, aren't we brave this year?" Amanda had asked. "You do know that my boyfriend is a football player and can crush you, right?"

"Yes, but I also know that my boyfriend is the captain of the football team and could snap your boyfriend like a twig. I don't think you want to get into a pissing contest with me. Get going." Milo had made witch cackling noises when Amanda turned and strode away in a huff.

"There's a crazed killer that seems intent on killing you," Amanda said, pulling me back to the present. "I'd call that trouble."

"Oh, that," I said, playing dumb. "It's nothing for you to worry your pretty head over. Thanks for checking on me though." I wanted her out of my store as fast as possible.

"Well, I admit to having ulterior reasons for stopping by." Amanda's face flushed prettily and she tilted her head down to look at the ground, but I could still see a wicked smile spread across her lips. When she raised her eyes to meet mine again they glittered with evil intent. She placed her hand over her stomach, splaying her fingers to cover as much area as she could. My heart sank when I realized what she was about to say. "I'm expecting," Amanda said excitedly. "Not many people know it, but Clayton and I are so excited about our little bundle of joy that's due to arrive later this year."

"That explains the sudden weight gain," my mom said. She placed her hand at the small of my back to remind me that she'd always have it through any battle.

"Mom," I said in a warning. As vapid and vain as Amanda was, I didn't want her starving herself and harming the baby because of something my mom said. We were better than her. "You look beautiful, Amanda. Congratulations to both you and Clayton."

Amanda had sneered at my mother's barb but flinched at my kindness. Had I found the way to beat her after all? "Thank you," she said cautiously. "Well, Clayton said an ordinary nursery wouldn't do for his baby, so I'm hoping you can help me find the perfect pieces. I want the room to be elegant, classy, and timeless."

"A child's nursery?" my mom asked. "Honey, there's nothing elegant or classy about changing shitty diapers, so it's best you prepare yourself for that now. You've come to the right place though. Maegan has the absolute best taste and can find almost anything your heart desires. She's also mature enough not to let the heinous way you treated her in high school interfere with conducting a business transaction. Right, Maegan?"

There was a not-so-gentle dig at Amanda and reminder that my business was more important than Amanda's shenanigans. She was right. I wouldn't allow Amanda to go around town telling people that I refused to help her. It would give my business a bad reputation and more ammunition for Amanda to use on me later. I'd be damned if I played another one of her games.

"Absolutely," I said to my mom before I kissed her on the cheek. "I love you."

"Call me later if you can tear yourself away from your man. Good luck, Amanda," my mother said dramatically.

"What did you have in mind for the nursery, Amanda? Did you have a theme or pattern in mind?"

"Uh…." It was obvious she expected me to refuse her.

"You don't want antique baby furniture because it doesn't typically meet today's safety standards and it lacks certain convenient features such as sides that lower or cribs that can convert to beds."

"Um…"

"However, there are manufacturers that specialize in making modern furniture that resembles vintage pieces. Beautiful stuff. I can help supplement whatever design you choose with lamps and decorative pieces. Oh! I found the most amazing collection of porcelain Beatrice Potter figurines, but I think I'm going to save those for my own nursery someday." Amanda looked at me like I had lost my mind, and before she could comment, I said, "There is more than one way to become a mother, Amanda. Surely you know this."

"Sure," she said, nodding her head.

Of course, I always knew that adopting kids was an option. I just didn't think I'd find a guy who could get past it. I had this idea in my head that men only wanted kids that carried their DNA. How misguided was that? It wasn't that Elijah told me something I didn't know, but hearing it from him made me want to heal that wound and live my life to the fullest. I didn't have to give up on being a mom, I just had to do it another way. I didn't have to wait for a guy to come around and approve my plan either.

"I'm going to adopt a houseful of rowdy kids." Visions of kids running through the house or back yard with barking dogs chasing them made me smile. Then I realized the house and yard wasn't my current residence, but it felt like home regardless. I didn't think I'd been inside the house with wide plank wooden floors, so why did it feel familiar. Then I realized that I had indeed recently seen those floors with my very own eyes. *Huh, I didn't see that one coming.*

"Do you smell something burning?" Milo asked, pulling me out of my thoughts. "Smells like sulfur." He sneered at Amanda. "I thought I saw your broom parked outside."

"Hello, Milo," she said.

"Should I grab a bucket of water?" he mock-whispered.

"Nah," I told him. "I'm helping Amanda pick out furniture and decorations for…" I wasn't sure she wanted people to know about her condition.

"Clayton and I are expecting a baby," Amanda told him. "Maegan is giving me some guidance."

"She is?" Milo asked.

"I am."

"You're a better person than I am," Milo said. "I still want to douse her with water for the way she treated you."

Amanda sucked on her teeth as she contemplated his words while she studied me. "She's a better person than me too. I'd have blasted me with both barrels."

"Too messy," I told her. "I've had enough drama this week. So, back to my original question. Do you have a color theme in mind?"

"We're waiting to find out the sex of the baby before we finalize the nursery, but I like your idea of choosing modern furniture that looks vintage and I love that chair." She pointed over to a Victorian style chair upholstered in beige striped silk fabric. It was one of my favorite pieces too. "And the matching ottoman." She walked over to the ottoman and ran her finger over the lid of the china teapot that sat on the sterling silver tray. "You've displayed it so beautifully that I want to buy the tea set and tray and I don't drink tea."

"Your mother does," Milo said from behind me. "Isn't her birthday coming up?" How Milo remembered all this stuff was beyond me.

"A few weeks," Amanda confirmed. "I'll take the chair, ottoman, the silver tray, and tea set."

"Step over to the register and we'll write it up and schedule a delivery date. Would you like to take your mother's gift home with you today?"

"Would the chair and ottoman fit in the back of my sport utility broom?" Amanda asked, winking at Milo.

"It fit in the back of my SUV, but I have a full-sized one for hauling big things," I told her. Amanda pulled her keychain out of her coat pocket. I took the keys from her and held them out for my brother. "Milo, will you kindly look to see if these items will fit?"

I don't know why I was suddenly so willing to put my turbulent past with Amanda in my rearview mirror, but it felt like the right thing to do. Milo wasn't there yet, but he accepted the keys and went outside anyway.

Amanda continued to walk around the store and comment on pieces that stood out to her, but swore she wasn't going to buy another thing until she knew if she was having a boy or girl. I wrote down some websites for her to look at for furniture while we waited for Milo to come back in. I needed to know if I had to tack on a delivery charge if they wouldn't fit in her SUV.

"What's taking him so long?" I asked out loud. "He better not be slashing your tires."

"I deserve worse," she said wryly.

"I won't disagree with you, but…" My words died in my throat when I saw what held him up. I smiled when Elijah looked up and met my eyes through the glass door. I opened it to let him and Milo in.

"Hi, Freckles," Elijah said affectionately.

"Hi there."

"I waved down some muscle when I saw that the chair and ottoman will fit in the back of her Sport Utility Broom. I may not like the Wicked Bitch of Blissville, but I have nothing against an innocent baby."

Elijah raised a brow at Milo's comment, but didn't remark on it. "Where's the chair and ottoman?"

"Uh…." Amanda stared dumbfounded at Elijah.

"Over there," I said, pointing. He dropped a kiss on my lips as he passed me. "Let me box up the silver and china for her while you guys carry out the furniture."

"Who's that?" Amanda said when we were alone again.

"His name is Elijah," I said, never taking my eyes off my task of wrapping the teapot and teacups with bubble wrap.

"Is he your boyfriend?" Amanda asked. I glanced up expecting to see disbelief in her expression, but I only saw curiosity.

"Um…." I wasn't sure how to answer that. First of all, I didn't know what was going on between Elijah and me, and second, Amanda wasn't someone I felt comfortable confiding in.

"Sorry, it's none of my business."

Milo and Elijah returned before I could respond. Milo handed Amanda's keys to her and nodded his head to the door in a not-so-subtle way. Amanda grinned and reached for the box holding her silver tray and tea set. Milo grabbed it before she could and headed toward the door.

"Take care, Maegan," Amanda said over her shoulder as she followed Milo.

"You know what it's like when you turn on a movie toward the end and you try to figure out what the hell is going on?" Elijah asked me.

"Yeah."

"That's how this feels right now. I can sense the roles you've all played, but not what led you to this big finale moment." He traced his finger along my jawline before he lowered his hand.

"I'll tell you everything you want to know," I told him.

"How about you tell me over dinner tonight? I was thinking I would make you my famous homemade pizza."

"Famous?"

"Not really," he answered ruefully. "It's not all that homemade either, but it is good. How does it sound?"

"Sounds perfect."

"What do you like on your pizza?" he asked.

"Surprise me," I replied. "I don't have any food allergies."

"It's great that I won't kill you, but I can go a step further and create something you'd actually want to eat."

"No anchovies," I told him.

"Be there at six, Freckles." He looked at me once he reached the door. "Don't bother bringing a nightgown. I like it when you sleep naked."

My focus and desire to stay at work disappeared in a poof after that. Luckily, the curious residents started pouring in after church to make the time go by faster.

Chapter Twenty-Two

Elijah

THE CAPTAIN HADN'T BEEN JOKING WHEN HE SAID FOR US TO be prepared for an early departure. Getting out of bed at five in the morning was not my idea of a good start, especially with Maegan sleeping so peacefully in bed. I wasn't used to navigating my bedroom in the dark and stubbed my toe on the corner of the bed.

"Fuck!" I whisper-yelled, hopping on one foot while my toe throbbed like a motherfucker.

"I'm not in the mood," Maegan drowsily mumbled from the bed. "Come back to sleep."

"Wish I could, Freckles, but duty calls."

"Well, tell it to call back in a few hours." I heard the comforter rustling as Maegan turned over then she patted the bed in the dark. "Come back here."

"Don't tempt me."

Maegan released a jagged sigh followed by a soft moan. "I guess I'll have to pleasure myself then."

My deep growl rumbled in the still of the morning. No fucking way I could ignore the need I heard in her voice. I just wouldn't be able to take my time like I preferred. Luckily, I didn't sacrifice another toe in the process of returning to my bed. Maegan held open the covers and I slid in beside her. My throbbing dick pulled my focus off my aching toe as I slid down her body and she parted her legs to make room for me. I much preferred to see her beautiful dips and curves but it was exciting to hear her breath hitch in delight as I trailed my fingers over her soft flesh or placed kisses on her bare pussy.

"Elijah!" Maegan threaded her fingers in my hair and raised her hips, telling me exactly where she wanted me.

If I wasn't pressed for time, I would've drawn out her pleasure and teased her, but I only had thirty minutes to rock her world, shower, shave, and meet Adrian. I was willing to skip the shaving part if I ran short on time, but I wasn't leaving that bed until I tasted Maegan's orgasm on my tongue. Damn, my girl was responsive as hell, so it didn't take long once I found that magic spot inside her sweet pussy while I sucked her clit into my mouth.

"Yes!" and "Elijah!" were two of my favorite words to pass through her delicious lips. I didn't think I'd ever tire of hearing them nor the way it felt when I slid my dick inside her tight, wet clench. "Harder!" was my third favorite word and I didn't disappoint her. Too fast, I was filling the condom and collapsing on top of her.

"I'm sorry if you're going to be late," she said. I didn't need to see her to know she was smiling from ear to ear. The way her pussy clenched my softening cock said that neither of them were sorry about what just went down between us.

"No, you're not," I whispered. I kissed the tip of her nose then pulled out of her. "Go back to sleep, Freckles."

"I'm wide awake now," she protested, but the drowsiness in her voice made me smile.

"Okay, then I'll take a nice hot breakfast before I go."

"Wake me when it's ready then," she replied cheekily.

She was fast asleep again by the time I got out of the shower, but I stopped to kiss her goodbye anyway. "Have a good day, Maegan."

She mumbled something indiscernible and snuggled deeper down in the covers. I knew there would come a day that I would whisper words of love to her instead. Yeah, the realization scared the fuck out of me, but I embraced it instead of pushing the feelings away. Scared meant that I was feeling something. It meant that I was alive instead of walking through life like an extra in a zombie movie. I'd been going through the motions of living ever since I found out that Brandy and Jack fucked around behind my back. Maegan made me realize that the life I lived wasn't enough. Damn, I didn't want to end up like Renzo's uncle—old and lonely. Not when I had a chance at something amazing with a woman who was unlike any other I'd previously met.

I knew it was too soon to be having long-term thoughts about a girl I'd known for less than two weeks, but my heart, gut, and brain all agreed that she was the one. We just needed to convince her of that, and we couldn't do it until the case was behind us. I wanted to take her on real dates and get to know her away from a crisis. I wanted to know the things that made her tick, made her mad, and made her fall apart in my arms. I had a jumpstart on the latter one, but the other ones were just as important if we were to create something special out of our mutual attraction to each other. I wanted Maegan to tell me about her battle with cancer, not hear it from someone else. That meant I needed to open up and talk about my past too. For her, I'd do it.

I expected Adrian to be waiting impatiently for me when I got to the station, but he wasn't there yet. He showed up five minutes late but didn't look remotely sorry. I didn't know him well enough to tease him yet, but I suspected that he was late for the same reason that I almost was. He probably couldn't make his lady sing as quickly as I could Maegan.

"Let's head out, partner," Adrian said.

He did most of the talking during the four-hour ride. He told me about the case that they referenced the day before with Adrian and the captain getting knocked out by a woman. He had me laughing hilariously when he talked about taking down the Christmas Bandits right after I was hired.

"You missed it, Markham. Gabe tackled Santa in his front lawn and I took down an elf that was as tall, if not taller, than you." He laughed at the memories.

"What the hell did the Christmas Bandits do?" I asked.

"They kicked off their reign of terror by vandalizing Santa's Village and hanging an effigy of Saint Nick from the flagpole."

"Brutal," I said.

"Then they started stealing Christmas decorations and cutting the electrical cords for exterior lights. They messed up when they hit the captain's house and Josh's salon though. The cap went all John McClane on their asses."

"Yippee-ki-yay and all that?" I asked.

"In glorious fashion," Adrian said.

"The town of Blissville is spunkier than I expected."

"The Christmas Bandits were from Goodville, not Blissville," Adrian corrected.

"I guess it's better than Whoville."

"That needs to be our next theme for the department's Christmas parade float. We were pretty lame this past year and I want to stomp the rest of the floats into dust." Adrian banged his fist against the steering wheel excitedly. "That's a great idea, partner."

"Glad I could help," I said with a chuckle.

We met Kentucky State Patrolmen Ralph Dennis and Mark Young outside of Thom Renzo's apartment complex at ten sharp. We didn't require a search warrant since Thom was the victim of a violent crime, not a suspect. The complex superintendent was on site to let us into the apartment since Renzo's keys found in his car were still considered evidence.

My good mood from the morning disappeared the second we crossed the threshold into his apartment. "You can wait for us outside," I told the super, shutting the door to prevent him from following us inside. There was no telling what we'd find.

Renzo's apartment was the clichéd bachelor pad. Cheap furniture, expensive television and gaming system, and empty takeout cartons, bags, and boxes everywhere. His bed was unmade, clothes were strewn all over the floor, and his bathroom looked like a hurricane had blown through it.

A feeling of dread and disgust permeated my body as we began to open drawers and look for any clue to the identity of Renzo's killer. It didn't take us long to figure out that the killer was most likely a victim of Renzo's sick, twisted mind. Every picture or magazine we found depicted his pleasure in seeing other's suffering. I'm not talking about rough sex or even BDSM. The expression on the women's faces told the story even if the article headlines didn't. In most of the photos, the women didn't look conscious.

"I'm going to fucking puke, Adrian." I wasn't lying either. That sausage biscuit I got from the golden arches drive-thru was about to come back up. What did this fucker do to women? Had he planned to do this to my Maegan?

"That makes two of us," Adrian said. He pointed to the laptop sitting next to the bed. "I'd rather you shove rusty nails under my fingernails than make me look at the content on the computer." There are things and images so vile and sick that no amount of experience on the force can prepare you to see.

"We have to do it," I said.

"Let me do this for you, partner." Normally, I would not have backed down, but I couldn't handle seeing anything about Maegan on that fucking creep's laptop.

I nodded my head and went into the living room to search the entertainment center. I pulled out one video after the other depicting sex crimes involving women on the covers. The titles were written crudely in black marker. How did anyone become so fucking sick? It didn't take long for Adrian to join me with the laptop tucked under his arm.

"Well? Did you have any luck finding our two blonde vigilantes?"

"I lost track of the number of blonde women I saw on his hard drive. This was one sick fucker," Adrian said with dread. "Um, his recent search engine activity did revolve around Maegan. It looked like he was trying to learn everything about her, but I couldn't find any type of journal that he used to detail his sick-as-fuck activities or the plan he had for her. There were plenty of photos of him with other women though."

"So this person did save Maegan's life by taking Renzo's?" I asked.

"I'd say yes." Adrian looked at the videos I pulled from the shelves and photographed them. "Jesus. Are those home movies?"

"I think so, but I can't be sure if they're his or something he bought."

Dennis and Young were just as sickened as we were, but all we could do was bag the evidence and remove it from site. It was almost lunchtime when we arrived at Renzo's employer.

The CEO and head of human resources for the small company met with us personally. "Thank you for taking time to meet with us, Mr. Titus and Ms. James," I said.

"We want to help you in any way we can. We were shocked to hear that Thom had been killed so violently," the CEO said. He gestured to the file on his desk before he pushed it across to me. "Here's Mr. Renzo's personnel file and Ms. James is prepared to answer your questions."

"Is this ours to take?" Adrian asked.

"Absolutely," Mr. Titus said. "Ms. James is available to answer any questions that arise later also."

"Yes," Ms. James said nervously. "I'll do what I can."

I narrowed my eyes and studied her body language. She sat straight and tall in her chair, exuding confidence, but her fidgeting hands and inability to maintain eye contact gave away how nervous she truly was. I didn't want to look a gift horse in the mouth, but the CEO was making things too easy. I started to suspect that the personnel file was a ruse on his part to cover something up. Smoke and mirrors. Look to the left so you don't see what I'm doing on the right.

"This is his complete file? It contains any and all complaints brought against him or disciplinary actions he received?" I asked Ms. James, but she wasn't the one who answered.

"Of course, Detective," Titus said, emphasizing his Southern boy hospitality.

I shifted my eyes to him and said, "Thank you, sir, but I wasn't asking you."

"Is this everything, Ms. James?" I asked more firmly.

"We need your help, ma'am," Adrian added, falling into the good cop role like he did when the captain had been his partner.

"Yes, I believe so," she said softly. She slowly raised her head and locked her gaze on mine. I knew she was lying when I saw the terror and shame in her blue eyes. I think she wanted to help us, but was afraid to do it. I didn't want to be a dick, but her losing her job was the last thing on my mind.

"The sexual harassment allegations that were filed against him are in this file then? Including the name of the employees who filed them?" I asked. I was completely shooting from the hip, but the way she flinched told me that I'd hit a bullseye.

"There were no harassment allegations made against Mr. Renzo, Detective. I'm not sure what you're talking…"

"Do not lie to me or I'll make things really ugly for your company, Mr. Titus. I want to know the name of the woman, or women, who filed complaints against Mr. Titus. I want you to start with ones who no longer work here."

Ms. James pulled out a sheet of paper from her briefcase and slid it to me. "Here's all of them."

"All of them?" I asked. "How many complaints of sexual

harassment does it take to get a guy fired?"

"More than ten," she said. "I wanted to fire that slimy asshole, but Mr. Titus wouldn't let me. My hands were tied."

"Yeah, so were the ladies that he sexually assaulted." I looked at the names on the paper and my heart broke for them. "Which one was the most outspoken about the ordeal?" We would interview them all, but I'd start with the one who seemed boldest in her attempt to get justice.

"Kayla Hanson," Ms. James stated. "Well, her sister Jessica, that is."

"Her sister?" Adrian asked. I was sure he was thinking the same thing I was.

"Her name isn't on this list," I said.

"Kayla didn't show up for work for a few days. I called her, but she never returned my call. Her sister finally retrieved the messages from her cell phone and called me. She explained that Kayla had been drugged and sexually assaulted. Kayla had refused to name her assailant after the police officer who responded seemed to blow her off. Asking questions about how much she had to drink or what she wore, as if either of those things made a difference."

"If Kayla didn't name her attacker then how did you know it was Thom?"

"She didn't tell the police, but she told her sister. Someone"—she tipped her head toward Mr. Titus—"wouldn't allow me to enter the complaint in Thom's file because Kayla herself didn't make it."

"Now wait a minute—"

I raised my hand to cut him off. "I'm not interested in hearing your excuses. I suggest you save it for your attorney." I turned back to Ms. James.

"How recently was Kayla's assault?" I asked.

"A month ago, maybe six weeks."

"So, he's escalating his attacks," Adrian said as he looked over the list of complaints and the dates they were filed against Renzo. "Do any of these women still work here?"

"No, but their contact info is on the sheet. Listen, Kayla has been a real mess since the incident. You might want to talk to Jessica first to arrange a time to speak with Kayla. I know where she works. We've become good friends." If Ms. James had blonde hair, I might've suspected that she was Jessica's accomplice.

"Where is that?"

Ms. James gave us the information we requested and we headed straight over to her office. The receptionist working the front desk looked at us in alarm but buzzed us in and told us how to navigate the maze of cubicles to find Jessica Hansen.

Jessica was the office manager and was afforded a small office in the back. The room was standard industrial white walls with beige commercial carpet and missing its sole occupant. The receptionist assured us that Jessica had just returned from lunch, so maybe she'd gone to the bathroom. It gave me the opportunity to learn a little about my prime suspect. The office was too small for all four of us to stand in, so the Kentucky patrolmen stood outside while Adrian and I entered.

The room was devoid of any character until you took in the potted blooming cactus plant and framed photos of two blonde women posing for selfies. Nothing about her office proved that she was my killer until I saw her Hellcat mousepad and an image of Captain Marvel as the wallpaper on her computer.

I looked toward the doorway when I heard someone approaching the office quickly.

"Hello, Officers," she said, greeting Dennis and Young. Jessica Hansen didn't even flinch when she stepped into her office and spotted Adrian and me. I could tell by the look on her face that she wasn't that surprised. It was almost as if she expected us.

"Ms. James called you, didn't she?"

Jessica didn't so much as blink. Nothing in her posture or her expression gave her away. Suddenly, she released a long sigh and swallowed hard. I was certain that I was looking into the eyes of Renzo's killer. She had saved Maegan from a horrifying fate, and I wanted to hug her. Instead, I said, "Jessica Hansen, you're under arrest for the murder of Thom Renzo."

She turned around and peacefully placed her hands behind her back for me to cuff. "It's okay. I have no regrets." I was pretty sure she was trying to make me feel better, but nothing about the situation felt right.

"You shouldn't say anything until your attorney is present," Adrian said.

"You haven't read me my rights, so nothing I've said so far can be used against me."

I thought it was quite possible that she would be acquitted of her crimes before a jury of her peers.

Adrian read her rights to her as we guided her out of the building and put her in the back of Adrian's car.

"I acted alone, Detectives," she said once he pulled out of the parking lot.

Adrian and I both knew different, but proving it might be difficult *if* we wanted to.

Chapter Twenty-Three

Maegan

"**T**ELL US *EVERYTHING* AND DON'T LEAVE ANYTHING out," Vanessa said when I walked into her house for Margarita Monday.

"Well, Amanda stopped by my shop yesterday. It sounds like congratulations are in order, Auntie Vanessa."

"Oh no!" Vanessa reached for my hand. "Did she go in there and start trouble with you? I'd hate to smack a pregnant lady, but—"

I cut her off with a wave. "Thank you, but it's not necessary. I think her goal was to rile me up, but she either gave up when she realized it wouldn't work, or finding out she's about to be a mom has softened her." I smiled when I thought about the amount of money she spent on the chair, ottoman, silver tray, and tea set. I definitely came out the winner after that battle.

"I'm glad to hear that Amanda can't upset you anymore, but that's not the *everything* that Vanessa was talking about. We want to know all about the new sexy man in your life."

"How do you know he's sexy?" Violet asked her.

"I'm a lesbian, Vi, not blind." April rolled her eyes. "Just because I'm not attracted to guys doesn't mean that I don't recognize a sexy

204

man when presented with one. Elijah is pure sex on a stick."

I hung up my coat and headed to the kitchen where I knew a margarita pitcher awaited me. I breathed the delicious, spicy aroma of Latin food baking in the oven and fought the urge to lift the lids off the pots on top of the stove to see what she had whipped up for us. Vanessa followed me into the kitchen and poured me a drink.

"Mmmmm," I said after a long drink. "Peach."

"It's your favorite," Van said. "I figured you could use it after the crazy time you've had. Are you really okay?" I'd be rich and could retire if I had a penny for every time someone asked me that the past two weeks.

I helped myself to the chips and salsa Vanessa had laid out for us to munch on before dinner. She waited patiently while I ate a few and washed it down with another drink. "I'm so hungry," I told her. "The shop was a zoo again today and there was no way that Bonnie could keep up with them on her own, so my lunch consisted of peanut butter crackers and Diet Coke." I looked at the large clock on the kitchen wall. "That was six hours ago." Trust me, I was glad the day went by fast so that I didn't have to worry about what Elijah was doing in Kentucky, but a proper lunchtime would've been nice.

"Let me get you something with a little more substance," Vanessa offered.

"It's not necessary," I told her. I didn't want her to go to any trouble.

"Maegan, you hate feeling buzzed and you've never been drunk. Let me grab you some cheese and fruit to help absorb some of the alcohol until the enchiladas, Spanish rice, and refried beans are ready in ten minutes." She pulled out a block of cheese and fruit from the refrigerator.

Van was right; I loved the taste of a mixed drink but not the side effects. I could already feel my face getting warm and that fuzzy feeling creeping in around the edges of my mind. My inner control freak started to panic, so I reached for a chunk of cheese.

"Delicious," I said.

Van pulled a bottle of water out of the fridge and placed it in front of me. She'd be the last person to admit how much she loved to nurture, but it was ingrained in her DNA. "Smoked gouda; it's silky and smooth." She tipped her head to the side and studied me.

April, Candace, and Violet entered the kitchen and poured themselves a margarita.

"What'd we miss?" April asked.

"Wait for us! We want to hear all about the sex too!" Violet exclaimed.

"No sex talk yet," Vanessa said. "I was just asking if she was really okay."

"I'm fine, Van. Really. Yeah, parts of the last two weeks have sucked"—all three of them snorted—"but other parts were…" My voice trailed off as I struggled to find the words.

"Orgasmic," April suggested

"Earth shattering," Violet added.

"Surreal," I told them. "I'm not going to give you gals the down-and-dirty details of what's been going on between Elijah and me." We weren't high school kids and Vanessa's kitchen wasn't the locker room. What I shared with Elijah was too special to cheapen by bawdy shop talk.

"So you're admitting that there's something going on?" Candace pressed.

"Of course, something is going on," I answered her.

"Something truly special from the looks of it," Violet said, wrapping her arm around my shoulders.

They were so disappointed that I wasn't going to give them a by-play of every orgasm Elijah gave me. A smile spread across my face when I realized I had lost count.

"Oh, would you look at that face," April said. "She's thinking about the orgasms she refuses to discuss. Lucky bitch."

"I spent quite a bit of time with Marley Kasey this weekend," I said to April, deciding that a change in narrative was in order.

"Oh, really," Vanessa said. "She's so lovely. Don't you think she's lovely, April?"

"Just because she's the only other gay woman in town doesn't mean that we're destined to be together," April said.

"How often do you tell yourself that?" I asked her.

"Every day that I look in the mirror," April admitted before she knocked back the rest of her drink in one gulp. She sounded miserable and I hated that for her. "Whoa!" She blinked a few times and set her glass back down with an indelicate *thunk*. She reached over and snagged a chunk of cheese off my plate.

"Hey! That's my cheese."

"Sorry," she said around a mouthful of smooth, smoky goodness. "God, I feel much better now. All tingly inside." I slid my plate over to share my cheese with April. I didn't want her to get too tingly, too fast.

"Why does Maegan get fancy cheese and fruit when the rest of us only get chips and salsa?" Violet asked. "The chips aren't even warm."

"This isn't a restaurant," Vanessa said. "I don't warm up my tortilla chips."

"Well, it's the least you can do if you're going to withhold the good cheese. I always knew that Maegan was your favorite," Candace told Van.

"Oh, for fuck's sake," Vanessa said, her lips quirked up into a wry smile. She began slicing off more cheese for April, Candace, and Violet. "Who said that I liked any of you?"

"You love us," April said, sounding tipsier by the minute.

"I do," Vanessa agreed.

"Oh!" Candace exclaimed. "I bet Maegan is the first of us to get married." Cut her off, bartender.

"Huh?" How'd we go from Vanessa loving us to me getting married? That was a big leap.

"Oh! I'll take that bet," Van said. "Twenty bucks says Maegan gets married first."

"That's not much of a bet," April hemmed.

"Fifty then!" Vanessa said.

"Not the dollar amount, silly," Candace told our host. "The point of a bet is to settle a disagreement between two or more people. No one here is disputing that Maegan is now most likely to get married first."

"Oh! You have a good point," Violet said. "We need to do a pool like they do when they guess the weight and inches of a newborn baby or predict the outcome of football games. Yeah, that's it!"

"Where's a notepad, Van?" Candace asked. Vanessa reached inside a kitchen drawer and pulled out a notebook and pen.

"We need to write it down. Everyone commits to twenty dollars and the one closest to Mae's actual wedding date gets all the money. One of us is going to win one hundred dollars!" April exclaimed.

"Where do you get that?" I asked. Hell, I hadn't consumed so much alcohol that I couldn't figure her winnings were skewed.

"There are five of us," April said.

"You think I'm entering?" I asked, trying to hold back my laugh. Candace snorted.

"Eighty then," Violet said, nodding her head. "I can buy a lot of books for that money."

"Try sixty," Candace corrected, shaking her head. "You'll get your twenty dollars back and an additional twenty from three other people. I wouldn't count your own cash as earnings."

"Must you be in CPA mode all the time, Candy Apple?" Violet asked.

"Really," April agreed. "So I was off a few bucks."

I raised my brow at Candace, but she just shook her head. "Okay, who wants what date?" she asked once she opened the notebook and poised her pen over a blank page.

"May twenty-fifth," April announced.

"This year?" I asked. "That's only a few months away!"

"Hot and heavy, Princess," April said smugly. "He'll snap you up before you have a chance to get away."

"No freaking way," I told her. I didn't yet know what hang-ups Elijah had, but I was sure they existed.

"Ignore her, Van. Write it down. I want May twenty-fifth."

"That's a Thursday," Violet said, looking at the calendar on her phone. "I'll take May Twenty-Seventh."

"You're both nuts," I murmured, but they were too busy squaring off to hear me.

"That's not fair!" April said. "This isn't the Price is Right. You don't just get to bid two days over mine to knock me out of the running."

"You're the idiot who chose a Thursday," Violet said.

"I'm not an idiot! You're a cheater," April countered.

"What are you talking about?" Violet stood taller and looked really pissed.

Vanessa, Candace, and I exchanged looks of confusion. What the hell was going on here and where was the source of hostility coming from? They'd been back and forth since the moment I walked through the door.

"You used a calendar," April replied accusingly. "That's cheating."

"Where was it stated that we couldn't take a minute to look at a calendar before we gave a date?" Violet asked calmly. "Oh, that's right. There were no rules, but you acted impetuously like you always do. Or maybe it was just 'the alcohol talking.' Does that sound familiar to you, April?" I would've known Violet was repeating words she heard by the tone of her voice alone, but her use of finger quotations added an impressive dramatic flair. Milo would've been proud.

April slapped her hands on the kitchen island. "I thought we got past this, Vi."

"Apparently *I* didn't." Violet closed her eyes and shook her head slightly to get herself under control. When she reopened them, she was once again the calm woman I was used to seeing. "Um, I think I'm going to head on home."

"No," Vanessa, Candace, and I said at once.

April started to follow Violet into the living room, but she was stopped by a scalding look. "Why are you following me, April?"

April swallowed hard, looking uncertain how to answer our friend. "You're my ride home, Vi."

I could tell that was the wrong answer by the way Violet's skin paled and her mouth popped open. "Call Marley Kasey to come get you." Violet turned and left without saying another word, only pausing to grab her coat. As if we didn't already know she was pissed, she slammed the door hard enough to rattle the frame.

"Oh my God. I've been such a fool." April covered her face and dropped in the seat next to me. I wrapped my arm around her while Vanessa and Candace circled the island to stand on the other side. We huddled together in an awkward group hug. April cried into her hands while Vanessa tried to communicate telepathically with me and Candace whispered soothing words in April's ear. Telepathy didn't work so well, so we resorted to body language.

Vanessa's widened eyes said, *Oh my God! What do we do?*

I tilted my head slightly and grimaced to say, *I don't have a fucking clue.*

"I've loved Violet for as long as I can remember," April finally said. "I never realized she had feelings for me too."

"What happened and when?" I asked softly.

"After her last breakup with that guy named Doug, Violet came over for dinner. She got a little tipsy and told me that she's been attracted to me for a long time. I wanted to believe her, but I was too afraid to trust my heart to her. She had only dated men, only expressed desire for men. I didn't want to be an experiment to her. I knew it would ruin our friendship if that happened, so I told her it was the wine and heartache talking."

"Oh, honey," Candace said. "When was this?"

"Six months ago," April said. "She kind of laughed it off and said I was right. Things were awkward between us for a few days, but we fell back into our old groove. I really thought it was a meaningless, drunken pass."

The timer on the oven chimed, interrupting us. *Wow!* All of that happened in ten minutes. Amazing how quickly a person's life could change. Vanessa pulled away to remove dinner from the oven. I just kept rubbing circles in the center of April's back.

"I'm sorry, April. I think it was my fault for bringing Marley up. I had no idea that Violet had feelings for you either. I never would have brought it up."

"It's not your fault, honey."

"I feel bad though."

"You know what?" Vanessa asked. We looked up and found her standing there with her oven-mitted hands on her hips. "We're going after her. You two are too drunk to drive. Let's pack this up and I'll drive us over to her house. You girls can talk things out. We can't let this continue."

"She doesn't—"

"No arguing," Candace said bossily. "Besides, I didn't get to pick a date for Maegan and Elijah's wedding."

"Me either," Van chimed in.

I groaned. "I was hoping we would forget about that."

"Fat chance," April said, rising to her feet. "I want a do-over now that I know I can look at a calendar." She looked me up and down. "Maegan isn't a summer bride anyway. She favors fall weather and colors."

"Dammit, I was going to pick fall," Vanessa said, zipping the casserole into a carrier. She looked at me. "Don't just stand there looking all in love and cute. Grab a damn storage container and start filling it with rice and beans. Damn, do I have to do all the matchmaking around here?"

"Don't hold your breath," April mumbled.

"Shut up!" Van, Candace, and I all said at the same time then burst into giggles.

God, it felt good to be with my girls and forget about murder and mayhem for just a little while.

Chapter Twenty-Four

Elijah

THE USUAL EUPHORIA THAT CAME WITH ARRESTING A murder suspect was missing when we processed Jessica Hansen back at the police station. We didn't walk through the station with our chests puffed out collecting high-fives as we went. There was nothing thrilling about arresting a woman who felt she had no other recourse but to take the law into her hands after the system failed her. In a turn of events, Jessica was the one who walked tall and proud through the precinct in Bowling Green, Kentucky, while Adrian and I looked like whipped puppies.

I didn't expect her to basically surrender and confess to us when we showed up at her office. I figured she would make us show hard evidence that she committed the crime, but maybe she knew it would just delay the inevitable. There was a high probability that her finger-prints were somewhere in Renzo's car or in the house. We also had the hotel clerk in Goodville who could identify her from a photo. If he identified her, he'd do the same for her sister, which we knew she didn't want. She couldn't protect Kayla from Thom Renzo, but she could save her from going to prison. I knew damned well that she saved Maegan from a similar fate—or worse—as Kayla.

We couldn't just put her in the back of Adrian's car and drive her back across state lines without going through official channels. The first of which was to take her official statement on camera where she waived her rights to have an attorney present. Jessica kept her eyes locked on mine as she detailed everything that happened from her sister's attack to the moment she bashed Thom's head in with a marble statue she found nearby. She denied her sister rode along with her and had a reasonable explanation for how she pulled it off by herself. She said anger and outrage made it possible for her to walk for miles in the frigid temperatures to retrieve her car that she'd hidden.

She didn't show any emotion until she circled back to her sister. "One day my sister is a vibrant, happy young woman and the next she's a ghost walking through life. Do you know she tried taking her own life, Detectives? She couldn't live with what that animal did to her. My little sister was on suicide watch for a month at a hospital. Do you know what it's like looking into the eyes of someone you love so much and not seeing them? Do you? How would you like seeing your sister's or *girlfriend's* wrists restrained to the bedrail so she couldn't end her misery? Where was her justice? Why wouldn't that cop listen to her?"

"Do you remember his name, Jessica?" I asked softly.

"Like you care."

"Oh, I do care," I countered. "I promise you that I'll do everything I can to make sure he never treats another victim in the same way." I wanted to assure her that he'd lose his job, but that was a promise that I couldn't make. It was her word against his. He had a union to back him, she had no one. Well, she had me, but my power was pretty limited. Her best bet would be to find a hungry journalist who wouldn't let up on the story until something was done.

Jessica relented and told us his name after a few minutes. Patrolman Dennis immediately left the room and I figured he was going to seek out the cop's supervisor. Jessica continued with her story, explaining that she didn't really plan on killing Thom. She said she started following the man to prevent him from hurting anyone else and hopefully catch him in the act that would open an investigation into his activity.

"There was no way a sick fuck like him didn't have a computer full of incriminating material," she said. "I knew that stealing his computer wasn't enough because you guys wouldn't be able to use it. I didn't have a concrete plan in place; I just needed to do something. Then I saw the look on his face when he tossed a black duffel bag in the trunk of his car." She closed her eyes and tears streamed down her face. "I knew he was going to hurt someone else and this sense of calm washed over me. I knew what I had to do. I don't regret it either." She scrubbed the tears off her face with her hands. "I only regret upsetting your girlfriend. I never intended for her to think she was the target of my anger. I just wanted to help."

There was so much I wanted to say to her but couldn't with the video rolling. We sailed through processing and interviewing her, but hit a snag when she refused extradition.

"I'm not making that easy on you, Detectives," she said with a wry smile. "I understand that I'm going to serve hard time, but I'd rather do it here so that my parents and sister don't have to travel so far to see me on visiting day. I'd like to call my parents so they can arrange for a good attorney."

I didn't think she'd have much luck avoiding extradition, but then I realized that maybe we could help her after all. We could talk to our county prosecutor and see if she was willing to allow her sentencing trial to occur in Kentucky. The crime may have occurred in our county, but both Thom and Jessica were Kentucky residents.

"Your parents and sister are already here," Patrolman Dennis said when he returned to the room. "I told them that we were about to wrap things up in here and they'd have a chance to speak with her before..." His words trailed off.

"It's okay, Patrolman Dennis. I didn't expect to get away with killing someone."

"I think we're done here," I said to Patrolman Young so that he could end the video. He nodded when it was off. "Listen, we'll talk to our prosecutor when we get back to see if she will waive extradition and allow you to stand trial here. You've admitted to the crime, but you can either retract your statement and insist on a jury hearing, or you can waive the right to a trial and go straight to a sentencing hearing where you'll be able to call witnesses to speak on your behalf in front of a judge. You have options."

"I will never ask my sister to testify to what that monster did to her. I'll spend the rest of my life behind bars if it comes down to that," Jessica said, raising her chin in pride.

"We'll see what kind of charges our prosecutor will want to file against you once he's had a chance to review the evidence we collected from Renzo's apartment," Patrolman Young said. "You're going to be our guest until you have a bail hearing though."

"That's fine," she replied. "Can I please see my family now?" Her chin wobbled slightly and I figured she was probably more scared than she wanted us to believe.

"Sure," Patrolman Dennis said.

The four of us rose to our feet and headed to the door. I looked over my shoulder before I left the room. Jessica lifted her head and met my gaze. "Best of luck to you."

"Thank you, Detective."

Making eye contact with her family was difficult, but I had to remind myself that I wasn't the one who committed a crime. I slowed down as I approached her mother and mumbled three words that I thought might help her daughter.

The four-hour drive back to Blissville was quiet as Adrian and I were both lost in our own thoughts. As sworn officers of the law, we could never encourage what Jessica Hansen did, but that didn't mean we couldn't understand her motivation.

"I doubt Prosecutor Buxton meets with us today, but we can try."

It turned out that she was eager to meet with us, thinking we carried good news. That changed when we told her that Jessica was fighting extradition. "What were her reasons? Did she just want to delay the inevitable?" she asked us.

"Ma'am, she wants to go to a prison closer to her family to make it easier for them to visit her."

Prosecutor Buxton snorted. "Seriously? She thinks that I'll agree to that?"

"I think you will when you find out the circumstances and hear about the evidence we found at Renzo's apartment. This guy wasn't some innocent victim cut down in the prime of his life. I'm sorry that his parents died, but not sorry they didn't have to see the animal their son had become."

The prosecutor sat back in her seat, looking less confident about her previous statement. "I'm listening, Detectives."

Adrian told her about the evidence he found on the laptop, and I shared details about the movies we suspected to be homemade. She looked as sick as we felt.

"Ma'am," Adrian said respectfully. "I saw the suspect's sister at the station, and I can confirm that she was in some of the photos we found on Renzo's computer. It looked obvious to me that she was drugged and not a willing participant in a consensual act."

"Oh," the prosecutor said. "I want to do the right thing here, Detectives. I just don't want to lose the confidence of the people who elected me."

She wanted to give in, but needed an incentive to force her hand. "Ma'am, the media is going to be all over this case when they get word of it." Thanks to me, I was pretty certain it would happen within twenty-four hours. "How do you think your constituents will feel when they find out that Thom Renzo had every intention of causing great harm to one of their favorite residents?" Hell, I'd only lived in Blissville a few weeks and I saw how much people loved Maegan.

"There are times when we need to pick a battle, and crusading against Jessica Hansen probably isn't the one I'd stake my career on."

Prosecutor Buxton crossed her arms over her chest and raised a brow. "Because I'm a woman?" I knew that Jessica's fate could be determined by my answer. She stood a better chance with a jury of local peers, people who could relate to her.

"Because you're human, ma'am."

She closed her eyes and breathed deeply into her lungs. "Okay, I'll make the necessary calls to law enforcement officials to let them know that we're waiving extradition so she can be tried there."

"Thank you," Adrian and I said in relief.

"You better hope this doesn't come back to ruin my career." She made shooing motions with her hands. "Get on out of here so I can prepare a statement. I want to go public with my decision before the details of the case are leaked to the press."

We left her office at once.

"Media, huh?" Adrian asked once we were back in his car. "Is that what you said to the mother?"

"Yeah, I told her to call a reporter." I released a breath of relief. It had been a long fucking day, but I was glad to have the case behind me. It was too bad that I couldn't say the same thing for Jessica and Kayla.

I got to go home and hold Maegan in my arms knowing that she was safe and healthy. It could be a very long time before Jessica breathed as a free woman and Kayla would never be the same. I prayed like hell that she took comfort knowing that Renzo couldn't hurt her or anyone else again, but she'd never get over what happened to her. I hoped she could find peace and realize that her life was worth living.

"I thought it might give her a fighting chance at a lesser sentence and bring shame down on the officer who allowed Thom to continue on like nothing happened without even talking to the guy," I explained.

"We can hope that Mr. Titus gets hit with a class action lawsuit," Adrian said. "What a fucking douche." He shook his head in disgust then said, "I can't wait to get home and hug my wife and kids. They remind me why I do this job."

"Same here," I replied. Adrian's brow rose high on his forehead. "Well, not the wife and kids part; I'm not living a double life. I meant I'm ready to give Maegan a tight squeeze." And so much more. "She's doing dinner with her friends tonight though, so it will be a while."

"You want to come over and have dinner with us? You can borrow my wife," Adrian offered. It was my turn to give him a questioning look. "Not like that, jackass."

"Nah," I answered. "I really appreciate it, and I'll definitely take you up on that offer another night, but I think I'll just decompress and sort out how I want to break the news to Maegan. I can't let her read about this in the paper or see it on the news."

"Town gossip is a terrible thing. Hell, news of Jessica's arrest probably beat us back to Blissville," Adrian told me.

"Let's hope not," I replied.

When we got to the station, we gave the captain a quick rundown of everything that transpired. He agreed with the prosecutor's decision to let Jessica be tried in Kentucky. He too offered to feed me when my stomach growled loudly to protest the way I neglected it, and I declined his invitation also.

I could heat up soup or leftover pizza from the night before and bide my time until Maegan got back from visiting with her friends. Now that the threat against her was past, I knew we'd return to living separately. I was going to miss her like hell on the nights we slept apart, but I wanted to do right by Maegan.

I saw the lights on in the back of my house as I pulled into the driveway. I knew that I hadn't left them on and Maegan's SUV wasn't in her driveway. My first thought was that someone wanting to get even on Axel Washington's behalf was paying me a visit. I wouldn't expect them to leave the lights on and advertise that, but criminals weren't always the brightest people in the galaxy.

I pulled my gun out of my holster and kept it trained in front of me until I got through the front door. Lulu bounded over to me happily, wagging her nub and barking out a greeting. I holstered my gun when I heard Maegan humming in the kitchen at the rear of the house. I sniffed the air and my mouth watered over the delicious aroma of Mexican food wafting through my house.

I found Maegan doing a cute little dance when I entered the room. She was wearing a pair of pajama pants that had roosters all over them. When she turned around, I was too busy staring at her unbound breasts to realize what her shirt said right away. In the middle of her chest was a big rooster and the words above it said: Cock Addict.

"Hey there, handsome," she said, smiling happily. She looked beautiful with her curly hair hanging loose and soft over her shoulders and not a drop of makeup on her face. Both her smile and pert nipples welcomed me home, and I realized just how badly I wanted to get used to finding her in my house after a long day.

Chapter Twenty-Five

Maegan

ELIJAH CLOSED THE DISTANCE BETWEEN US IN A FEW STEPS then backed me up against the counter. "Hello, Freckles." He buried his hands in my hair and kissed me like he hadn't seen me in days. "Damn, I like you in my space."

My heart raced over his confession. I feared my presumptuous actions would have the reverse effect. Hell, it wasn't that long ago that he completely flaked on me. Would he do it again once the case was over?

"I like being in your space, Elijah." His stomach growled ferociously making me laugh. "Hungry?"

"Famished." He turned loose of me to lift the lid off the containers. "Oh my God," he said on a low groan. "Enchiladas, refried beans, and rice."

"Dinner kind of went tits up, so I decided to bring leftovers ho... here to you." I laughed nervously hoping he didn't catch my slipup.

"What happened? How'd you get here? Your SUV isn't in your driveway."

"Well, I was too tipsy to drive, so Van dropped me off here. I'm not sure where to begin with how wrong our night went."

"Start anywhere you want as long as you do it while we eat."

"Deal," I said, heaping food onto a plate and handing it to him.

We settled at the small table in the kitchen and Elijah practically dove into his food. I would've thought he was consuming it too fast to taste it, but his moans and groans said differently.

"Oh, Maegan. This is so damn good. I can't get enough."

Those were things he usually said when I had possession of his cock—either in my mouth or pussy—or he had his head buried between my legs. I was suddenly in the mood to push back from the table and throw myself at him. Only his obvious need to eat stopped me. *Let the man refuel, Mae. He's going to need it.*

"God, who made this?"

"Vanessa made it," I told him.

"Which one was she?" he asked before he shoveled another bite in his mouth.

"Why do you ask?"

Elijah's head snapped up and he met my suspicious gaze with widened eyes. He shook his head. "Just curious."

"It's the one thing she knows how to make," I told him. "A man can't live on enchiladas every day."

Elijah dropped his fork and wiped his mouth. He looked a little skittish. "I didn't imply that I was going to ask her on a date or anything. I was just curious which of your friends made this dinner."

"Which one of my lovely friends, you mean?"

"They are lovely women," Elijah said. "I'm not going to pretend I didn't notice." He licked his lips nervously. "Are we fighting?"

I burst into laughter then because my reaction—or overreaction—was ridiculous. "No, Elijah. I'm sorry."

"It must've been some night with your friends, Freckles."

"You have no idea." I told him about everything that happened at Vanessa's house, minus the wedding talk, of course. "Then we all climbed into Vanessa's car—she's the tall brunette, by the way—and went over to Violet's house."

"Which one is Violet? I'm guessing that didn't go well either?" he asked.

"Violet is the petite blonde with the pixie haircut." It was clear he had no idea what kind of hairstyle I was talking about, but there was only one other blonde in the mix. "She wasn't home or at her parents' house either. We're not sure where she went. She wouldn't answer her phone."

"So which one is the redhead and the shorter brunette?" he asked. "Sometimes people just need some quiet time to lick their wounds."

"Candace is the redhead and April is the shorter brunette." I tilted my head to the side and studied the gorgeous man who sat adjacent to me. "You sound like a man with experience," I said softly. I was dying for him to tell me about the shadows I saw in his eyes from time to time.

"You can say that again," Elijah replied. "Let me tell you about a naïve fool who trusted his heart to a woman who cheated on him with his brother while he was serving his country."

I gasped. "No!"

"It happens a lot, Freckles. I just never thought Brandy would do that to me." Elijah shook his head like he still couldn't believe it. "Imagine the horror of finding my wife pregnant with my brother's baby when I returned home. It not only destroyed my relationship with my brother and father, but has made my mom's life hell."

"I'm so sorry, Elijah." I knew it had to be hard when your man went off to war, but on what planet was that an acceptable way to treat someone? "You do realize that their behavior is a reflection on their character, not your worth. Please tell me that you know that."

Elijah nodded slowly. "It's a recent epiphany." A slow smile crept across his face. "Sitting here with you makes me glad that I wasn't ready to trust again until now. I'm sure I met some real nice girls over the past ten years, but not a single one of them made me want to tear down the walls I built around my heart until you."

"Me?" I asked pointing to my chest.

"You, Freckles." He reached for my hand and brought it to his mouth. "You're genuine and honest, loving, and so loyal to those you love. You keep a man on his toes without using manipulation to accomplish it. You make me want to believe in forever again."

"Wow." Hearing that was sweeter than any three-worded declaration.

"You wow the hell out of me, and I can't believe that you're still single. How the hell is that possible? That loser Clayton couldn't be the only guy in this town interested in you."

I'd already told Elijah about my biggest hang-up, but it was time I told him the entire story. "I told you that I couldn't have kids, but I didn't tell you why." I released a shaky breath. "When I was seventeen, I developed a large bruise on my leg. At first, I thought I got it from playing soccer, but couldn't recall an incident that would have caused it. Then it wouldn't go away. I started feeling run-down and weak, so my mom took me to the doctor. They thought it was mono, but decided to do a blood panel to be sure nothing more serious was going on. I had leukemia, Elijah."

"I'm sorry, Freckles." He ran his hand over my hair again, then pulled me to him for a kiss.

"It was horrible, and I pray every night that I never know sickness like that ever again." I offered him a smile because he looked so miserable on my behalf. "I wouldn't trade the experience for the world though. Um, prior to that, my mother and I fought constantly. Nothing I did seemed good enough and I felt like she wanted me to be someone I wasn't. That all changed when I got sick. She just wanted me to be healthy. She said it over and over, sometimes when she wasn't aware that I heard her." I took a deep, shaky breath so I wouldn't cry. "I never want to put my parents and Milo through that kind of pain again. I used to think that not being able to have children was the end of the world. I think that the sting will always be there, but you helped me realize that I can have the life I've always wanted. I just have to go about it in a different way."

"Did some dickhead say that you weren't good enough because you couldn't have kids?" he asked me.

"Not directly to my face, but there were whispers and rumors." He looked like he was ready to rough someone up, so I covered his hands with my own. "You weren't the only one with a recent epiphany. Maybe some of the guys I dated would've been okay with adopting kids, but I wasn't willing to take a chance to find out."

"Maegan, I'm beyond rusty at dating since I spent the last ten years trying to avoid it. I'm going to fuck up, piss you off, and probably drive you nuts at times, but I'm hoping that you'll take a chance on me."

"Well, how could I refuse with a ringing endorsement like that?" I asked. "I have one favor to ask."

"Name it."

"Please don't start treating me like I'm made of fragile glass. Never stop dirty talking to me either. God, Elijah, it makes me crazy and melts my insides."

"Yeah?" he asked eagerly. "You're going to regret telling me that."

"No, I don't think that I will." I smiled ruefully. "There's a saying that men want a lady in their parlors and a harlot in their beds. I don't think women are all that different. I like a gentleman in the parlor and a filthy-mouthed man in my bed."

"Really?" Elijah didn't sound too sure.

"I'm sure there are some women who won't agree with me, but we don't care about what pleases them. I prefer to hear all the things you want to do with my tits and cunt."

Elijah blushed profusely, and I thought perhaps I'd gone too far, but he tossed me over his shoulder and hauled me upstairs to his bedroom where I practiced being his harlot while he put his filthy-fucking-mouth everywhere on my body. We both took what we wanted—immense pleasure from each other's body. Although neither of us declared love to the other, there was no doubt that there was a deeper connection and meaning in everything we did together.

Much later, Elijah cradled me against him on the couch and told me about his day. I shook hard in his arms when he confirmed that Renzo most likely targeted me as one of his victims. My heart broke for Kayla and Jessica Hansen. I knew that we wouldn't solve violence with more violence, but I couldn't imagine the hell that Kayla had lived through. Was I capable of harming someone who hurt Milo or one of my friends like that? Yeah, I thought I could. I hoped like hell that I never had to test the theory though.

"I think it was the first time I hated arresting someone for the crime they committed," Elijah said.

We sat together for a long time taking comfort from each other without talking. It was nice to know that we didn't have to fill every second with chit chat. I glanced at the clock on the wall and was surprised at the late hour.

"I need to go home and get some sleep. It's my turn to open Books and Brew tomorrow morning."

"Stay here," Elijah said, tugging on my hand when I got to my feet.

"I can't. I think it's best I go back to my own house so that you don't get sick of me."

Elijah pinned me with a dark look. "That's not likely to happen, but you should probably make me court you properly."

"Court me?"

"What's wrong with that term?" he asked.

"Nothing if you're a duke looking for a future duchess," I teased. "We call it dating these days. I was thinking it's best to ease you back into dating. Besides, you've had all of me, so it's not like playing hard to get now would get me anything. And as you pointed out, I don't play games."

"I haven't had *all* of you, Freckles. I need to earn that though."

My face flushed hot when I realized what he meant. "Oh, honey.

226

We ladies don't give that up unless it's for birthdays, anniversaries, or we're trying to talk you into buying a new car."

Elijah threw his head back and laughed heartily, causing me to place my hands on my hips. "I was talking about your heart, but it's good to know what I can expect next week."

"Next week?"

"It's my birthday." He waggled his eyebrows and rubbed his hands together gleefully like he was already picturing parting my ass cheeks and sliding his cock inside me.

I cupped his face in my hands and lowered my lips until they hovered above his. "You can stay over tomorrow night. I take Wednesdays off and I always make French toast and crispy bacon for breakfast."

"Being your neighbor sure has perks that the landlord never told me about."

"I might not be your neighbor much longer," I told him.

"Where are you moving to?"

"This historical home is about to go on the market, and I'm pretty sure I can get it for a good price."

"You're not seriously thinking about buying that Scooby-Doo haunted house."

"I will if I can get the price that I want and Andy tells me the renovations won't exceed what I want to spend. Will you be too afraid to visit me if I do?"

"Can I pour a circle of salt around the bed?" Elijah countered. "There's no ghost or ghoul that can keep me away from you, Freckles."

"Dinner tomorrow?" I asked. "I make amazing spaghetti and meatballs."

"I wouldn't miss it."

Elijah walked me and Lulu to our front door. The goodnight kiss he gave me was long, soft, and full of promise, longing, and so much hunger that I nearly changed my mind. I knew if we were going to do this right, then we needed our relationship to be healthy. That meant we needed to take a few steps back, possibly even start all over.

He took a step backward after our kiss ended. He smiled softly at me and said, "The lady rocked my world, but in all the right ways."

Chapter Twenty-Six

Elijah

I HAD BEEN SERIOUS WHEN I SAID I NEEDED TO EARN MAEGAN'S heart, but I was woefully uneducated about what people did on dates these days. Was going to the movies still a thing? There were so many streaming services out there, and although I had subscribed to a few, that wasn't how I wanted to impress Maegan. I knew damn well that we wouldn't get past the intro on whatever movie we picked on Netflix or Hulu because I'd be all over her. She deserved more from me than my horny groping.

I found a movie theater close by that had reclining loveseats and sold beer and wine. That sounded like a perfect setup to me. I took her out for dinner before we went to see the next biggest superhero movie. I tried really hard not to get jealous of her lusting over Superman by teasing her pretty pussy beneath the blanket she brought because theaters were "always cold." I wanted her to think about me, not him. I noticed it was the same blanket I let her borrow the night we met. I started calling it my lucky blanket because I seemed to get lucky whenever it was near.

Maegan had picked the reclining loveseat in the farthest corner at the top of the movie theater and I was starting to get suspicious that she'd had ulterior ideas when she brought the blanket and picked a secluded seat. I was even more convinced when I slid my hands beneath the waistband of her yoga pants and found her completely bare. If that wasn't enough, the sultry smile on her face would've told me that my lady had a filthy mind. God, I loved it.

After the movie, Maegan directed me to drive around and park behind a closed store then straddled my lap in the cab of my truck and rode me ten ways to Sunday. Let me tell you, it wasn't that Henry guy's name she was calling out when she came hard enough for her greedy pussy to put a chokehold on my cock. There was no sense in pretending that we weren't hot for each other, when we couldn't keep our hands off one another. That didn't mean I couldn't show her that she meant more to me than just sex.

Maegan had given me the most memorable birthday I'd ever had. She treated me to a delicious steak dinner on the Ohio river and a country music concert featuring my favorite bands. Instead of driving back to Blissville, we stayed at a hotel and Maegan gave *every* single part of her body to me.

I had flowers delivered weekly to her at Curious Things so that she'd know I was thinking about her. I took her dinner on nights she worked late. Maegan treated me to a French toast brunch every Wednesday before I went to work and sent me charming or sexy texts every day. My favorite nights were the ones where we stayed in. We had developed such a tranquil relationship in such a short time.

There were plenty of nights that Maegan read a book or took a bath while I watched television or tinkered with one of the clocks my grandfather was working on when he passed away. We were happy to be together, but didn't need to be in each other's faces all the time. I fell deeper and deeper in love with Maegan every single minute that I spent with her, yet I hadn't found the courage to say the words yet.

Many times, I opened my mouth to tell her but no words came out. Maegan must've seen my struggle because she would brush her hands across my cheek or kiss my lips then say, "I don't need the words, Elijah. I know how you feel."

Maegan took me home to meet her family and they welcomed me with open arms. It was easy to see how Maegan and Milo turned out to be such great people. It also made me miss my family more than I had in years. Talking to my mom over the phone wasn't enough, I wanted to hug her. I wasn't sure that my dad and I would ever be the same, but I found myself wanting to try. I would never get over what my brother did to me, but I needed to stop hating him. I figured it was necessary for me to heal old wounds to be the best man I could for Maegan. I wasn't sure when I'd reach out to my folks, but I knew that I would soon.

Valentine's night rolled around and I wanted to do something special with her, but she and Milo had already arranged a special event at Books and Brew. She felt torn between her responsibilities to her work and me, so I joined her at the bookstore. They called it a Blind Date with a Book. They took several dozen books and wrapped them up in brown paper and tied them with twine. On the front, they wrote a few clues about the book on the paper in red marker, such as the era it was about, or if it was adventure, horror, or romance. They also drew hearts and flowers, or some other symbol associated with the book to jazz it up a bit.

One book had a martini glass and another had a skeleton key. I bought one that said: World War II and Action Adventure. They added a drawing of an old war plane used in that era. They put a lot of thought into the event and I ended up having a lot more fun than I anticipated. It might've had something to do with the coffee, hot chocolate, and cookies, but I was pretty sure it was the woman who radiated joy in that fiery red sweater dress and knee-high black leather boots.

You know very good and fucking well that I couldn't wait to see what she wore beneath that sexy little number. I couldn't wait to put her booted legs on my shoulders and make her mine over and over again. I decided to assist Milo with beverages while Maegan and the other employees helped ring up sales of blind book dates. I figured it was better to keep my mind busier on things that didn't include getting naked.

My little wildcat had an entirely different idea. Once everyone left, she led me to her office and let me do all the filthy things to her that I wanted to the first time I visited her there. I thought for sure that antique desk was up to the task, but then it started groaning and straining beneath my wild thrusts. I carried her to the door and gave her a good wall-banging, hard fuck.

"Maegan, you're making it really hard for me to prove that I'm not in this for the sex," I told her, resting my forehead between her glorious breasts while I tried to catch my breath and wait for my heart to stop pounding.

"Are you saying you want us to abstain from sex?" she asked in a disbelieving tone.

"No, but I'm attempting to be a gentleman."

"Elijah, who asked you to be a gentleman? I love how raw and real you are with me, and you have never disrespected me—not one time. I love looking at you and knowing that you want to be between my legs more than you want your next breath. No one has ever made me feel the way that you do. I love that you don't try to change a single thing about me. You make me proud to be a sexual woman." I lifted my head and looked at Maegan. Her luminous eyes and soft smile made my heart kick back up. "We learned just how fleeting life could be and how much it could all change in a blink of an eye. I was really lucky, Elijah."

"We were lucky," I corrected her because goddamn, I couldn't imagine life without her in it.

"I love you, Elijah Markham. You might not be ready to say the words, but you're going to hear them. I. Love. You. I want to make you as happy as you make me."

The lady was a thief, plain and simple. She robbed me of my ability to think, stole my breath, and snagged the heart that I thought had been long gone. I madly loved her.

"I love you too, Freckles. I really do. No one has ever made me as happy as you do, and I thank my lucky stars every single night for you."

She was brave, fearless, and more courageous than most men I've known in my life. *And the lady is mine.*

Epilogue

Elijah

Four months later...

I WALKED THROUGH THE FRONT DOOR OF THE HOUSE THAT SAT at the end of a secluded lane at the edge of town. I looked up into the two-story entryway and hardly recognized it as the same house that I entered the night Thom Renzo was murdered. It looked like I stepped back in time to when the house was first built.

The hardwood floors gleamed beneath a crystal chandelier, and the wide curving staircase that led up to the second-story landing had been refinished as well. My heart's desire stood looking over the balcony railing at me with her hands on her hips.

"There you are," she said. "I was starting to think that you got lost."

Maegan had stripped the old wallpaper off the walls and painted them in soft neutral colors that would act as a backdrop to her art and furnishings, allowing the original, restored woodwork to shine. Well, that was what she said would happen anyway, and I had no reason to doubt her. My lady of the manor knew what the hell she was doing. You'd never guess that the house had been in horrible shape just a few months prior.

"Nah, you can't lose me that easily," I told her. "I backed the moving truck in the driveway to make things a little easier. Your mom, dad, Milo, and Memphis are heading over in a bit. They promised to bring pizza and beer."

"What do you think of the place now that she's finished?" She didn't let me come over the last week because she wanted to surprise me. I was surprised all right.

I had been really skeptical of her buying the place because so much mystery surrounded it. I wasn't sure that I believed in ghosts, spirits, and whatnot, but Anthony Bliss's disappearance and Thom Renzo's murder had to leave an imprint on the place. Right? Maegan called a local resident named Emory Jackson who claimed to be a psychic. Hell yeah, I was disbelieving until I researched him on the internet and saw all the cases he assisted law enforcement officers with over the past five years. It helped to find out that Emory was good friends with the captain and Adrian. They told me he was the real deal and vouched for his character. Then I felt like a real asshole when I learned that he was also Memphis's cousin.

Emory seemed like a great guy and I liked him the moment we were introduced. Before Maegan bought the house, she had Emory come over and give his impressions. "I'm not detecting any negative energy present, but there is a ghost here." A door had randomly slammed upstairs as if to punctuate his statement with an exclamation.

"I'm telling you that's Anthony's ghost. I don't believe he just disappeared," Maegan said. "This is his beloved home, but I think it's sad that he's trapped here," she had told me. "I have a feeling the answers are in that cellar and I'm going to find them."

Maegan hired someone to haul every single thing the Renzos had owned after she made sure that none of the Bliss family's belongings were mixed in. Only a few of the Bliss treasures, as Maegan called them, were discovered upstairs, such as the pearl necklace Renzo had told Maegan about, and a very old, elaborate smoking pipe carved out of dark wood and ivory. She just knew it was Anthony's and the source of the random tobacco smell we caught on occasion. Most everything else remained in the cellar waiting for her to explore.

"I think I know someone who can help you if you're interested," Emory told her. "He's a paranormal investigator. You might've heard of him, Lyric Willows."

"Oh! Oh my God! Are you kidding? That's the guy that Memphis lusts after!"

"I know, and I offered to introduce them but…" His words trailed off.

"Memphis only likes the bad boys," Maegan had finished for him.

"Elijah," Maegan said, pulling me back to the present.

I walked further into the foyer and shut the door behind me then walked to the bottom of the steps. "It's almost as beautiful as the lady who owns it."

"Awww," Maegan said, walking toward the top of the steps. Instead of walking down, she hopped onto the banister and slid down into my waiting arms. "That never gets old."

"You know what else never gets old?" I asked seductively.

"I have an idea. How much longer will we be alone?"

"Not long enough for me to fuck you proper."

"You say the sweetest things, Elijah." She slid out of my arms and headed to the front door. "I guess we better get started moving boxes in now so that we can get to the more pleasant activities quicker. That gigantic copper bathtub will do wonders for our tired bodies tonight." That damn thing was big enough for three people, but I promised that it would only get used by two.

"Now you're talking, Freckles." I started to follow her outside, but stopped when my cell phone rang. My heart seized in my chest when I saw who was calling me. There could only be one reason for my old captain from the Columbus Police Department to call me.

"Detective Markham," I said into the phone.

"It's Captain Barker calling, Detective. I'm afraid I have some bad news. I just learned that—"

"Axel Washington is a free man," I said, finishing for him.

"An hour ago," he confirmed.

"How?"

"Evidence and witnesses went missing. There were issues with juror intimidation also. The judge declared a mistrial and that animal is walking free until the prosecutor can decide if they want to retry him."

"If?" I asked.

"They like to win, Detective."

"Fuck!"

"My sentiments exactly," the older man said. "I don't have to tell you that you're in danger if Axel Washington ever learns your true identity. Be careful, Detective."

"Thank you, sir."

I hung up just as Maegan walked in with her family and Memphis behind her. "Look who's here." She saw my thunderous expression and the smile slid from her face. "What's wrong?"

Telling Maegan that a psychopath might show up in our lives someday served no point right then. Axel didn't know my identity yet, and I just had to pray it stayed that way. I finally had everything I ever wanted and no scumbag was going to take that away from me.

"Just took a call about an old case that I worked. There's nothing for you to worry about, Freckles." I could tell that she wasn't one hundred percent sold on my answer, but I saw the moment she decided to trust me.

I just hoped she didn't live to regret it.

Maegan and Elijah's story continues in *The Lady Stole My Heart*.

Other Books by
AIMEE NICOLE WALKER

Only You

The Fated Hearts Series
Chasing Mr. Wright, Book 1
Rhythm of Us, Book 2
Surrender Your Heart, Book 3
Perfect Fit, Book 4
Return to Me, Book 5
Always You, Book 6
Any Means Necessary, Book 7

Curl Up and Dye Mysteries
Dyeing to be Loved
Something to Dye For
Dyed and Gone to Heaven
I Do, or Dye Trying
A Dye Hard Holiday

Road to Blissville Series
Unscripted Love
Someone to Call My Own

Coauthored with Nicholas Bella
Undisputed
Circle of Darkness (Genesis Circle, Book 1)

Acknowledgments

First, I need to thank my husband and children for their constant support and encouragement. It's not easy living with a writer who often disappears into a fictional world for long periods of time. They do so many things to help me out so that I can realize my dream. I love you guys more than words can ever express.

Many thanks go out to my three best friends, Annabella, Deena, and Kerry. They've stood by me, cheered me on, picked me up, and held my hand through some rough patches. I love you girls so very much. I wish everyone had friends like you because the world would be a much kinder place.

To my creative dream team, thanks seem hardly enough for all that you do. Pam Ebeler of Undivided Editing thank you for your tireless work, feedback, and many laughs while editing. Jay Aheer of Simply Defined art is just an incredible artist, and I love how she brings my words to life. Stacey Blake of Champagne Formats is also an amazing artist who does incredible interior formatting and designing for e-books and paperbacks. Let's not forget Judy Zweifel of Judy's' Proofreading. She does an amazing job of finding the tiniest details that make a book shine.

I would like to thank my beta readers for all the honest feedback they gave me. I appreciate you gals so much. Aimee's ARC Angels are Racheal, Abbey, Jodie, Kim, and Laurel. Thank you for all that you do!

About
AIMEE NICOLE WALKER

I am a wife and mother to three kids, four dogs, and a cat. When I'm not dreaming up stories, I like to lose myself in a good book, cook or bake. I'm a girly tomboy who paints her fingernails while watching sports and yelling at the referees. I will always choose the book over the movie. I believe in happily-ever-after. Love inspires everything that I do. Music keeps me sane.

I'd love to hear from you.

You can reach me at:

Twitter—twitter.com/AimeeNWalker

Facebook—www.facebook.com/aimeenicole.walker

Blog—AimeeNicoleWalker.blogspot.com

www.ingramcontent.com/pod-product-compliance
Lightning Source LLC
Chambersburg PA
CBHW071304250626
47159CB00004B/1308